DON'T TELL
A SOUL

Books by Kirsten Miller

Don't Tell a Soul
How to Lead a Life of Crime
The Eternal Ones

Books by Kirsten Miller and Jason Segel

The Last Reality Series

Otherworld
OtherEarth
OtherLife

DON'T TELL A SOUL

KIRSTEN MILLER

DELACORTE PRESS

Text copyright © 2021 by Kristen Miller
Jacket art copyright © 2021 by Dan Quintana

All rights reserved. Published in the United States by Delacorte Press, an imprint of Random House Children's Books, a division of Penguin Random House LLC, New York.

Delacorte Press is a registered trademark and the colophon is a trademark of Penguin Random House LLC.

Visit us on the Web! GetUnderlined.com
Educators and librarians, for a variety of teaching tools, visit us at RHTeachersLibrarians.com

Library of Congress Cataloging-in-Publication Data
Name: Miller, Kirsten, author.
Title: Don't tell a soul / Kirsten Miller.
Other titles: Do not tell a soul
Description: New York : Delacorte Press, [2021] | Audience: Ages 14 and up. | Audience: Grades 10–12. | Summary: "Bram moves to the small town of Louth in order to help her uncle start his new inn, but when she discovers a legacy of silenced women tied to her new home, she sets out to investigate the truth behind the town's 'Dead Girl' myths"— Provided by publisher.
Identifiers: LCCN 2020007149 (print) | LCCN 2020007150 (ebook) | ISBN 978-0-525-58120-8 (hardcover) | ISBN 978-0-525-58121-5 (library binding) | ISBN 978-0-525-58122-2 (epub)
Subjects: CYAC: Mystery and detective stories. | Ghosts—Fiction. | Hotels—Fiction. | Uncles—Fiction.
Classification: LCC PZ7.M6223 Don 2021 (print) | LCC PZ7.M6223 (ebook) | DDC [Fic]—dc23

The text of this book is set in 11.75-point Adobe Caslon Pro.
Interior design by Andrea Lau

Printed in the United States of America
10 9 8 7 6 5 4 3 2 1
First Edition

For my aunt Virginia, who knows (as do I) that ghosts are real

DON'T TELL A SOUL

One

There was no one at the station when I arrived. I'd slept for most of the three-hour ride, while the train had barreled its way through a blizzard. When it stopped at Hudson, I stepped down from the car and sank into snow that was already shin-deep. I'd barely reached the platform and set down my suitcase before the train sped off again, leaving me all alone with the darkness.

The lights were out at the station house, and when I hurried to the door, I found it locked. We'd pulled away from Penn Station over two hours late. Looking around at the buried town, I could tell it was a miracle we'd reached Hudson at all. I left my bag by the door and stepped out into the night. There was little to see but the swirling snow. I'd never known a world so quiet or so dark.

The warmth of the train car slipped away, and the cold crept through my buttonholes and under the collar of my coat. There were no lights in the buildings and no cars on the road. I was alone in a town I'd never visited, and I was convinced that I'd been forgotten. Fear coiled around me, squeezing the air from my lungs. The courage that had driven me north had vanished. I knew I shouldn't have come—and now I had nowhere to go.

Then the glare of headlights appeared in the distance, blinding me as a car approached. A taxi pulled up within feet of me and stopped. Then I heard the mechanical hum of a window lowering, followed by a man's gruff voice.

"Howland?"

The name threw me at first, and panic tightened its grip on my chest.

"Howland?" He shouted it the second time, impatient for an answer. Then I remembered I'd be using my mother's maiden name.

I wiped away the tears that had welled in my eyes and hoped he hadn't seen them. "That's me," I called back.

The driver's door opened, and something that looked like a bear emerged. As it waded through the snow and into the headlights' beams, I saw it was a giant man in a brown fur coat. He passed by with a grunt.

"Get in," he ordered. "I'll grab the bag."

I reluctantly climbed into the backseat of the cab, which was blistering hot and smelled like whatever beast the man must have murdered to make his coat. As he returned to the car with my suitcase, I was able to get a good look at him. He seemed old, though exactly how old was hard to say. A bramble of gray whiskers sprouted from his nostrils and covered his face from the nose down. He opened the door on my left and tossed my enormous suitcase onto the seat beside me. Whatever his age, he was clearly very strong. I didn't want to be alone in a car with him. If there had been any alternative, I would have jumped at it. I pulled my backpack closer on my lap. Hidden inside were the weapons I'd ordered online for protection—a box cutter and a can of bear repellent.

"That your only suitcase?" the man asked.

"Yes," I said. He slammed the door in response and opened his own.

I waited until he'd wedged his massive body into the driver's seat before I asked, "Do you know where I'm going?"

"That I know," the man said. "Whether we'll get there is anyone's guess. Plows haven't been able to keep up with the snow." He turned and glared at me over his shoulder. His eyes were so narrow that he seemed to be squinting. "You couldn't have waited till morning?"

"I didn't know it would get this bad," I said. Though

even if I had, I wouldn't have waited. Staying in Manhattan was no longer an option.

"Storm's gonna get worse before it's all over," he informed me. "I'd strap on my safety belt if I was you."

I noticed his own seat belt still dangling from its hook as he backed the car out of the station. The dashboard warning bell chimed a few times before giving up. We picked up speed, snow hurling itself at the windshield, trying to push us back where we'd come from. There was no road ahead, just a seamless expanse of white.

"How long will it take to get there?" I asked nervously.

"No telling," the driver said. "Gotta get over the river and up the hill. Outside of town, the roads are bound to be brutal." He clearly considered it just short of a suicide mission.

"Maybe I should stay in Hudson."

"I was told your uncle wants you at the manor tonight," he said. "I suppose he has his reasons."

"So you know James." That made me feel better. Not a lot, but a little.

"I live in Louth." The man peered at me in the rearview mirror, and something in his look gave me the feeling he didn't care much for my uncle. "Everyone knows everyone in Louth."

The backseat windows had fogged up. I wiped a circle clear with my coat sleeve and rested my forehead against the glass. No light broke through the darkness around us, and I assumed we'd left civilization behind, until we passed a car idling on the side of the road. I saw its owner shoveling it free from a snowbank, and I realized we were still in town.

"The electric's out," I noted. Seventeen years in Manhattan, and I'd only lived through a single blackout.

"Happens," the man said. "It's out on the other side of the river, too. You'd better hope they have a fire waiting for you up there at the manor. You're gonna freeze to death in that place if they don't."

"There are worse ways to go," I muttered.

"What did you say?" he demanded. In the rearview mirror, his eyes were wide open, and I could see they were blue.

"Nothing," I said, holding his gaze. I knew he'd heard me. And he'd understood.

We didn't speak much after that.

I don't know how long the trip took. As soon as I was convinced that death wasn't imminent, my mind returned to the life I'd just left. But at some point, I heard the car's engine begin to strain as we started up an incline. I'd only been to my uncle's house once, right after he moved in, but I'd never forgotten the sight of it sitting on top of its hill.

The first time I'd laid eyes on it, I'd thought it looked lonely. There was no better place to hide from the world.

The steeper the climb got, the more our progress slowed, until eventually the car crawled to a stop. Within seconds the wipers were overcome and the windshield was covered with snow.

The driver got out to investigate, and I pushed open my door and followed him.

"What happened?" I asked, wrapping my arms around myself in the sudden cold.

"We're stuck," the driver grumbled, as if it were somehow my fault. He pulled an ancient flip phone out of his pocket and tapped in a number. "It's me," he informed whoever picked up. "Nope, didn't make it. . . . 'Bout fifty feet from Howland's drive. . . . Yep. . . . Thanks, Joe. 'Preciate it."

He snapped the phone shut. "Get in and get comfortable. We'll have to wait. I just gotta make sure the tailpipe is clear so we don't die while we do. A plow should be through in a couple hours. They'll give us a ring when they're close."

My chest tightened. I wasn't going to wait. I couldn't be trapped in a car with a man I didn't know. My anxiety was building, and I knew a full-blown panic attack could follow.

"I heard you say we were right at the drive." I looked around. Nothing seemed familiar. "The house can't be too far from here, can it?"

The man raised a hand to shield his eyes and squinted

at the snow-covered hill ahead of us. "Half a mile. Maybe more."

"That's not so far," I said. "We can walk and wait for the plow at the house."

"No," he said. Just that—*no.* He didn't offer an explanation.

"It'll be a lot warmer—" I started.

"No," the man interrupted me. "This car is my livelihood. I'm not gonna leave it."

"I don't understand," I persisted. "What could possibly—"

"No," he said again. Third time was the charm. We both knew that the car would be fine. The man didn't want to set foot in my uncle's house.

"Well, I'm going," I announced. I'd take my chances in the storm. "Can I leave my bag here?"

He snorted. "Can't take it with you. I'll bring it round once the roads are clear. You sure you won't get lost?"

I pulled my phone out of my pocket. "GPS," I said. "No one ever gets lost anymore."

I typed in my uncle's address, and with my headphones on, I followed my map app's directions. Even beneath the trees, the snow was building, and I waded through drifts that buried me to my knees. Without the phone's flashlight I wouldn't have found the entrance to the drive. Everything around me was covered, its true nature hidden. There was no way to tell the road from a ditch.

I knew half a mile was roughly ten city blocks. Before I set out, I thought I could take ten blocks of anything. As it turned out, I was wrong about that. By the time I reached the crest of the hill, I was certain I was going to die. I began to wonder what people would say if a photo of my frozen corpse popped up on social media. It was nice to imagine that I might be mourned. But New York had made it clear that I wouldn't be missed.

I stopped at the top of the hill to catch my breath. The wind was wild and it clawed at my lungs. I knew I couldn't rest long or I'd freeze to death on the spot. Somehow I chose the right moment to pause, though I'm not sure I'd call it luck. For just a few seconds, the storm seemed to clear and the moon peeked out from the clouds, casting a pale silver light onto the landscape. Ahead of me, tall white figures stood in two straight lines. They were covered in snow, but I knew what they were, and they sent a chill down my spine. I'd seen pictures of the house and its grounds that had been taken just after the renovation. My uncle had trimmed the century-old topiary hedges that lined the drive into humanoid shapes. A dozen design magazines had called them masterpieces. But I thought they looked like monsters. Even the photos were terrifying. I wondered if the sight of them would turn guests away.

Waiting for me in the distance was the house. It seemed even more massive than I remembered. Three stories of stone crawling with ivy, with a dozen dark windows on every floor. Two wings branched off a central hall. I knew one wing had recently been destroyed in a fire, but from where I stood, it was impossible to tell which one was damaged. The snow had stitched the house back together. It sat there, still and silent. I had the sense it was watching, like a camouflaged beast stalking its prey.

I'd come to Louth in search of answers, but I wasn't sure I was ready for what I might find. My feet refused to take another step—either forward or backward. Then I saw something dart across the drive a hundred yards ahead of me. It rushed from a hedge on my right to its twin on the opposite side. It must have been an animal, but it was far too big to be anyone's pet. And if my eyes could be trusted, it was almost entirely white. I was alone in the wilderness with something large—something that could see me better than I could see it. My heart pounding, I switched off my phone's light and remained perfectly still, waiting for the creature to step out from behind the hedge. It had to be a deer, I told myself, but I wasn't sure I believed it. There was something strange about the way it had moved. The creature had seemed to be walking on its two hind legs.

I was trying to come up with an explanation when the hedge suddenly shook, shedding piles of snow. Then, just as the thing was about to make its next move, the phone in my hand rang. I glanced down instinctively, and my eyes landed on a brightly lit screen with the word "MOTHER" in the middle. My hand shaking, I hit ignore, and the screen went dark. But when I looked up again, I realized I'd been blinded. I could hear something moving, just off to my left. The beast had gotten closer, but the only thing I could see was the hulking silhouette of the house at the end of the drive. I turned my flashlight back on and ran as fast as I could toward the house, certain there was something behind me.

I sprinted to the front door of the house and pounded on it with my fist. Then I spun around and pressed my back to the wood, ready to confront whatever was out there. But there was nothing, and I felt like a moron. Then the door opened and I fell flat on my butt.

A woman dressed in a flannel robe towered over me. "You must be the niece." She was standing safely in the center of a circle of candlelight. I scrambled to my feet, embarrassed and still catching my breath.

She was forty-something and pretty in an *I grow my own kale* kind of way. The candlelight accentuated her chin, leaving dark shadows beneath her eyes that gave her an air of fatigue. I was grateful she wasn't laughing.

"I'm Bram," I said, pulling myself together. I took the hand she offered and shook it.

"I'm Miriam Reinhart. Your uncle will be happy you

made it here safely." Then her brow furrowed. "Where are your things?" She stepped past the door's threshold and peered out into the night. "Where's Boris?"

I didn't even need to ask. Only someone named Boris could have rocked a fur coat the way my dear driver had. "His car got stuck at the bottom of the drive. He's waiting for the plow to come through. For some reason he didn't want to walk up to the manor."

Miriam shivered as she closed the door. Then she looked back at me with her eyebrows raised. "You *walked*? Alone? Up the hill through the blizzard? People die in weather like this."

"It wasn't the best decision I've ever made," I admitted. "I saw something on the way here. Some kind of animal, I think. It was big. And white. What do you think it could be?"

"You're in the country now. It could have been anything." My eyes must have widened, because Miriam seemed to take pity on me. "I wouldn't be too concerned," she added. "There aren't many animals around Louth that would go after a human. And those that would aren't smart enough to pick the locks on a door." Then she cocked her head toward the mansion's grand staircase. "Come along and I'll show you up to your room. After your trip you must be exhausted."

As I followed her across the entrance hall toward the

stairs, I noticed that the stone floors were pockmarked, and the plaster walls had been patched but left rough in places. I knew that was how Uncle James had wanted it—imperfect. When I was little, he told me that true beauty is flawed. I was an ugly duckling, so people said that kind of thing to me all the time. But I knew James actually meant it, and his house proved him right. It was a masterpiece. Above our heads, the crystals of a massive chandelier caught the candlelight. The impression the room gave was one of great age and dignity. Having greeted thousands of guests in its time, it was far too splendid to be bothered with an outcast like me. As I climbed the stairs, I searched for signs of fire damage. I didn't see any, but there was still a faint stench of smoke in the air.

"Do you live here?" I asked Miriam.

"I stay overnight when I'm needed. James asked me to be here to welcome you. Then the blizzard hit and the lights went out. So I'll be sleeping in one of the guest rooms tonight."

"Is James away?" I asked.

"No, he's here," she replied. "Since we're getting to know each other, I have a question for you, too."

"Okay," I said, steeling myself for the worst.

"'Bram' is an unusual name for a girl, isn't it?"

I relaxed a bit. It was a question I was often asked. "My

father's name was Abraham," I said. "I look like him, so they nicknamed me 'Bram.' He's dead now."

"Oh," Miriam said. "I'm sorry to hear that."

I said nothing. People had been telling me the same thing for years. It had taken me a while to figure out that it was just what people were supposed to do—pretend that they cared. No one ever really meant it.

At the top of the stairs, there were doors on either side of the landing. When Miriam and I hung a right and entered a long corridor, I knew it was the opposite wing of the house that had burned. She guided me past the first two doors in the hall and then stopped at the third, which she opened.

The first thing I saw was the crackling fire. It drew me in, and I suddenly realized how cold I still was. My clothing was sopping wet from melted snow, and I'd almost gone numb from the knees down. Then I noticed the room's décor—a four-poster bed with a duvet decorated with tiny pink buds. A vanity stood beside a plush armchair covered in rose-colored velvet. The room's windows hid behind matching curtains, and dark green paint covered the walls.

"I'm just putting you here for the night," Miriam assured me as I made my way toward the fireplace. I wondered if she worried that the girly décor might offend me. I was thrilled just to have a place to sleep. "With the power out, it would be too cold in the room James chose for you. This one has the best fireplace in the house. But I promise—first thing tomorrow, we'll move you."

"This room is fine," I told her. My skin prickled from the heat of the fire. Pleasure and pain mingled together.

"It should do for now. We'll get you into the right room in the morning."

I glanced over at Miriam. She was still standing in the hall. She seemed reluctant to enter. "Seriously, this one's fine," I assured her. I didn't want anyone making a fuss over me.

"Oh good," she said, though she still seemed agitated. "Here—" She fished two items from the pocket of her robe and headed toward me with an arm outstretched. One of the items was a yellow candle, and the second was a box of safety matches. "Just in case."

"It's okay. My phone has a flashlight," I said, holding up the device. But when I clicked the screen, it was dead. The flashlight app had drained the battery, and my charger was back in Boris's car. I reached for the candle and matches.

"Thank you," I told her.

"Be careful with the candle," she warned me. "Don't fall asleep with it lit. You know—"

I nodded. "Yes. I'll be careful."

When her smile returned, it was far less convincing.

"What would you like for your welcome breakfast?" she asked. "How about bacon and eggs?"

"Sounds perfect," I told her, hoping she'd just leave me be.

"Then it's settled. I'll see you in the morning," Miriam said, heading back to the door. As she reached it, she seemed to hesitate for a moment with her hand on the knob, as if there were something else she wanted to say. But she held her tongue. I turned back to the fire and heard the door close behind her.

I enjoyed the heat for a few more moments before I set the candle on the bedside table and dragged a chair from the vanity to the fireplace. I stripped out of my wet clothes and hung them in front of the blaze to dry. Then I stood there in my underwear, rotating slowly like a pig on a spit. As feeling finally returned to my limbs, I realized that the room's walls weren't a uniform green. In the dim light, I could see the outline of trees painted on the walls all around me. I imagined myself lost in a dark forest, scared and alone, with no hope of rescue, and the fear from my walk up the hill returned. I bolted for the bed and burrowed under the covers. They smelled like smoke, but I didn't care. I pulled the blankets up over my head. Some people run when they're terrified. Some people scream. I'd learned to hide and hope it all went away. It was a habit I knew I needed to break.

When I woke in the middle of the night, I wasn't even sure that my eyes were open. The fire had died, and the room was so dark, it was as if I'd been swallowed. But I knew that I wasn't alone. I held my breath and listened. I could hear the faint sound of footsteps nearby. That was enough. I was wide-awake in an instant. My hand shot out from beneath my blankets toward the nightstand and landed first on my lifeless phone. I was teetering on the edge of panic when my fingers finally located the candle and matches Miriam had left me.

When I struck a match and lit the candle, I saw that my bedroom door was open. It wasn't open a crack as if the latch hadn't caught. It was standing wide open, and I could sense something lurking just out of sight. For a moment, I sat there frozen, like a doomed girl in a horror movie, watching for whatever it was to step out of the darkness and into my room.

Then the spell broke, and a burst of energy shot through me. If something was coming, I wasn't going to sit there and wait for it. I threw back the blankets, bolted to the bedroom door, and slammed it shut. My fingers didn't fumble when I turned the lock.

I took a few steps back and stood there in my underwear, facing the door, gulping down air as my skin turned to ice. My fingernails dug into the candle, and wax dripped down my hand. I expected to hear a rap on the wood or to see the knob twisting. Everything remained still and the room stayed silent. But I knew what I'd heard. Someone was out there. And I had no intention of ever sleeping in the rose room again.

Two

With the door shut and locked, I wrapped a blanket from the bed around my body and started a fire. It was cold, and my hands were shaking so badly that I kept snapping matches in half. Thankfully, there were embers hidden beneath the ashes, and the twigs that I'd tossed onto them caught fire quickly. As soon as the blaze had pushed the darkness into the corners of the room, I took a look around. There was no sign of an intruder. I checked beneath the bed. Then I threw open the curtains in case someone might be hiding behind them, and discovered French doors with a Juliet balcony on the other side of the glass. The storm had passed and the moon was shining. My windows looked out over the gardens in front of the manor—and the hedges that lined the drive. They were shapeless mounds at that point—nothing human about them—and the world outside seemed perfectly safe and serene.

But I didn't doubt myself. I knew what had happened. My mind wasn't playing tricks on me, and I hadn't let my imagination run wild. I dug through the vanity until I found some paper and a pen, and with my bottom half tucked under the bedcovers, and a tattered cashmere throw wrapped around my shoulders, I wrote everything down. I wanted to make sure I had a record. I knew that without one, details would blur, facts might get twisted, and the story could spiral out of control.

Hours later, I woke to a blinding light. I'd set my writing aside and fallen asleep with the curtains open, and now the sun's rays were bouncing off the white blanket that covered the world outside. As my eyes gradually adjusted, I was pleasantly surprised by what I saw. In the daylight, my room didn't feel frilly or fussy. The furnishings were fit for a princess—but one who'd died ages earlier and left them behind. The velvet on the chair was threadbare in places, and the finish on the vanity had worn thin. On their own, every piece would have looked slightly shabby, yet they came together beautifully. If my written account of the night's events hadn't been lying there right beside me, I could have convinced myself it had all been a dream.

But it hadn't. I remembered being scared out of my wits,

and I would have asked to move to another room—if not for the painting on the walls around me. The forest that had frightened me the previous evening had transformed into fruit-filled trees and flowering meadows. The artist who'd painted the summertime landscape had been gifted. The plaster was damaged in places, but what remained of the artwork was impossibly lovely. At first, I thought the paint must have darkened over the years. Then I spotted the moon high on the wall and the stars on the ceiling, and I realized the mural showed a night scene.

My attention was drawn to an image directly across from the bed, and I climbed out from beneath the covers for a closer look. A small white boat was crossing a wide blue river. The name on the side of the boat was printed in letters too tiny to read, and there didn't seem to be anyone inside the vessel.

I circled the bedroom, studying the rest of the mural. In the distance there appeared to be mountains. Eventually I found a few houses—clustered together as though they belonged to a town. Nearby was a tiny storefront with a sign that read MAXWELL & MASON, GENERAL MERCHANDISE, LOUTH, NEW YORK. I searched for signs of life in the village, but the windows were all dark. There were no dogs in the yards or birds in the trees. The only living creature I spotted was a girl in a long white dress on her way to the village. She seemed eager to get there. Her long hair flowed behind her as though she'd broken into a run.

I leaned in to study the girl more closely and saw that her face had been drawn in remarkable detail. She didn't appear that much older than me. It was odd to see her there, all alone on a dark country road in the middle of the night, wearing a dress that wasn't made for running. Her cheeks were flushed and her eyes were wide with excitement. Wherever she was going, I thought, it was somewhere she longed to be.

That was the moment I decided I needed the room to be mine. It didn't make sense, and I couldn't explain it. A few hours earlier, I would have rather been anywhere else. But with the sun shining, the room felt right—like it wanted me there. Like I wasn't crazy for coming. For the first time in ages, I almost felt hopeful. My life in Manhattan was over, but I might have a reason to keep going in Louth.

The clothes I'd left hanging by the fire were damp but wearable. I pulled on my jeans and sweater and set off down the stairs in search of my uncle. But when I reached the bottom of the grand staircase, I paused. The urge to explore was too strong to resist.

I opened a door that I knew must lead to the burnt wing of the house, and stepped into a parlor. I lifted the collar of my sweater up over my nose, though the wool couldn't mask the stench of smoke. The fire had spared the room's floor and walls, but a dark black stain crawled across the ceiling as if searching for the door. The temperature plunged as I walked from room to room, and the damage grew worse the farther I went. Eventually, it was impossible to tell what function the rooms had once served. The plaster had burned off the walls, exposing the stone underneath, and the ceiling was little more than a matrix of charred wood. In places I could see into the floors above. At one point I came across a small mound of snow in the middle of a room. I looked straight up and caught a glimpse of the sky. At the far end of the wing, the glassless windows were all boarded up.

"Good morning," someone said, and I nearly leaped out of my skin. I spun around to see Miriam standing there, her hands shoved into the pockets of a long denim skirt. Her graying brown hair was pulled back in a no-nonsense ponytail, and her sweater bore several prominent holes. She may have been smiling, but the expression seemed forced. I didn't blame her for being a bit wary of someone like me.

"I didn't mean to startle you," she said. "I guess you figured out that the power's back on. The plow came through early this morning, and Boris dropped off your things. I went upstairs to let you know, but you'd already set out to have a look around."

"Sorry—" I started nervously.

"It's okay," she assured me. "I would have wanted to

check it out, too." Then she paused for a moment to take in the room. "It may be hard to believe, but this was once the most beautiful library. I saw a picture of it in a magazine. The walls were lined with shelves filled with leather-bound books. Your uncle had built quite a collection." She stopped, her mouth twisted as if the library's destruction were too much to bear. "Do you know what happened?"

"There was a fire," I said, stating what would have been obvious to anyone with eyes or a nose.

"Yes." Miriam caught my gaze and held it. She was waiting to see if I'd heard the rest of the story.

"My uncle's second wife died," I added.

"Did you know her?" Miriam asked.

"No," I told her. "James and my mom—it's complicated."

Miriam nodded. "It often is," she said.

"Did *you* know her?" I asked.

"Of course," Miriam told me. "Dahlia and I both grew up here in Louth, and my son went to school with her daughter, Lark."

The mention of the name sent my heart racing. "Lark was here the night of the fire, wasn't she?" I inquired as casually as I could manage. "How is she?"

Miriam grimaced. "She was hurt. I'm afraid she's still unwell."

What a nice way of putting it, I thought. My mother hadn't been quite so kind.

"You have a son?" I asked. I was just being polite. Miriam's son didn't interest me. I was thinking of a school photo of Lark that had been published in the paper after the incident. I'd seen a pretty girl who'd done everything she could to hide her looks with ghoulish black makeup. I had a million questions—but none I could ask without seeming morbid.

"Yes, my son's name is Sam. He graduated from high school last summer, and he's been taking care of the manor and its grounds to earn money for college. If you see someone working on the property, that's probably him. I'm sure he'd love to show you around."

Miriam seemed to think I might need a companion. I hadn't come to Louth to make friends, and I didn't need a social life getting in my way.

"I know your uncle will be glad to see you," she added awkwardly when I didn't respond. "How long do you think you'll be staying?"

"I have no idea," I told her.

Miriam frowned. That clearly wasn't what she'd wanted to hear. "I see," she said. Then her voice dropped an octave, and I figured something important was coming. "It's not my place, but I feel I should warn you. I know you've been through a lot, but this may not be the best time for an extended visit."

Miriam had been so discreet until that point. But her

warning left little doubt. She knew about me. I crossed my arms over my chest, but I still felt exposed.

"There's nowhere else for me to go," I told her. It was true.

"You have no other family?" Miriam seemed skeptical.

"No, I don't," I said bluntly. She had no right to interrogate me. "Everyone but my mother and uncle is dead. I'm surprised James didn't tell you that, too."

Miriam took in the information and released a weary sigh. "James hasn't been himself since the fire."

"Oh really? Who has he been?" I asked, my anger rising. In my experience, people never really changed—they just removed their disguises.

Miriam attempted a smile. I think she assumed I was joking. "You'll see what he's like now," she told me. "Don't act shocked when you do."

"Okay," I agreed, though it seemed a bit silly to promise that I wouldn't be shocked when I had no clue what to expect. "Is he up yet? I should say hello."

As I turned to head back the way I'd come, Miriam's hand flew out and grabbed my forearm. "One more thing before we go." I looked down at her hand gripping my arm. She had my attention, but she paused as if reluctant to continue. "I want you to come to me if anything . . . unusual happens during your stay here."

"Like what?" I asked, my curiosity piqued.

"Anything." Miriam let go of my arm. "Anything at all."

I figured I'd test her. "As a matter of fact, something happened last night," I said. "I woke up and found my door wide open. I'm pretty sure it was closed when you left. Was there someone in the house last night aside from you, me, and my uncle?"

Miriam's face aged twenty years in ten seconds. The creases in her forehead grew deeper and the color drained from her cheeks. "Not to my knowledge," she said. "Did you see anyone?"

I shook my head, watching her carefully. "No," I told her.

"Then I wouldn't let it worry you. Old houses behave in strange ways." She said it as though she were trying to convince herself as much as me. "But please let me know if it happens again."

"I will."

"Let *me* know," she repeated. "Don't worry your uncle. James already has far too much on his mind."

"Okay," I said. If she was trying to set me at ease, it wasn't working. I was suddenly much more concerned than I had been.

"So," Miriam said with an unconvincing smile. "Are you ready for some bacon and eggs?"

Three

I followed Miriam out of the burnt half of the house and into the manor's south wing, where a formal dining room sat empty. High above my head, the gilded ceiling had been lovingly restored. A white drop cloth still covered the room's chandelier, and in the dim winter light, it looked like a phantom hovering in midair. In the corner was what had once been a butler's pantry. It hid a servants' staircase that led downstairs to a kitchen—an enormous Victorian food factory built to feed a few lucky masters and an army of servants. The appliances were modern, but the room still belonged to the past. The ceiling was low, the pots were all copper, and the floors were made of stone. Snow sealed the little windows that lined the walls above our heads, and the room was lit by the blaze in a fireplace large enough to roast a whole ox. A long wooden table ran almost the full length of the room. Miriam pulled out a chair for me.

"You might want to watch. This stove can be tricky. Your uncle still hasn't figured out how to use it." Then she paused and listened. "Speak of the devil. I think I hear him coming down now."

I couldn't help but feel a rush of excitement. I'd been devoted to James when I was little. My father had worked long hours at his architecture firm, and my mother hadn't taken to motherhood the way she'd hoped. I'd been a lonely child, and James had been the ideal playmate. Born seven years after my mother, he was everything she wasn't—charismatic, exciting, and fond of children. My grandparents had died in a car accident the summer James graduated from high school, and he'd taken his inheritance and set out to wander the globe. My mother once told me that she'd seen him twice in the five years between their parents' funeral and the day I was born. After that, he visited regularly. He brought me presents from faraway lands—giant fighting beetles, creepy dolls—each gift chosen to delight me and mortify his sister. A few times a year, he would whisk me away on a Saturday, telling my mother we were off to the library or the movies. Instead we'd head to the amusement park at Coney Island and gorge on hot dogs and cotton candy.

By the following Monday, James would be off again, and I would be left alone, eagerly waiting for his return.

I was nine when James came back to New York to stay. He married a young woman named Sarah, bought a town house a few blocks from ours, and started calling himself a businessman. My mother was thrilled that her baby brother had stopped burning through his inheritance and was finally getting serious. I was confused. It seemed like the person I'd known my whole life was pretending to be someone he wasn't. Before long, James's business started to struggle, and I barely saw him. When I did, he spent most of the time on his phone. My aunt Sarah did her best to make up for him. She had a job of her own, but she always found time for me. I thought she pitied me for losing the uncle I'd adored. I didn't realize that she'd lost him, too.

Then one day Sarah and my father died. Within a week, James was gone. He'd closed his company, sold his house, and disappeared. My mother was furious. I didn't hold it against him at first. Every night I prayed James would come back. We didn't hear from him for years.

Next thing we knew, James had bought an old mansion in the middle of nowhere and announced he was opening an inn. I begged my mother to take me to see him. We drove up for a visit and discovered him living in a hollowed-out ruin. I remember herds of mice stampeding down the halls and a goat living in one of the bedrooms. James and my mother fought at dinner, and she accused him of being selfish and irresponsible. That was the last time I saw him. My mom and I didn't even go to his second wedding. After our visit, she rarely even mentioned his name. She seemed determined to forget she'd ever had a brother. In my darkest moments, I'd wondered if the uncle I remembered had ever really existed.

Now the sound of footsteps was growing louder. I stood up straight and watched the doorway. I had no idea who I'd see. My whole body was buzzing with a blend of excitement and terror. When James finally appeared in front of me, I was glad Miriam had warned me that he'd changed. I'm not sure I'd have known who he was if she hadn't. His black hair was shot through with gray, and the scruff on his chin had gone white. I'd always thought of him as a giant. Now he appeared hunched over and hollowed out—like something was feeding on him from the inside. I couldn't help but notice that he'd added extra holes to his belt. Without them, the pants he was wearing would have collapsed around his ankles. In the years since I'd seen him, James had become an old man. Miriam was right. It took me by surprise. I hadn't expected to pity him.

"My God, you've grown up gorgeous." James drew me into a hug, and I was startled to feel ribs jutting out from his back. "I can't tell you how happy I am to see you."

I'd spent years daydreaming about this moment—the uncle I'd adored saving me from my mother and welcoming me into his home. But now that it was happening, it didn't feel right.

"Thanks for letting me stay," I said once I'd managed to break free.

"I'm delighted to have you, Bram. In fact, I'm sorry it's taken so long. I would have had you up here ages ago if your mother had allowed it. You know how difficult she is."

I did, which was why it had always been so hard to believe he'd abandoned me. I watched as James eased his body into a chair. When he looked up at me, he was practically beaming. He did seem happy to have me in his home.

"I'm making Bram some eggs and bacon," Miriam said. "Would you care for some?"

"No, thank you, Miriam," James replied. "I'll be fine with coffee."

I walked around the table and took a seat across from him.

"I spoke with your mother this morning," he announced. His tone made it clear that the conversation hadn't been pleasant. "She said you haven't been answering her calls."

"My phone died last night," I told him, remembering the creature I'd seen seconds before the word "MOTHER" had flashed on my phone's screen.

"Ah," he said as Miriam set a mug of coffee down for

him. "Well, give her a shout as soon as you're able, before she drives me completely batty."

"I will," I promised. *When I'm ready,* I added to myself.

"How did you sleep?" he asked, raising the mug to his lips.

Before I could answer, Miriam chimed in nervously. "I was meaning to tell you—I had to put Bram in the rose room last night."

James glanced up from his coffee to look at Miriam for the first time. His thick black eyebrows cast shadows over his eyes. "The rose room?"

"I'm sorry, James. The power was out. It was the only room I could get warm enough. I didn't want Bram to freeze to death."

James's eyes remained locked on the housekeeper. The only sound was the bacon sizzling on the stove. Miriam didn't cower or turn away from his glare. There seemed to be another conversation taking place—I just wasn't able to hear it. But one message came through loud and clear—there was something weird about the rose room.

"I know you had another room in mind for me," I said, "but I was wondering if it would be all right if I stayed put."

James's attention returned to me. "Isn't the rose room a bit frilly for you?" he asked. "You used to be such a tomboy."

"Did I?" I couldn't really remember what I'd been like

before he left New York, and I didn't know if it was the right time to tell him that tomboys were no longer a thing.

"Now that the power's back on, I do think the blue room would be better, Bram," Miriam hastened to say. "I've got it all ready for you."

"Sounds like she's already fallen in love," James said. "Don't forget your eggs, Miriam. It would be a shame if they burned."

Miriam took the hint to mind her own business and turned back to face the stove.

"What is it about the rose room that appeals to you?" James asked me.

"The painting on the wall," I told him. I saw Miriam freeze with her spatula in midair. For a moment, she and James remained perfectly still. They didn't even appear to be breathing.

Finally James spoke. "The painting? What about it?"

My mother always said I had a knack for finding trouble. I'd been at the manor for less than twelve hours, and I'd already crossed some invisible line. "I don't know," I said. "It's unusual. When I saw it this morning, it made me feel happy."

James had just taken a sip of coffee. "*Happy?*" He choked on the word. Miriam was approaching the table with my bacon and eggs on a plate. Her eyes were wide, and I knew I'd surprised her as well.

"Is that strange?" I asked.

"Did you tell her?" James asked Miriam.

Miriam seemed startled by the question. "No," the housekeeper said solemnly, placing a hand over her heart as though taking a pledge. "I didn't say a word."

James nodded. "Will you excuse us for a minute or two, Miriam? I think I should speak to my niece alone."

"Certainly." Miriam set the plate of food down on the table in front of me and scurried out of the room.

"What's going on?" I asked, my discomfort growing by the second. It was way too early for me to be rocking the boat.

James held up a finger and waited until Miriam's footsteps faded in the distance, before he finally continued. As I watched his finger, I could see it trembling, and I wondered if James might be ill. "I was hoping I wouldn't need to tell you until you'd settled in. There's a story about the mural in the rose room," he said. "If you live in Louth, you're bound to hear it. You might as well hear it from me."

I almost laughed at my luck. *Of course* there was a horrible story. I should have expected it.

"There's a girl in the painting," James said. "Did you see her?"

"Yes," I said, bracing myself. "Who is she?"

"Her name was Grace Louth."

"Louth? Like the town?"

James nodded. "Her father built the manor. The town is named after him. The rose room belonged to Grace while she lived here. In 1890, she drowned herself in the Hudson River. She was only eighteen years old. It was a terrible tragedy."

That was the last thing I'd been expecting to hear. "She killed herself? *Why?*" I could picture the girl's radiant face. I'd imagined her racing toward something wonderful. I was devastated to learn that she never made it.

James shrugged. "Why did girls drown themselves in rivers back then?" he asked, as if the answer were obvious. I couldn't figure out what it might be.

"I don't know," I said. "Why did they?"

"Heartbreak," he informed me. "Grace was planning to elope with a lover, but her father found out and bribed the fiancé to leave town. According to the legend, the painting shows Grace in her wedding dress, heading for the river the night she died."

I sat back in my chair and closed my eyes. If it was true, I'd been wrong about everything. The Grace Louth I'd seen on the wall was euphoric. Everyone else saw a desolate bride rushing toward her death. Either something was wrong with me—or with them.

"So don't be surprised if you hear people claim that the manor is cursed."

I cleared my throat and blinked my eyes. I could hardly believe the word had just left my uncle's lips. "Cursed?"

"A few days after Grace drowned, her father, Frederick Louth, was found dead of a heart attack in the rose room. People say Grace's ghost came back for revenge, and some believe this house has been cursed ever since."

"I don't believe in curses," I told him. I didn't believe in ghosts, either.

"Nor do I," James agreed emphatically. "I want you to know that. But there's been a great deal of gossip in town since Dahlia died. People think the curse was responsible for the fire that killed my wife. It wasn't, of course."

He paused for a moment, and I assumed that was the end of it.

"But her death did have something to do with the mural," he said.

That got my attention. "How?"

James stared down at the table before looking back up at me with red-rimmed eyes. "My stepdaughter, Lark, chose the rose room when she came to live here with her mother."

I felt a rush of excitement. We'd chosen the same room.

"Her father came from a family with a history of mental illness, and Lark had already begun to show signs of it when I met her. After Dahlia and I married, Lark's condition deteriorated. By the time of the fire, she'd gone mad."

"*Mad?*" The word caught me off guard. I knew he meant

"crazy," but outside of a nineteenth-century novel, I'd never heard anyone actually use the word "mad" that way before.

"I'm sorry," James said. "I know it sounds old-fashioned, but I don't know how else to describe her condition. Lark was always a little . . . unusual. But she didn't show many outward signs of mental illness until the end. About a month after she moved to the manor, she became obsessed with the girl in the mural. She spent hours and hours locked in her room, writing about Grace Louth. At night, she'd come out and wander the house. It was all so macabre. Eventually, Dahlia decided to send Lark to live with her father. We both hoped her mental state would improve after she left the manor."

"But it didn't?" I asked.

"No. The night the north wing burned, Lark broke into the manor while her mother and I were sleeping. The fire department believes the blaze started when a candle she was holding ignited a pair of drapes."

"So the fire was an accident?" I asked.

"It was ruled an accident, but I have my doubts. All we know is that the fire trapped Lark in a room in the north wing. Dahlia—" He stopped for a moment, too choked up to continue. Tears flowed freely down both sides of his face. "While I was phoning 911, Dahlia must have heard Lark's cries and run to help. Lark jumped from a window to escape the fire, but Dahlia never made it out. She died of smoke inhalation. The firemen found Lark wandering the grounds, raving about dead girls. When her condition didn't improve after she was released from the hospital, her father was forced to have her committed."

I took a moment to think it through.

"You think your stepdaughter burned your house down?" I just wanted to confirm that that was his account.

"I wish there were another explanation, but that's the only one that makes sense."

"I'm very sorry to hear that, Uncle James." I was. Very sorry.

"Thank you." He wiped his tears on his shirtsleeve before reaching across the table and taking my hand. "It helps to have you here. I know you have a lot on your plate, Bram, and I know bad things have happened. Your mother told me her side of the story, and I'm sure you have yours. I don't want you to think you have to deal with my worries, too. This should be a time of healing for both of us."

I didn't know what to say. I hadn't come to heal. The damage that had been done could not be reversed. Still, I nodded.

"You can choose any room you like. After everything I've told you, are you sure you still want to stay in the rose room?"

I nodded. "I am." I wanted to be where Lark had been.

James frowned. He'd hoped for another answer. "Then

you have my blessing to stay. There's only one thing I have to ask."

"Okay."

"Let's focus on life and let the dead rest peacefully in their graves. There's been too much tragedy in our lives, Bram. I don't think I can bear anymore. How about you?"

"No," I told him. "I've had enough, too."

He brushed my cheek with a knuckle. "You were always such a sweet little thing. I wish your father could be here to see you so grown-up and mature," he said. Then he took my hand. "I think we're going to get through all of this together, don't you?"

"I hope so," I told him. It wasn't a lie. There was honestly nothing I wanted more.

"Then I'll let Miriam know that the rose room is yours. You don't need to explain yourself—or tell her we had this conversation. In fact, the less you say to Miriam the better. The locals here love to gossip—and most of them are not fond of outsiders. There are a million crazy stories floating around about this place."

That was something I had no trouble believing.

Four

After breakfast, I went for another wander. This time, I checked out the devastation on the top floors of the north wing. The third-story rooms appeared to have sustained the most damage. The floorboards seemed so brittle that I worried I might plunge right through them. But the second story seemed safe for exploring. Pieces of charred furniture still stood where they had the night of the fire. But everything was black—as if the rooms had been hosed down with an industrial paint sprayer. So, when I entered the final chamber, my eyes were instantly drawn to a splash of yellow on what must have once been a small table. A fresh box of safety matches lay beside it.

All candles look alike, but the moment I picked it up,

there was no doubt in my mind that the candle was the same one that Miriam had given me the previous night. I could see the half-moon marks where my fingernails had dug into it. It wasn't until that moment that I remembered falling asleep with it lit. The candle should have burned all the way down. But it hadn't. Instead it had found its way to the other side of the manor.

Someone *had* been in my room—and they'd returned after I had fallen asleep. I'd known that coming to Louth might not be safe, but I'd figured I would have a few days to settle in before things got dangerous. The candle felt like a warning, and the sight of it made my skin crawl. I left it right where I'd found it, and told myself I'd have to be more careful. But I didn't even consider changing rooms. The rose room was where I needed to be.

As I made my way back out of the burnt wing, I stopped in a room with plywood panels nailed to the wall where a pair of French doors should have been. The wind whistled through a thin crack between two of the panels, and a thin sliver of daylight cut across the floor. I put my eye to the opening and saw that the snow had resumed falling. Fat, lazy flakes settled on the railing of a little balcony on the other side of the plywood. It was a twin of the balcony outside the rose room. Six months earlier, Lark Bellinger had jumped from that very spot.

I knew all about Lark. I had for months.

I'd been under house arrest in Manhattan when the manor had burned. My mother hadn't said a word. I'd had to read about the tragedy in the *New York Times*. The story was too juicy to be passed up—even by the most serious newspapers. I suppose I should have been grateful. If not for all the lurid details, I never would have known.

Even the *Times* coverage read like the plot of a movie. A wealthy former Manhattanite spends years restoring an old Hudson Valley mansion. He marries a beautiful local woman, and she and her teenage daughter move in. A few months later, the mansion catches fire, and the new bride tragically dies trying to save her daughter. The girl is later discovered outside on the grounds, raving unintelligibly. Police claim she sustained a serious head injury after jumping from a balcony on the second floor. No one could explain why she was at the mansion in the middle of the night when she'd recently been sent to live with her father nearby.

I'd studied the pictures that accompanied the articles. I even pulled them off websites and made my own file. The makeup and piercings didn't fool me. Lark had tried so hard to make herself look tough. That wasn't what I saw at all. What I saw was a girl just like me.

The newspapers never mentioned what happened to Lark after the fire. I had to ask my mother. "The girl lost her mind," I was told. "She started a fire that killed her mother. They had to send her away."

That was when I knew there was something wrong with the story. It sounded like a million old tales I'd been told—simple and tragic with a clear villain and victim. But in the real world, girls don't just lose their minds. If they kill their mothers or beat up their boyfriends or burn down their houses, they tend to have reasons. So when it became clear I couldn't stay in Manhattan, I suggested that my mother send me to Louth. She would have preferred I go to a boarding school where no one had heard of me. I knew that would be pointless. No matter where I went, my shame would soon follow. My own innocence would never be proven, and my reputation couldn't be salvaged. But I thought maybe, if I went to Louth, I could find out what had really happened to Lark.

I was still standing with my eye pressed to the crack between the boards when I heard footsteps enter the room. I figured it was Miriam coming to find me. I wasn't going to let her startle me again. I stayed right where I was.

"Do you need something?" I asked.

There was no answer. I heard the footsteps stop and turn back the way they'd come. As I listened, a strange thought entered my mind. The footsteps sounded softer than they should have—as though the person behind me weren't wearing shoes. I spun around to look, but there was no one there.

Five

At lunchtime I pulled on my boots and headed outside, toward the town of Louth. Even with all the snow on the ground, it took less than twenty minutes to see all the sights. The manor sat on top of a hill. The Hudson River flowed in the valley below. Between the hill and the Hudson were five streets that ran parallel to the river, each one no more than a few blocks long. The first streets I strolled down were lined with old houses. Most were in various states of disrepair, but every fourth or fifth house looked like something you'd see on Instagram. And there were always a couple of houses on each street that were under construction. It was like a virus was spreading through all the old wood, slowly turning the town into a rich people's retreat. When I hit the fourth street, I saw just how far the disease had progressed. Grace Street (named after my new dead friend, I later discovered) was Louth's sad excuse for a commercial thoroughfare—three blocks long, with little shops on both sides. Half were the sort of shops you'd expect to see in a tiny town on the banks of the Hudson River—stores that sold crap people might actually need. The rest of the storefronts showcased pine-infused chocolate bars and cashmere pajamas that cost four hundred dollars.

I stopped outside a bakery that looked like it had last been decorated in the 1950s. The sign above the door read COLUMBO in a swooping cursive font, and the white lace curtains in the window were yellow with age. Some of the pastries behind the glass looked like they might date from the fifties, too. But the aroma wafting from the shop was delightful, and I could see a plate of fresh croissants on the counter. That was exactly what I was after.

I opened the door to the sound of laughter. No one was manning the register, but I could hear two women chatting away in the kitchen at the back of the store. "Hello?" I called out.

"Right with you!" a cheery voice replied. Then a woman in a hairnet and apron emerged, wiping her hands on a paper napkin. She and her co-worker must have been having their lunch. "What can I—" she started to say. Then she froze and came to a complete stop. I'd inspired some pretty dark feelings in my day, but I'd never had anyone refuse to look at me. The woman kept her gaze fixed on a point just over my left shoulder.

"What can I get for you?" she asked, her voice chilly but polite.

I wanted to leave, but I refused to let her get the better of me. "A croissant, please." I could feel my hands shaking inside my coat pockets, and I hoped she couldn't tell.

"For here or to go?"

I'd planned to sit at one of the café tables near the window. "To go," I said.

She dropped the roll into a little brown bag and took my money. As soon as the transaction was over, she disappeared into the kitchen, leaving me alone in the shop. Soon I could hear two women whispering.

My cheeks flushed with humiliation, I started for the door. Then I stopped. Standing just on the other side of the bakery's window was a guy my age. He wore a long, black coat and held a steaming cup of coffee in one hand. He looked amused, and I realized he must have been watching the entire time.

I wasn't going to stand there and let him mock me. I stomped out of the bakery.

"Don't take it personally. The locals don't like people like us," he said as I brushed past him on the sidewalk.

"Excuse me?" I paused and spun around to face him. He was handsome, with floppy black hair and dancing dark eyes framed by expensive glasses. My first impression was that he seemed reasonably intelligent and extremely rich. I'm sure most girls would have been thrilled to have him strike up a conversation. I was not one of those girls.

He pointed to the bag in my hand. "There's a café called JOE just down the street. You can get some coffee to go with that. Want me to show you?"

"No, thanks," I said. "I can find it on my own."

As I walked away, I heard only the crunch of my own boots on the snow. I didn't let myself glance over my shoulder, but I knew he was still standing there watching me.

I couldn't have missed JOE if I'd tried. The café looked like a tornado had picked it up somewhere in Brooklyn and dropped it down in the middle of Louth. The barista, with his designer flannel shirt rolled up to display his tattoos, was clearly a transplant. There was only one other customer inside the café—a girl in a black fur coat and black sunglasses. Her lips were painted a brilliant red, and they'd left a crimson smudge on the teacup in front of her. She sat so still that she could have been mistaken for a mannequin. I couldn't see the eyes behind her glasses, but I could sense them staring at me. I'd been in Louth for less than twenty-four hours, and I'd already become the town freak.

"Hey!" The barista greeted me like I was his long-lost best friend, and I almost backed out the door. "What can I get for you?"

"Coffee," I said, hoping the conversation would end there. It didn't.

"You in for the weekend?" the guy asked as he filled my cup.

"Yeah. And all the weekends after that," I said. Out of the corner of my eye, I saw the girl lift the teacup to her lips.

"Ah," said the guy, nodding and grinning like he'd been hitting the peyote before I arrived. "Gotcha. So where are you staying?"

"Up at the manor. With my uncle."

"So you're the niece! James mentioned you were coming to visit."

"He did?" That seemed very unlike him. It was hard to imagine my frail-looking uncle leaving the manor to make small talk with the locals.

Suddenly there was a loud clatter in the dining area. I glanced over to see that the girl in the fur coat was mopping up spilled tea. The barista rushed over to her table with a handful of napkins. As they cleaned up the mess, he said nothing to the girl, and she said nothing to him.

"You know James?" I asked once he'd returned, trying to imagine my uncle befriending a guy with a man bun and a tattoo of Dolly Parton.

The guy snorted. "Sure. James is a legend—a pioneer. Dude practically discovered Louth. I don't think there was anyone for miles around when he got here."

"I don't understand," I said, frowning. "The town's been here for over a century."

"Oh yeah," the guy said. "There were *people* here for sure. I was talking about folks like *us*."

"Folks like us?" I asked. The guy outside the bakery had said something similar. I'd never considered myself a "folk," and I couldn't wait to hear what I had in common with Paul Bunyan's hipster brother.

"You know—from the city. There are a bunch of us here now—and all over the county. In the summer you'll probably see everyone you know."

God, I hoped not. "In *Louth*?"

"Well, in Hudson anyway. Louth's still a bit off the beaten path," he said. "But once your uncle's inn opens, that ought to change. We were all thinking it was going to happen this summer. But I suppose it's gonna take a little more time now."

A little more time. Ha! "Yeah, I think that's pretty safe to say," I told him. "The place is a wreck."

"You up here to help James get it back into shape?"

"Sure," I told him as I picked up my coffee. "That's exactly why I'm here."

I chose a table on the other side of the café from the girl in the fur coat—and a seat facing in the opposite direction. Just as I was taking my first bite of croissant, the chair across from me was dragged out, and suddenly the girl was sitting in front of me.

"Hello," she said as she took off her glasses. She wore no makeup aside from lipstick. She didn't need to. Her eyes were a startling green. I wondered if she always kept her secret weapons hidden behind shades. "I'm Maisie."

I swallowed the lump of croissant in my mouth and washed it down with coffee. "Bram," I said. I didn't know what she wanted, but I knew she was after something. Girls like Maisie didn't usually sign up for the welcoming committee.

"I heard you talking to Jeb. You're the girl who's going to be living up at the manor." It wasn't a question. She knew who I was. They all did.

"Word gets around fast," I said.

Maisie smiled flirtatiously. "Welcome to our little fishbowl," she said. Then she pointed a red-tipped finger at my lunch. "How'd you get that? Jeb told me he was out of croissants."

"I bought it at the bakery. The lady there wasn't very

nice to me, so I came here to eat it. Apparently, the locals don't like people like us."

"I'm a local," said the girl. Her smile widened.

"Really?" I found that hard to believe.

"Born and raised." She leaned back in her chair and crossed her legs. Her fur coat parted, and I saw she was wearing what looked like a silk nightgown underneath. Above her tall snow boots, her skin was bare and exposed to midthigh. She gave the impression of someone who'd fled disaster in the dark of night. I imagined her arriving on the Hudson's shore in a lifeboat, the only survivor of a luxurious ship that had sunk to the bottom of an icy sea.

I glanced up at a clock on the café wall. "Do you go to school here?" I asked. People our age were usually fully dressed by noon on a Monday.

"Not when it's midwinter break," she replied. "School's out for the rest of the week. How come you don't know that?"

"I'm done with school," I informed her.

"You graduated?"

"Not exactly," I said. "But I'm not going back."

"Interesting. So how long are you planning to hang out here in Louth?"

I wondered if there was an answer she was hoping to hear. "I have no idea," I told her.

"Hmmm," she said meaningfully. I waited for her to say more.

"What?" I asked when she didn't.

"You're not scared?"

"Scared?" I asked. So she wasn't there to welcome me, after all. She had another motive.

"You must know what happened up there," Maisie said. "A woman died a few months ago. Dahlia Bellinger."

"Yes, I know," I said. Did she really think that fact had somehow escaped me? "She was my uncle's wife."

"She wasn't the first."

"No, she was his second wife," I said.

Maisie cocked her head as if I'd accidentally let something slip. "I meant Dahlia wasn't the first person to die in the manor."

James had warned me about the stories floating around. I hadn't expected to hear them on my first day in town. "Are you talking about Grace Louth?" I asked.

"Among others," Maisie replied.

Now this strange girl had my undivided attention. "What others?"

"Including Lark Bellinger's mother, three women have died at the manor over the years."

Suddenly I was much more intrigued by the living. "Did you know Lark?" The diva and the goth would have made an odd pair, but I could see how they might get along. Morbid girls have a way of finding each other.

"I've known her since kindergarten," Maisie confirmed.

"Were you friends?"

"Were?" The word had a bite. "*She's* not dead. But we haven't hung out much since she got locked up in Hastings. That's a hospital for the mentally ill, in case you didn't know."

I did know. I also knew what had put a tremor in Maisie's voice and why she kept her hands clasped together to keep them from shaking. It wasn't fear that made her jaw quiver. It was rage. What had happened to Lark infuriated her.

"You don't think she should be there?" I asked carefully.

"Lark Bellinger is as sane as I am," Maisie insisted. "At least, she was until she moved into that house."

"What are you saying?" It sounded to me like something had happened to Lark at the manor. I wondered what Maisie knew.

"I'm saying you need to be very careful, Bram Howland. I don't know why you've come here, but you'd be better off back in Manhattan. Louth isn't a good place for people like us—and the manor's the worst place of all." Maisie rose from the table and slid her sunglasses back on.

"Us? I thought you were a local," I said, looking up at her.

"I meant *female*," she said.

I hadn't expected the conversation to take that particular turn, but if Maisie had been hoping to shock me, she must have been disappointed. I wasn't easy to shock.

I waited for Maisie to stomp away then, but she didn't. She stood there frozen, staring past me, as though she were engaged in a silent argument with someone I couldn't see. When she spoke again, the anger in her voice had been replaced by fatigue. "There are three houses down by the water. I live in the second one. If you ever need help, come and find me."

I watched from the window as she trudged outside. Stray flakes dislodged by the wind collected on her black hair and coat. Then I picked up my empty coffee cup and made my way to the trash can.

"Wow, that sounded intense," the barista said as I walked past the counter.

"Excuse me?" I'd never heard anyone confess so casually to eavesdropping. "Were you listening to our conversation?"

"Couldn't help it. Small place, small town. Listen, don't let Maisie scare you away. She's known around Louth for being . . . troubled."

I could see the need on his face. He wanted so badly for me to ask. He couldn't wait for an opportunity to share all the juicy tidbits he'd gathered.

"Good," I told him. "Troubled people are the only ones you can trust."

I walked a few blocks to the river and stood at the end of a dock that stretched out over the water. The first time I saw a picture of Manhattan island surrounded by ice, I was convinced it couldn't be real. Then my father told me it used to happen most winters. You could walk all the way across the frozen Hudson River from Manhattan to the mainland. The winter my dad died, I kept my eyes on the Hudson whenever I rode down the West Side Highway. I swore to myself that if it ever froze over, I'd spring out at a stoplight and make my escape. It never happened.

In Louth, the same river seemed impossibly wide, and despite the fact that the air was bitter cold, the water in the middle was still moving freely. Floating along the banks were circular patches of ice that resembled translucent lily pads. It was tempting to think you might be able to hop from one to the next. But I was already starting to suspect that escaping from Louth would be no easy feat. I believed Maisie when she'd said that the place was dangerous. But it made no difference to me. I wasn't going anywhere until I had the answers I needed, and I had absolutely nothing to lose.

When I finally turned back toward home, I noticed three gorgeous old houses perched on a hill looking over the river just north of town. Though none of them were as big or seemed quite as old as my uncle's manor, they'd weathered the years with far more grace. The first house on the row looked empty, but smoke billowed from the chimneys of the other two. Maisie had mentioned she lived in the second one. A figure in a black coat was walking down the riverside road. It was the guy I'd seen outside the bakery. There was nothing else in that direction. Perhaps he was paying my new friend a visit—or maybe he called the other house home.

Six

The sun had briefly peeked out from behind the clouds while I stood on the dock, but as I made my way back to the manor, the wind picked up speed and dark clouds gathered over the forest. The weather was growing wilder and the temperature was plunging. I realized I needed to get home in a hurry.

The road narrowed outside of town, and trees crowded together at the edge of the asphalt. A sharp crack echoed like a gunshot in the woods, and I heard a branch plummet to the ground somewhere out of sight. Others followed as trees sacrificed limbs to the ice, snow, and wind. I had almost reached the drive to the house when I heard a vehicle approaching from behind. I stepped to the side of the road, and a battered pickup rolled past. Three large men had crammed themselves into the cab. The truck slowed almost to a stop as the men craned their necks for a look at me. I suddenly realized where I was—out in the middle of nowhere all alone. My panic surged when I remembered I'd left my phone charging in the rose room. I couldn't even call for help if I needed to.

When the truck disappeared around a curve in the road, I slipped into the woods to hide. A few seconds later, it returned, just as I had suspected it would. It came to a stop right where I'd been standing.

"Hello!" a man shouted. "You out there? You need a ride?"

I was crouched behind a snow-covered stump a few feet from the road, shivering and praying they wouldn't spot my frozen breath.

"You think it was one of the dead girls?" I heard one of the other men say. The other two didn't laugh. It wasn't a joke.

"Don't be stupid," the first responded. "That was Howland's niece."

The window went up, and the vehicle drove off. I waited until I heard nothing but the wail of the wind and the crackling of the icy forest around me. Avoiding the road, I trudged through the snow between the trees until I reached the manor's drive.

Maisie had said Louth was no place for people like us. I wondered if she'd had men like that in mind. My heart was still battering my ribs, and my mouth had gone dry. The metallic taste of fear coated my tongue. Maybe they hadn't intended to scare me. Maybe they'd only meant to get me out of the cold. Maybe I could have trusted them. But I knew that there was a dangerous gap beneath every leap of faith. I'd fallen in once. I wasn't going to let it happen again.

The weather only got worse while I climbed the hill. When I reached the top and saw the manor waiting, I felt almost giddy with relief. I didn't believe in curses, and I didn't give a damn if the house was haunted. The man in the truck had spoken of dead girls with a respect I doubt he'd have shown to any living young woman. I assumed he was referring to the girls Maisie had mentioned. If so, he was scared for the same reason that I wasn't frightened at all. The living terrified me, but I didn't fear ghosts. The dead are supposed to be buried and dealt with. But they don't always go away. That's what I was counting on—and what terrified him.

As I walked toward the house, the sun began to dim. There didn't appear to be any lights on inside, and it occurred to me that there might be no one home. I tried the front door, and it was locked. For the first time, I noticed the number of keyholes along the edge of the door. A few appeared to be brand-new—as did the digital keypad above the bell. It seemed unusual for an inn to have so much security. The whole idea was to invite people inside. I wondered who my uncle was trying to keep out.

I pressed the bell and waited, but no one answered. I hadn't explored the mansion enough to know where the other entrances could be. I stepped back from the doorway and looked up at the house. The ivy clinging to the façade seemed to writhe in the wind. Where the snow had fallen away, I could see that its serpentine vines remained a vibrant green. I was reaching out a hand to touch it when movement on the far side of the grounds caught my eye. A bulky figure in a dark down coat was heading toward me. He wore a knit cap and a scarf pulled up over his nose.

There was nowhere to go. I looked around for a weapon, and all I could find was a snow shovel leaning against a wall. I grabbed it and turned. "What do you want?" I demanded.

He pulled his scarf down, revealing the chiseled jaw of an old-school superhero. "I'm Sam," he said.

"Miriam's son?" he added when he saw that the name hadn't registered. "I watched you come up the drive. Mom's at the store and your uncle is out. I figured you might not be able to get inside." He pulled out a ring of keys so large, it resembled a medieval weapon.

I relaxed a little, but not completely. "Why do you have keys to my house?" I asked, wondering if he'd been the one I'd heard sneaking around the manor the previous night.

"I work here," he said politely, but in a tone that made it clear I was out of line.

"Sorry." I felt like an ass. "I'm Bram."

"Yeah, I know," he replied. He seemed to have no interest in me. I liked that about him.

"I'm a little on edge. Some local guys scared the hell out of me on the way here."

Sam left a key dangling in the third lock and looked over at me. "What did they do?" he asked.

I hesitated. I knew how it was going to sound. "Offered me a ride."

He nodded and got back to work. "On a freezing cold day in the middle of winter. Definitely serial killers," he said with a perfectly straight face as he continued to open the door one lock at a time.

"Are you making fun of me?" I really wasn't sure.

"I'm just kidding. This isn't New York City. No one from Louth is out to get you." He made me feel ridiculous.

"That's not what I heard," I shot back. I didn't appreciate being treated like an idiot.

"Oh yeah? From who?"

"A girl named Maisie. She told me I should be careful."

"That's probably good advice," said Sam. "Maisie knows

a thing or two. But so do I, and I stand by what I said. You don't have to worry about anyone from Louth. I can't speak for anyone else, though."

Sam opened the last lock, tapped a code into the security pad, and opened the door. "Here you go," he said, holding a cluster of keys out to me. "Keep them until you get your own set. The code for the door is ten-oh-eight-eighty-two. He changes it every week."

I felt the blood drain out of my face. "What was the code?"

"Ten-oh-eight-eighty-two." His eyes widened and he reached out an arm to steady me. "Are you okay?"

"That was my aunt Sarah's birthday," I said. Why would he have chosen that number, though? Was it meant to be an expression of love? Or was it a message? And if so, was it meant for me?

"Was Sarah James's first wife?" Sam asked. "Were the two of you close?"

"I'm really sorry," I told him, pulling my arm free from his grip. "I need to go."

"Hey, wait!" he called out as I walked away.

I turned back, thinking maybe he knew something about Sarah.

"You should leave the shovel here," he said. "If you ever get snowed in, I'll need it to dig you out."

I'd forgotten all about the shovel. I went back and set it

against the wall. The last thing I wanted was to be sealed inside.

I ran up the stairs to the rose room, but stopped just inside the door. The suitcase I'd left standing against the wall was now on the floor. The zipper was open less than an inch. I'm sure most people wouldn't have noticed, but I'd spent seventeen years with the world's biggest snoop, and I always knew when someone had been through my things. I spotted my phone charging on the bedside table. I'd left it face-down as always. Now it was lying faceup. When I opened my suitcase, I could tell that the contents had shifted ever so slightly. I picked up a bra that I knew for a fact had been tucked into the side of my suitcase. Someone had moved it while I was gone. I looked back at the open door that led to the hall. Once again, I felt the strange sensation that some-one was watching me.

The phone rang, and I jumped up and rushed for the door. I slammed it, locked it, and stood there staring at it while the phone continued to ring. I didn't need to look at the caller ID. There was only one person it could be—everyone else had been blocked. I caught my breath and then answered.

"I've been phoning all day! Why haven't you called me?" my mother demanded.

"I'm sorry," I told her. "My phone was dead, and I've been getting to know my new home."

"After everything that's happened, when you don't let me know you're okay, I imagine the worst," my mother answered.

And what would *that* be? I wanted to ask her, but I didn't dare. My mother's voice was my kryptonite. No matter what words she chose, the message was always the same. I was incompetent, immature—a danger to myself and everyone around me. "I'm sorry," I said instead.

"Well, I spent last night worried about you when I should have been networking. The gala was a big success, by the way. We raised over five million dollars for abandoned pets. Can you believe it?"

"Congratulations," I said. "I know your pets are like children to you."

"I hope you're not being funny," she said.

"Of course not," I insisted. "I would never joke about my siblings."

She seemed to accept this. "Everyone was there," she said. "We didn't have a single no-show."

"Not even the Lanes?" I asked.

"Not only were the Lanes there," she said, her voice swelling with pride, "but they were among the night's biggest donors. They gave a hundred and twenty-five thousand dollars."

"So does that mean I can come home when I'm ready?"

During the pause that followed, I dug my nails into the palm of my hand.

"Bram—"

"Never mind," I said. "Forget I asked."

"Bram, darling, I promise things will be back to normal eventually. But the wounds are still fresh, and all the old temptations are still here. You're going to need more time. We all need more time."

"More time without me."

"Bram—"

I'd only been yanking her chain. I hadn't been serious. But now I could feel hot tears trickling burning trails down my cheeks. I tried not to sniffle. To keep my voice steady. I didn't want her to know she still had that kind of power over me.

"By the way, I think James has told people why I'm really here," I said.

"Told them *what*?" My mother's tone of voice could turn on a dime.

"All of it," I lied.

"He has?" I imagined the look of horror on her face, and I grinned.

"Yep. I think he even told the maid."

"The *maid*?" Then the panic left her voice. I'd pushed it too far. "Very funny, Bram."

I wiped my face. "Maybe I'll tell them all."

"Don't you dare," she whispered. "Don't tell a soul."

Those were the words I'd been waiting for. I didn't plan to tell anyone. I just wanted to hear her say it again.

"The Lanes agreed not to press charges, Bram. But that could change. This is your future we're talking about, darling."

"I know," I told her.

I was only playing along with her game. We both knew I didn't have a future.

Seven

After that phone call, I just wanted to be alone. I was sick of the living, so I spent the rest of the afternoon with Grace Louth. She might have been dead for more than a century, but she'd clearly left an indelible mark on the town that bore her name. By all accounts, Lark had found her fascinating, which meant I needed to get to know Grace, too.

According to countless "Beyond the Grave" websites, Grace Louth drowned in the Hudson, just as my uncle James had told me. Over the years, I'd read a hundred stories just like hers. Grace was secretly engaged to a boy who'd "stolen her flower." When her father found out about the impending nuptials, he paid the young man to leave town. Just as her father had predicted, the young man then outed himself as a scoundrel by immediately marrying another woman. So Grace did what any self-respecting girl would have done. She put on her wedding dress, ran into town, and threw herself into the river. Her bridal veil was discovered days later, tangled up in a tree branch that had washed up onshore twenty miles south of Louth.

I found a dozen versions of the tale, but all agreed on the cause of death. Heartbreak had led poor Grace Louth to suicide. Judging by all the spooky stories I'd read over the years, that seemed to be how lots of ladies kicked the bucket back in the day. At least that's what people liked to believe. Driven insane by betrayal, girls got gussied up in their wedding dresses and threw themselves into rivers. Afterward, they'd curse the houses where they'd suffered so horribly. It was a simple tale readers could all wrap our heads around. No one ever asked what had really happened, of course. The truth always got buried along with the girls.

Grace's story took an unusual turn following her fatal plunge. Shortly after her death, a sharp-eyed mourner noticed something odd about the mural in her bedroom. In the summer, weeks before she'd died, Grace's father had hired an artist to decorate the walls with a pastoral scene. That's how the mural in my bedroom had been painted. Apparently, when the artist had finished, Frederick Louth had found the nighttime scene a bit odd, but the artist's work was so lovely, he hadn't complained. Long after the artist had finished, and days after Frederick Louth's only daughter had died, a guest pointed to a small figure in the otherwise deserted landscape. It was a portrait of Grace. Dressed in a white gown, she was running down the hill toward the river, her long blond hair streaming behind her. No one doubted that the mural showed the girl on the night she died.

Some said the portrait, painted weeks before Grace's death, had been a prophecy of the tragedy yet to come. Others swore up and down that the girl didn't show up on the wall until after Grace died. Many attempts were made to locate the artist, but the person appeared to have vanished into thin air. Over the days that followed, the manor's servants became convinced that Grace's restless spirit remained in Louth Manor. They claimed she would emerge from the painting after dark and roam the halls. Then, late one night, Frederick Louth was found dead in the rose room. The doctors said he'd suffered a heart attack trying to pry the plaster off the walls.

Aside from the mural, which I'd seen for myself, there was one more thing that made Grace's story different. Photographic evidence. On the day of Grace's funeral, a newspaper sent a photographer to capture the manor. There was no one home at the time the picture was taken—the residents and staff were all at church. And yet there seemed to be a fuzzy figure standing behind the rose room windows.

When I squinted, it almost looked like a young woman in a wedding dress.

Is this the ghost of mad Grace Louth? asked the caption. That's when I put down the phone and stopped reading. *Mad.* The word hadn't left my head since James had used it. I liked it. It was such a shame, I thought, that the term had gone out of fashion. I couldn't think of another that fit me so perfectly.

I was mad that everyone had called me unhinged. I was mad I'd been told I couldn't trust my own eyes. I was mad that I'd ever questioned myself. I was mad that they might have gotten away with it all. But I wasn't crazy. And I was convinced that Lark and Grace hadn't been, either.

I slid off the bed and found Grace's portrait on the wall. I stood there and studied it. I still could have sworn she looked thrilled. I didn't know her real story. And no one knew mine. But I suddenly didn't feel quite so alone. There were three of us now.

Three mad girls.

Eight

Around six that evening, I heard a knock. My eyes moved to the door, and I watched the handle twist back and forth in vain. I knew the door wouldn't open. I'd locked it and wedged a chair under the knob.

"It's Miriam," the housekeeper called through the wood. "I came to see if you'd like some dinner."

I looked out the windows. It was dark outside. The croissant at the café was the last thing I'd eaten. I'd been so immersed in Grace Louth's legend that I hadn't realized I was famished.

"Give me a sec to get dressed, and I'll be right down!" I shouted. There were only three people who could have rifled through my stuff while I was in Louth that afternoon.

Miriam was my top suspect. Number two on the list was her son. The Reinharts weren't to be trusted, and I didn't want Miriam to hear me removing the barricade from my door.

Downstairs the kitchen was lit by the flames from the fireplace. Miriam had taken the seat closest to the stove. Sam sat silently at the head of the table. The browned carcass of a chicken claimed center stage.

"Where's my uncle?" I asked as I pulled out a chair.

"He and his business partner had a meeting in the city," Miriam informed me. "They said they would be back later."

"His business partner?" It was the first I'd heard that such a person existed.

"A man named Gavin Turner," Miriam said, passing me a bowl of roasted potatoes. "He's an investor in the inn. James made him a partner not long after the fire."

"Why would James need investors?" I asked. My mother always said her brother hadn't been born with a head for business. But he *had* been born rich, and so had Sarah. After she'd died, he'd left the city with a sizable fortune.

Sam regarded me with a bemused expression as I served myself some of the chicken. "We don't know. We're just your uncle's servants," he said bluntly.

It was such a strange thing to say. James had some

notable faults, but snobbery had never been one of them. I almost wondered if we were talking about the same person. I realized I must have rubbed Sam the wrong way that afternoon. Maybe he'd heard me on my call with my mother. Or maybe he just didn't care for outsiders.

"How was your first day in Louth?" Miriam asked, to change the subject. "Did you do anything interesting?"

"Well, let's see," I said, pausing for dramatic effect. "I got snubbed by a lady at the bakery, had two people warn me that Louth isn't a good place for me, got scared by some guys in a pickup who wanted to either help me or murder me. I also found out that the manor might be cursed and that the ghost of Grace Louth killed a man in my room. So, yeah, I'd say it was a pretty interesting day."

Miriam and Sam shared a look. I suppose they'd been expecting typical chitchat. They would learn soon enough that there was nothing typical about me.

"Why didn't anyone tell me that the manor's so famous?" I pressed them. "No wonder Lark was fascinated by Grace Louth."

Neither of the Reinharts uttered a word. Miriam kept her lips primly sealed, and Sam glowered at me as if I'd gone somewhere I didn't belong.

"Sorry, but we've been asked not to speak about what happened to Lark or her mother," he said. "James doesn't want any more gossip, and we don't want to lose our jobs."

I looked at his mother and lifted an eyebrow. If that was the rule, she'd already broken it.

"James wouldn't fire you for something like that. Besides, I'm family."

"Your uncle didn't make any exceptions," Sam said.

"Then how about Grace? Can you talk about her?" I was growing frustrated.

Sam opened his mouth, but before he could speak, his mother laid a hand on his forearm. She had something she wanted to say. "The manor is not cursed, if that's what you're wondering," she told me.

Sam shot her a side-eye.

"How can you be sure?" I asked, interested to hear what she'd say.

"Members of my family have worked in this house from the day it was built to the day it was abandoned over a hundred years later. No one ever saw any evidence of a curse."

I figured I'd play devil's advocate. "You were the one who demanded I come to you if I ever saw anything unusual. Now you're telling me this place *isn't* cursed or haunted?"

"A house doesn't need ghosts to be haunted," Sam said.

That caught me off guard. I wasn't sure what he meant.

"Can we *please* find something a little more uplifting to discuss?" Miriam sounded frazzled. "I think I've had more than enough death for one lifetime."

The good subjects were always the ones no one wanted

to discuss, of course. I could tell by the look on Miriam's face that I was definitely onto something. If the Reinharts didn't believe in curses or ghosts, what *did* they think had happened to Lark? I knew I wasn't going to find out anything more that night. We tried a few other topics, but none of them seemed to stick. A half hour later, dinner was over and cleanup began. I cleared the table while Miriam loaded the dishwasher and Sam put the leftovers away. No one spoke a single word.

While Miriam and Sam stayed behind in the kitchen, I took a nighttime tour of the top three floors of the manor. I couldn't bring myself to explore the basement. I had a deep-seated fear of underground spaces, and the thought of what might lie beneath the old house repelled me. I knew I couldn't avoid the basement forever, but I planned to save that adventure for daytime. After leaving the Reinharts, I started on the first floor and worked my way up. I explored thirty-six rooms in all—from the formal dining room to the servants' quarters on the third floor.

The south wing of the manor wouldn't have looked out of place in a palace. The wooden floors featured intricate inlays. James had chosen the finest carpets and papered the walls with richly colored prints. No expense had been spared when he'd purchased the furnishings. The rooms were as lush and luxurious as they must have been in Frederick Louth's day. I imagined young Grace twirling under the chandeliers and racing down the grand hallways. It was hard to believe the entire mansion had been home to a family of three. I'm sure from the outside, Grace Louth looked like a princess. But I knew just how empty a big house can feel to a little girl.

As I moved through the mansion, I kept count of the rooms that were locked. There were four, including my uncle James's bedroom. Inside the chambers I was able to visit, I opened wardrobes and peeked into closets. The only sound was that of my footsteps on the floorboards. Some of the rooms were only dimly lit, and when I reached the north wing, there were no lights at all. I'll admit I was a little bit frightened—though not of curses or ghosts. There were times when I was sure I wasn't alone. I felt a presence in the manor, but I kept on going. The house knew the truth about the girls who'd lived there, and I was determined to make the manor share its secrets with me.

Eventually I ended my tour in the conservatory on the ground floor. The walls and ceiling were composed of thousands of perfectly cut pieces of antique glass set in a cast-iron frame so delicate that it looked like it could have been spun by a spider. The décor was vaguely Indian, with teak furniture and raw-silk upholstery that had faded a bit in the light. It seemed like no one had visited in the months since the fire. The plants in the boxes along the glass walls had all shriveled up and expired. The tall palm in the center of the room was as brown as a paper bag. Only a cactus in a concrete planter was thriving. Red flowers were bursting out of its prickly pads like little baby aliens.

Outside, the darkness pressed against the conservatory on three sides, and snow climbed its glass walls. The moon was out, and I could see the grounds behind the manor and the outline of the trees at the edge of the woods. The view couldn't have been lovelier. Then I noticed a line of strange holes that led across the snow-covered lawn from the woods to the manor. They were footprints—and they looked fresh.

A pinpoint of light drew my eyes to the forest. As I watched, it seemed to brighten and dim like a star or a flickering flame. Someone had recently come to the manor. And someone—or something—was still out there in the woods.

Nine

The next morning, before I'd even had breakfast, I set out to discover the source of the light I'd seen the night before. As soon as I slipped into the forest behind the manor, I realized it wasn't as wild as the woods on the way to town. The trees all appeared perfectly pruned, as if they were part of the manor's gardens. *In the summer,* I thought, *this must be a magical place.*

I shuffled through the snow until I reached a clearing. In the center, a stone mausoleum sat at the end of an ice-covered pool. Planters on either side of a grand wooden door held bouquets of frozen flowers that looked ready to shatter with a single touch. The snow surrounding the building had been shoveled aside, forming a tall white wall around it. As I watched, Sam emerged from the woods to my left with a bundle of twigs under his arm. He opened the door, and I saw that hidden windows lit the interior. I watched him arrange the twigs on a pyre and set them ablaze. The mausoleum's fire was the source of the light I'd seen the previous night.

I was planning to slip away unseen. I knew I hadn't made much of an impression on Sam, and the feeling was mutual. Then he emerged from the mausoleum and caught sight of me standing there. I saw him flinch—and watched the relief wash over his face when he realized who I was.

"I spotted the fire from the conservatory last night," I said before he had time to wonder if I'd been stalking him. "I thought I'd come find out what it was. Do you always keep it lit?"

"Twenty-four hours a day. You can see the light from town. Your uncle obviously wants everyone to know how much he loved his wife."

"How romantic," I said.

"Isn't it?" Sam replied flatly. "Want to have a look around?"

"Sure. Let's see if James's taste in graves has changed over the years." I glanced back over my shoulder at the sullen superhero. He didn't appreciate my dark sense of humor. "By the way, I consider myself an expert on mausoleums. Have you ever been to Green-Wood Cemetery in Brooklyn?"

"I've never been to Brooklyn," Sam admitted.

"Well, when you go, you should visit Green-Wood. It has the very *best* mausoleums."

One of them belonged to my aunt, Sarah. I used to skip school and take the train to the cemetery. I never saw anyone there, but I knew my uncle visited. The flowers were always fresh, and there was always a handwritten card that read *Love, James.* After I said goodbye to Sarah, I'd walk all the way to the other side of the graveyard to spend some time with my dad. My mother hadn't shelled out nearly as much as James had. Sarah had stately columns, a marble floor, and a statue of a weeping angel. My father rested beneath a simple tombstone with his name inscribed on the front. I tried to make it up to my dad. I'd sit with him for hours and tell him everything that he'd missed.

It had been months since I'd been able to visit the graveyard. Before I left for Louth, I asked my mother if I could go out there one last time. She was busy with the gala, she said. She didn't have time to escort me to Brooklyn, and she couldn't allow me to go on my own. It would have taken a couple of hours to let me say goodbye. She didn't want to go.

Now I stood inside Dahlia Bellinger's mausoleum. The fire kept the space warm, and its smoke rose from the pyre like a charmed snake and disappeared through a hole in the ceiling. Beyond the fire was an alcove where Dahlia's marble coffin lay atop a pedestal. The sides were carved in a pattern that resembled an explosion of petals. They belonged to the flower for which Dahlia had been named. Benches sat on either end of the alcove, but there was no space in the mausoleum for another coffin. Dahlia would be spending eternity alone.

"Does my uncle come here?" I asked.

Sam's answer surprised me. "Every day," he said. "Sometimes he sits here for hours."

"He really loved her," I said.

"Everyone loved Dahlia," Sam said, coming to stand next to me. His manner had changed. Outside it had been as brusque as ever. Inside the mausoleum, he seemed almost reverent. I had a hunch that if I asked the right questions, he might break the rules and tell me about Dahlia and her daughter.

"Why did everyone love her?" I asked.

"She was kind," Sam said. "We knew she'd had a rough time, but she was always doing whatever she could to help other people. My mother says she wishes Dahlia had spent just a fraction of that time on herself."

"Why did she need help?" I asked.

Sam shook his head. "I don't know," he said. "Anyway, it's a shame you never met her."

It was among my biggest regrets. But I didn't say that. "What about Lark? Was she a saint, too?"

"God, no." Sam laughed. "Lark's nothing like Dahlia.

She's a born troublemaker. Even when we were little, she never wanted to be told what to do. Apparently, she gave your uncle so much grief that he made her go live with her dad."

That wasn't quite the tale James had told me. "I heard Lark was losing touch with reality," I said. "They had to get her out of the manor because she'd become obsessed with Grace Louth. Is that true?"

Sam glanced over at me, and I knew I'd pushed it too far. "You know I'm not supposed to talk about any of this. I can't afford to get fired."

"Just give me a yes or no," I pleaded. "Is Lark mentally ill?"

"I have no idea what she is now," Sam admitted. "Losing your mother like that would be enough to make anyone lose it, don't you think? But the girl I grew up with seemed perfectly healthy."

"So you don't think she went berserk and burned the house down?"

Sam wouldn't bite. "All I can tell you is that Lark was always one of the smartest, nicest kids I knew. She wasn't for everyone, but I liked her a lot. I think you would have liked her, too."

"I have a feeling you're right," I said.

For the first time since we'd met, Sam smiled. "Come on," he said. "I'll give you a tour of the grounds."

In February, there wasn't much to see. The manor's glorious gardens were nothing but vast stretches of snow with a few prickly lumps protruding here and there. "You'll have to use your imagination," Sam kept saying. By the time we'd walked all the way to the front of the house, it had become a running joke.

I'd decided I liked him. Sam didn't seem to want anything. The tour wasn't an excuse to spend time alone with me. He was obviously proud of the work he'd done—even if most of it was hidden under a foot of snow. I felt so comfortable in his company that it wasn't until we were walking between the topiary bushes that lined the drive that I remembered I hadn't been alone with a guy my age in months. I shivered at the thought and put my guard back up.

"These are some creepy-ass bushes," I said, looking up at the topiary. The wind had swept away much of their snowy coats, and misshapen monsters were beginning to emerge. The humanoid hedges had been intimidating enough when they were being kept perfectly pruned. Now that they were returning to their natural state, they were truly disturbing.

"Yes, this is the one spot where I don't recommend using your imagination," Sam said. "I keep asking James if I can trim the hedges, but he always tells me to wait. I have a hunch he likes them this way. Maybe he thinks they scare off unwanted visitors."

I remembered how they'd looked in the dark the night I'd arrived. They'd almost succeeded in scaring me away, too.

"Speaking of creepy, I saw something out here the night I arrived," I said. "Whatever it was walked on two legs. I watched it run across the drive from one bush to another."

I saw Sam stiffen. He looked out into the trees. "Lot of deer around here," he said. "They come out at night and eat everything they can find. It's a constant battle to keep them from destroying the gardens."

"Do the deer here walk on two legs?" I asked.

"They can if they want to," he said. I sensed he was on the verge of clamming up, so I stopped asking questions. Then, as I turned to look back at the manor, Sam asked one of his own.

"Why are you here, Bram?" he said. "And why have you been asking so many questions about Lark?"

If he'd asked me a moment earlier, I might have told him. But by the time the words were out of his mouth, I was unable to answer. My eyes had been drawn to movement on the balcony outside the rose room. Someone was standing there. A figure in white, watching the two of us. I was too far away to get a good look at her. Her features were little more than a blur, but I knew it couldn't be Miriam.

"Look." I pointed to the house, my voice rising. "Who's that standing on my balcony?"

"I don't know what you're talking about," Sam answered.

I glanced over at him to see that he was staring straight at me. His face was blank, but all the color had drained from it. He looked as if he'd just seen a ghost.

"Come on! Let's see who it is!" I grabbed Sam's arm, but he wouldn't budge. "What are you waiting for?" I demanded.

"I don't see anything," he said. "Are you sure you're feeling okay?"

"Oh my God, what's wrong with you?" I cried. "Are you blind? She's standing right there!"

I'd taken my eyes off the balcony for a split second. This time, when I looked back, she was gone. I dropped Sam's arm, and everything went silent. Either my eyes were playing tricks on me—or Sam was. I honestly didn't know which was worse. I'd been alone with him for well over an hour, and I'd started to trust him. Now I realized I didn't know him at all.

I felt the panic welling up inside me.

"I gotta go," I told him; then I broke into a run, and I didn't stop until I was back at the house.

Sam never tried to stop me.

Ten

I was racing up the stairs to the second floor when I was ambushed by my uncle. I'd passed his Land Rover in the drive, where I'd noticed heat waves radiating from its hood. He'd just driven up. Where he'd come from was anyone's guess. I could see he'd had a haircut, and he was wearing one of his old suits. I remembered how handsome James had been when I was little. He was only forty years old now, but he looked like that younger man's grandfather.

"What happened to you? Where have you been?" he asked, staring in horror at my snow-covered clothes.

"I was just having a look around the grounds," I told him. I didn't know how he'd feel about my visit to the mausoleum, and I was eager to get upstairs to the rose room.

I saw a flash of annoyance in my uncle's eyes, but it vanished as quickly as lightning.

"Go put on something dry. I can't have you catching cold your first week in town." Then he caught himself and laughed. "Wow, that was terrifying. I sounded just like my father. What I *meant* to say is that I've invited my business partner for breakfast. If you don't mind, I'd like to introduce you to him. Wear whatever you like—although, I suspect you'll be much more comfortable if you're dry."

"You have a business partner now?" I knew the answer was yes. What I couldn't figure out was *why*.

"After the catastrophe, I had to find a partner," James said. "It's going to take a fortune to repair all the damage."

"Shouldn't your insurance cover the restorations, though?" I asked.

The look James gave me let me know I was pushing it. "The insurance had temporarily lapsed when the fire took place," he said.

"Really?" I was genuinely surprised. Without insurance, a fire could have destroyed him financially. My mother always said James was irresponsible, but letting the insurance lapse was completely insane.

James lifted an eyebrow. "Do you know who *you* sounded like just now?" he asked.

"Sorry," I said. That was enough to put an end to my questions. I was *not* going to turn into my mother.

"The truth is, I wasn't well when it happened, and I'd lost track of the payments."

"What was wrong with you?" I couldn't help myself. I had to ask.

"Please, Bram." James shook his head in exasperation. "Go get dressed. Gavin is on his way. Do your old uncle a favor and make a good first impression."

As I bounded up the stairs, taking them two at a time, I wondered who James wanted his partner to see. What kind of girl should greet our guest? Should her handshake be strong and confident—or limp and timid? Whoever met Gavin Turner at the door, I knew one thing for certain—it wouldn't be me. In my experience, first impressions weren't to be trusted. I'd learned the hard way that you never see the real human being the first time you meet someone. You're lucky if you ever do.

When I finally reached the second floor, the figure I'd seen on the balcony was long gone. I hurried down the hall, peeking into every room, but there was no sign of anyone. I started to worry that Sam might have been right. My mother had told me I couldn't trust my own eyes. In my weakest moments, I'd almost believed her. Then I stepped into the rose room and felt a chill in the air. I walked to the French doors and saw the snow had been disturbed outside on the balcony. A small puddle had formed on the floor inside.

I checked under the bed and in the closet to make sure there was no one still lurking in the room before I changed into a warm, dry outfit. When I heard a car pull up in front of the house, I peeked outside. A black Mercedes-Benz SUV had appeared in the drive below. I stepped back as the driver's door opened, and a handsome man in his mid-forties emerged. His immaculate blue suit fit his tall, muscular form perfectly. Though his bald head gave him gravitas, he wasn't that much older than my uncle. In fact, he was what James might have looked like if he'd stayed in Manhattan. I was sure my uncle had made the same observation.

I was still watching the man when the front passenger door of the SUV opened and a much younger male stepped out. He had a full head of hair, but otherwise the resemblance to the older man was uncanny. There was no doubt they were father and son. It wasn't the first time I'd seen the younger of the two. He was dressed in the same long black coat and black glasses he'd been wearing outside the bakery. The top button of his coat was undone, and he hadn't bothered with a scarf or hat. A pair of tall black boots appeared to be his only concession to the cold. I'm sure my jaw was still dangling when the guy's head tilted back and his eyes met mine. He didn't look anywhere else—just up at my window, as if he'd been expecting to see me there all along. When he smiled, I turned and walked away.

I eavesdropped from the second floor as James chatted

with the guests in the entrance hall. I gathered from the conversation that the son went to a famous prep school in Connecticut and was home for midwinter break. My uncle hadn't been expecting a second guest. He sounded perfectly gracious, but I knew he was annoyed.

"When will we be meeting this fascinating niece of yours?" James's partner inquired.

"Bram should be down shortly," James told him.

The other man lowered his voice. "It's kind of you to take her in. Are you certain you're up to the challenge so soon after the tragedy? Even the easiest teenagers can be difficult to handle."

"I don't expect any trouble at all," James assured him. "Bram's been perfectly lovely since she arrived. I know I have a challenge ahead of me, but I think rescuing Bram from my sister's toxic home has already done her a world of good."

"If anything goes wrong, it will fuel the rumors about the manor," his partner pointed out.

"And if everything goes well, it will prove them all wrong," James replied tersely.

I chose that moment to make my entrance, and their conversation paused as I walked down the stairs. All three of them turned to gaze up at me, and I felt like I was being presented in some creepy, old-fashioned ritual. All I was missing was the virginal white dress. It occurred to me then that grand stairways were designed for grand entrances like mine. How many times had Grace Louth in her fancy dresses been forced to put on the same show?

"Gavin Turner, I'd like to introduce you to my niece, Bram Howland," James said when I reached the first floor.

I waited for the man to hold out his hand, and when he did, I shook it. I figured I might as well play along. "A pleasure to meet you, Bram," said my uncle's partner. "I've heard a great deal about you. But your uncle neglected to mention how lovely you are." His gaze was so penetrating that I felt like I was being appraised on a cellular level.

"How do you do?" I stared back—and didn't look away until he was the first to blink.

"This is my son, Nolan," he said, and the younger man stepped forward. "I believe you're both the same age. Nolan will be eighteen in June."

"Hi," I said.

"Hello," he replied, with the same smile he'd worn outside the bakery. He was very handsome, but I knew plenty of guys like him back at home. I'd discovered that those blessed with both looks and money were often stunted in ways that weren't always obvious to the naked eye. Some lacked personalities or consciences. The rest were garden-variety assholes.

"Excuse me, gentlemen," said a voice. I turned to see Miriam standing in the entrance to the formal dining room.

"Breakfast is ready downstairs in the kitchen." Her voice sounded cold—almost icy—and she wore a servant's stoic mask. It wasn't the same Miriam who'd greeted me my first day.

I was already dreading the meal with our guests, when Nolan spoke up.

"Why don't we let the old people talk business?" he said. "You and I can go grab a coffee in town."

"Nolan," his father scolded. I couldn't tell if he was truly angry. It all seemed a little rehearsed. "They've prepared breakfast for us here at the manor."

"What would *you* like to do?" Nolan asked, beaming at me as though my opinion were the only one that mattered. "Lady's choice."

"I could use some more fresh air, I suppose." And a chance to pick Nolan's brain to see what he knew about the manor. But truth be told, I would have gone anywhere with anyone to get away from that breakfast.

"The forecast is calling for bitter cold," James warned darkly. I could tell he didn't want me to go.

"She'd better get used to the cold if she's going to live here," Nolan replied with a laugh.

"I'll be fine." While it was kind of amusing to see James playing the role of a father figure, before I'd arrived at the manor, I hadn't gotten so much as a birthday card from him in years, and I wasn't going to let him control me here.

92

"Okay," he relented. "Just be careful. Stay out of the woods."

"Let me grab my coat and boots," I told Nolan and flashed my uncle a smile. I ran back up the stairs to my room and slipped on my winter wear. Into my left coat pocket went my phone and wallet. Into the right went my mini can of bear repellent and my trusty box cutter. After the incident with Sam, I wasn't planning to trust anyone anymore.

James and Gavin had vanished by the time I returned. Nolan stood alone under the chandelier in the entrance hall. Dressed in black and lit from above, he looked like a character in a play.

"Thanks for getting me out of breakfast," he said. "This is supposed to be my vacation, and my dad keeps dragging me to business meetings. I think he's trying to bore me to death."

I forced myself to smile. "I'll do my best to be entertaining."

"I don't think you'll need to try very hard," Nolan said. "I'm already quite entertained."

He was flirting with me. I giggled the way I'd heard other girls giggle, while my fingers fiddled with the box cutter in my pocket. "Then let's go." I opened the front door and winced when a blast of cold air slammed into me.

We strolled in silence until we were past the hedges.

"So—how did your father end up working with James?" I asked, attempting casual conversation.

"The way my dad tells it, James made him an offer he couldn't refuse. Plus, my dad has fond memories of the manor. He spent his summers and holidays in Louth when he was growing up. My family has owned our house by the river since my dad was a little boy."

"Does he like it here?" I asked. Gavin Turner hadn't struck me as someone who would be a fan of country living.

"Doesn't everyone?" Nolan joked as we walked down the hill. "Have you made any new friends since you got to town?"

"It's only my second day here," I replied, careful not to say too much. "And to be honest, most of the people I've met don't seem much friendlier than that lady at the bakery."

Nolan laughed. "I'm not surprised. I've been coming up here my whole life, and they still treat me like I'm a serial killer who's just waiting for a chance to murder them all and steal their children."

"You've been coming to Louth your whole life?" I asked.

"My grandfather loved to sail on the Hudson. That's why he bought a house in Louth. Our family's summered here ever since."

"So you're kind of a local," I teased.

Nolan laughed even harder. "As far as these people are concerned? Not even close. They used to tolerate us. But ever since my dad invested in your uncle's inn, things have gotten pretty tense. The locals *really* don't like the inn."

"Why?" I asked, truly confused now. "Isn't it Louth's main attraction?" Its *only* attraction, I could have added.

"You've seen all the houses being renovated in town?" Nolan asked, and I nodded. "Those are all owned by city people now. The locals know the inn will bring even more outsiders to Louth, and some of those outsiders will want to stay. In a few years, the whole place is going to turn into an outpost of New York City. The locals realize their days are numbered. When the manor burned, I think a lot of people in town were secretly relieved. I bet half of them would have happily set the fire themselves. Then my dad swooped in to help James pay for the repairs, and suddenly the locals were right back where they'd started—on the verge of extinction. So don't expect to get anything but a cold shoulder from the people of Louth."

I wasn't in Louth to socialize, but it was still depressing to find out I was already hated here, too. I'd already been banished from my hometown. My so-called friends had shunned me. My mother couldn't bear to be in my presence. My school had requested that I not return. I'd fled a city of eight million people, only to find myself trapped in a podunk town where everyone thought my family was out to destroy them.

"Hey." Nolan stopped me just before we reached the end of the manor's drive. "I didn't mean to upset you. I'm really sorry. Don't worry about being all alone here in Louth. If you like, I'll be your friend."

I almost laughed at his presumptuousness. "You don't even live here," I reminded him. "You're only in Louth for midwinter break. After that, you'll have to go back to school."

"Then I shall come to visit you every weekend," he pronounced theatrically, his hand raised as though taking an oath. "As well as all national holidays."

I couldn't help myself. It was hard not to like him. Inside my coat pocket, I let the box cutter slip from my fingers. It was a relief to let down my guard for a bit.

"Seriously, though," Nolan said as we resumed walking. "We'll make your stay in Louth a thrilling, once-in-a-lifetime adventure."

The road curved and the town appeared below us. Cottony smoke rose from chimneys on snow-covered roofs. Framed by trees, it was a Christmas card scene.

"Believe it or not, it's been pretty exciting so far," I said, keen to keep the conversation going.

"Oh really?" Nolan replied. "Was there another escaped goat on the loose in town? That was the highlight of last winter."

"Nope," I said. "I think there was an intruder in my house this morning. I saw her standing on the balcony of my room."

"Really?" He turned to look at me and seemed appropriately impressed. "What did she look like?"

"I was on the other side of the grounds, and I couldn't see her clearly, but it looked like a girl in a white dress."

Nolan whistled. "A white dress? Do you think it might have been the infamous Grace Louth?"

I rolled my eyes. "I don't believe in ghosts."

"Wearing the dress she drowned herself in," he added in a spooky voice. "Now I'm jealous. My house doesn't have any ghosts."

"Don't get jealous," I said. "There's a chance it was all a mirage. I was with someone at the time. He insisted he didn't see anyone."

"That's weird," Nolan agreed. "Who were you with?"

"A guy named Sam Reinhart. He works for my uncle, and he was giving me a tour of the grounds."

"Ah, good old Sam. Clark Kent's dull brother. Well, that explains why he didn't see anything. Sam's far too boring to see a ghost." He smiled when I laughed. "It's funny 'cause it's true. Have you heard that Mr. Personality is the town hero? I think it's some kind of football thing. He was the team quarterback, if I'm not mistaken."

"You know him?"

Nolan looked at me with one eyebrow arched. "This is Louth. Everyone knows everyone here. That's one reason why my dad recommended that your uncle hire outsiders after the fire. Instead James decided to employ one of the town's biggest gossips and her son, the prom king. He said they were too cheap to refuse."

Nolan had to be exaggerating. I couldn't imagine plain, practical Miriam Reinhart as a town gossip. But I didn't bother to challenge him. I wanted to get back to the girl on the balcony.

"Do you really think the manor might be haunted?" I asked just as we reached café JOE.

"Honestly?" Nolan's smile faded as he answered. "I have no idea. All I know is that the place is weird."

He pulled the café door open and held it, waiting for me to enter. I hesitated. A thousand new questions were suddenly bouncing around in my brain. The first had made it all the way to the tip of my tongue when a familiar voice called out, "Nolan! Bram!"

The barista with a man bun was waving to us from behind the espresso machine. I sighed and stepped inside the café. Nolan snickered. "I can tell you've met Jeb. Give me your order and go save yourself," he whispered, coming to the rescue once again.

I left Nolan standing at the counter chatting to the hipster barista while I navigated around the coffee bar to find a table out of sight. Occupying the seat I would have chosen was a girl in tortoiseshell sunglasses—Maisie. This time she was wearing an oversized camel-hair coat with its collar turned up and purple lipstick that made her lips look like fresh bruises.

"Hi," I said.

"You're with Nolan," Maisie noted darkly. She held her teacup with both hands, and I saw that her nails had been painted to match her lips. "Things are worse than I thought."

"I just met him," I said. "His father came to the manor for a business meeting. We walked down here for a cup of coffee."

"I told you this place wasn't safe," Maisie whispered. "Why didn't you listen?" Then she sat back in her seat as though someone had just appeared behind me.

"Hello, Maisie," I heard Nolan say. "You're up early."

"So are you," Maisie hissed. "You usually don't crawl out from under your rock until noon."

I looked back at Nolan and found him smiling. He handed me a cup of coffee. "You know what I love most about the country?" he asked me. "How people here mind their own business. What do you say, Bram? Shall we continue our walk?"

I glanced down at Maisie. I couldn't see her eyes, but I could feel her glare. I stuck my right hand into my pocket and ran my thumb over the box cutter's handle. "Sure." I followed Nolan back around the counter.

Jeb looked surprised to see us. "Leaving so soon?"

"One of your customers wasn't pleased to see me," Nolan said.

Jeb smacked his forehead with the heel of his hand. "Oh man," he said softly. "I'm sorry about that. She's been camped out for so long that I forgot she was back there. Otherwise I would have warned you."

"No worries," Nolan assured him. "We all need people like Maisie to keep us on our toes."

I led the way to the café door, and outside Nolan and I walked side by side through a tunnel that had just been cleared by a kid with a snowblower. "So how long have you and Maisie been sworn enemies?" I asked.

Nolan found the question amusing. He seemed to find the humor in pretty much everything. I wondered if he took anything seriously. "Since she moved into the house next door a couple of years ago."

I remembered seeing him down by the water the day I met Maisie. "So you two are neighbors. That must be awkward."

"For her, maybe," Nolan said, as if he couldn't summon the energy to care. "Maisie hates me, not the other way around. I don't know what I ever did to her, but she's had it in for me since day one. If anything, I feel sorry for the girl. Her home life is seriously screwed up. How did you meet her, anyway?"

"She introduced herself to me at the café yesterday. We

talked about Lark. I think Maisie is still pretty upset about what happened to her."

"We all are," Nolan said.

"You knew her, too?" I asked, surprised.

"Lark was one of the few people in Louth who was always nice to me," Nolan said. "I thought she was smart and interesting. We hung out a few times. I guess you could say we were friends."

"I know Lark is in an institution now, but Maisie told me that she was totally sane before the fire. Sam Reinhart said pretty much the same thing. What do you think?" I worried Nolan might feel like I was interrogating him, but I couldn't stop myself.

Nolan shrugged. "I'm not a psychiatrist," he said. "And I hate to gossip. I'm too used to being the one they all talk about. I never questioned Lark's sanity for a second. But there is something I can show you if you don't mind walking a little bit farther. It might explain why some people are so willing to believe she had problems."

"Okay," I agreed. It didn't matter how cold it was. I would have trekked across the north pole in pursuit of more information about Lark. I hesitated only once—when we reached the edge of town. The pavement turned to gravel, and the trees leaned together over the road, blocking sight of the sky.

"Don't worry." Nolan said, seeming to sense my discomfort. "It's only a short walk from here."

Inside my coat pocket, my thumb worried the box cutter's button. I'd come to Louth for a reason, I reminded myself. I couldn't run the second I got scared. As we walked down the lonely road, all I could hear was the sound of our boots on the snow-covered gravel. Aside from tire tracks, there were no signs of civilization. I felt the familiar panic ignite inside my chest. I knew it would be my fault if something happened. I'd accepted the risk, hoping there would be a reward.

Then suddenly Nolan stopped. We were standing at the top of a driveway that ended with a gate fastened with at least ten padlocks. A giant red No Trespassing sign was fixed to the front of the gate. Along the drive, every tree for as far as I could see had at least one warning sign nailed to its trunk. TRESPASSERS WILL BE SHOT! PRIVATE PROPERTY! KEEP OUT! I OWN A GUN AND A BACKHOE! IF YOU CAN READ THIS, YOU'RE IN RANGE! I SHOOT FIRST AND ASK QUESTIONS LATER!

There were at least a hundred signs, some red and some yellow.

"What the hell are we looking at?" I asked, even more on edge.

"This is the entrance to Ruben Bellinger's farm. This is where Lark's father lives."

It was hard to wrap my head around. Lark's father. "*Here?*

This is the place where Lark was staying at the time of the fire?"

"Yep. What do you think?" Nolan replied, contemplating the scene.

It made no difference what words had been printed on each of the signs. They all screamed the same thing in unison. The person who'd posted them to the trees was not well.

"Mr. Bellinger doesn't seem interested in making new friends." I tried to sound diplomatic. "If I had to make a diagnosis, I'd say he's a little bit paranoid."

"A bit?" Nolan smirked. "The signs have been up for ages, but Lark told me her dad wasn't always this way. Then when she was in fourth or fifth grade, Ruben stopped taking his medication and his problems got worse. Her mom tried to stick it out, but she ended up leaving Ruben a couple years later. She and Lark moved across the river to Hudson. That's where they were living when Dahlia met your uncle. Apparently, Ruben wasn't happy about the marriage. He was still obsessed with his ex-wife."

"How do *you* know all that?" I asked.

"Your uncle told my dad," Nolan said. "James claims Ruben used to watch the manor at night. I guess that was the reason why James put new locks on all the doors. I don't know if it's true, but if it is, it's creepy as hell, don't you think?"

Before I could answer, I heard a sound somewhere deep in the woods. "Did you hear that?" I asked Nolan.

"Hear what?"

Until that moment, I'd never heard a shotgun cocked in real life, but the sound was unmistakable. Someone with a gun was lurking among the trees.

"I should get back to the manor," I told Nolan. I didn't give him a reason, but I figured it was best to hit the road before Ruben Bellinger put two bullets into our backs. Maisie hadn't been joking. Louth *was* a dangerous place.

"Want to take a shortcut?" Nolan asked. "We're actually not that far from the manor. If we walk through the woods, we could be back in ten minutes."

I didn't know him well enough to tell if he was joking. "Have you lost your mind?" I pointed at one of the Keep Out signs.

"Nope," Nolan said with a laugh. "Just making sure you haven't, either."

When we finally crested the top of the manor's hill, I could see James standing in the driveway with Gavin Turner. I couldn't hear what they were saying, but I saw my uncle's jaw clench as he listened to Nolan's father. They were arguing. That much was certain. I got the impression that their business relationship wasn't quite as rosy as Nolan had made it seem. Then James spotted the two of us coming up the drive. As he waved, a smile took the place of his frown.

"I enjoyed our walk," Nolan said while we were still out of earshot. "Let's take another one sometime soon."

I couldn't read his face. There was no knowing look in his eye, no smile lifting the edge of his lips.

"I should warn you—I don't date," I informed him.

Nolan grinned, and I realized I'd been too quick with my answer. "Okay, good to know. But you do *walk*, am I right?"

I felt myself blushing. I'd been silly to jump to conclusions. "Of course," I said. "Another walk would be nice."

"Great! There's a place up in the mountains I'd love to show you sometime."

"Sounds good." I was so embarrassed that I probably would have agreed to anything when I should have just said no.

A few minutes later, I was standing beside James, waving at the back of the Turners' SUV. The instant it disappeared, my uncle slid an arm around my shoulder and squeezed.

"Did everything go okay with Nolan?" he asked.

"Yeah," I said. "He's not too bad."

"I'm sorry if you thought I was being too protective before. I didn't know if you were comfortable spending time with young men yet. I wasn't expecting Nolan to join us this morning, and I didn't want you to feel pressured to entertain him."

My uncle's concern made me uncomfortable. I wasn't used to people worrying about my feelings. "It's fine. We had a nice walk," I answered.

That's when James's voice changed. "The truth is, Bram, I don't know Nolan very well and I can't vouch for him. It's not been very long since the . . . incident. I don't want anything to happen that might impact your recovery."

I squirmed with discomfort. He was edging near the one subject I didn't care to discuss. "Nolan and I just went for a walk," I said. "It wasn't a date."

"He seemed quite taken with you," James pressed.

"I'm not interested in Nolan," I told him. "I have no intention of dating anyone."

My uncle squeezed my shoulder. "I'm glad to hear it, Bram," he said. He seemed pleased. "I really do think it's for the best for the time being."

Something inside me shifted, and I felt the anger rising. *When did you decide to care?* I wanted to ask him. Why weren't you there when I really needed you? Why didn't you save me before it was too late? But I didn't say anything.

Instead I swallowed my words, as I'd always done. I felt them melt back into the molten pit inside me that had been churning and bubbling for five long years, waiting for the right time to explode.

I went upstairs and took a cold shower. Then I stayed in the rose room for the rest of the day. I did what I could to keep it together. The right time was close, but it hadn't yet come.

Eleven

In my dream, the whisper was soft and cajoling—the kind you'd offer a whimpering pet or a crying child. Lips brushed against my ear, and feverish breath scalded the side of my face. I couldn't see a thing. I felt a flaming hot hand on my thigh. I couldn't speak. I couldn't call out for help. Something was horribly wrong with my voice.

Then I found it. I sat up, wide awake, and screamed until my throat was raw.

"Bram! Bram!" The bed bounced as someone plopped down onto the mattress. An arm curled around my shoulders and shook me until I recovered my senses. I could feel Miriam's heart pounding inside her chest. She was panting as though she'd sprinted all the way to my room.

"Sorry," I croaked.

"Sweetheart, it's okay." Then she leaned closer to my ear. "What happened? Did something scare you?"

I shook my head to spare my voice. I wasn't scared. I was sorry for dragging her out of bed in the middle of the night.

"I think she's going to be okay," Miriam assured someone.

I looked up to see James standing in the doorway, swathed in the pajamas of the bigger man he'd once been. He knew what he'd heard. I hadn't been screaming in fear. Rage sounds different. I know my mother must have warned him it would happen, but I could tell by the look on his face that he wasn't prepared. He thought I was crazy.

"Was it a bad dream?" Miriam asked me.

It had all the elements of a bad dream. Monsters. Terror. Darkness. But it was more than a dream. It was a memory— one that had lodged itself in the back of my head.

I cleared my throat. "You guys can go back to sleep," I told them both. "I'll be fine. I have the same dream all the time. It's nothing new."

"You're sure? You're as red as a beet," Miriam said, though she was looking at James, not me.

"Positive," I said, swinging my legs over to the other side of the mattress and standing up. "I'll go splash some cold water on my face." I walked to the bathroom and paused at the door. Neither Miriam nor my uncle had budged. "Thank you," I said firmly. "You can both go." I waited until Miriam crossed the room and James stepped aside to let her out. Then the door closed behind them. James hadn't said a single thing.

I stood in front of the bathroom sink with the water running. My face was still a deep red—like that of a newborn baby who's just discovered her lungs. That's what the dream felt like. A shock, followed by terror. And then finally, freedom.

When I returned to the rose room, the door was standing wide open. The only light in the room came from the embers glowing in the fireplace. I was sure James had closed the door when he'd left with Miriam, but I hadn't had a chance to lock it. Now the empty doorframe stood like a portal to a darker place. I could sense someone there, standing just out of sight. Whoever it was had been summoned by my screams.

This time, I didn't run or slam the door shut. I wasn't going to hide anymore.

"Hello?" I said, careful to keep my voice low. "Who's there?"

I waited for an answer. Then the outline of a girl appeared in the doorway. She was small—almost dainty. While her face stayed in the shadows, her satin dress glowed faintly.

It was drab and dingy, no longer white. The skirt appeared sodden and the hem had ripped. Clutching the fabric were pale hands with long, thin fingers.

I hadn't touched drugs in a year, and I'd been so sure of my sanity. Now I was seeing something I knew couldn't exist. Ghosts lived in people's heads, not in their houses. My own skull was full of them. Now it felt like one of them had broken free. My mind hadn't been strong enough to hold her.

"Am I going crazy?" The ground was disintegrating beneath my feet. It was a sensation I knew all too well. When you aren't sure what's real, it feels like you're falling.

I tried closing my eyes. When I opened them, the girl was still there, and I started to cry. My faith in my sanity was the only thing I had left. It had saved me from hopelessness and given me purpose. Without it, I knew I'd be lost.

"Please," I begged the girl. "Don't do this to me."

I watched her fingers begin working the fabric between them. It seemed like something a real girl would do.

"If I start seeing things, they'll send me away," I told her. "I'll never find out what happened here."

She said nothing, but I saw her fingers freeze.

"Do you have any idea what it's like, not knowing what's real?" I felt my chin quivering. The tears were now falling freely. "It feels like you're trapped in a place where nothing means anything. I came here to escape, and I won't let you stop me."

I couldn't see her anymore, but I knew she was there. "Go away," I sobbed. "Please. I have too much to do."

Blind from tears, I turned my back to the girl in the doorway, crawled into bed, and cried until I fell asleep.

Twelve

I woke to the sound of someone opening the door. The room was flooded with sun, and the combination of bright light and noise made my head throb.

"What are you doing in here?" I demanded as Miriam made her way to my bedside.

By the time the last word left my lips, I was fully awake. "Was my bedroom door open just now?"

"No. I'm sorry. I knocked, but you didn't answer." Miriam waited for a response, but I was struggling to make sense of what I recalled of the previous night. I was *sure* I'd fallen asleep with the door wide open, but now it seemed that I hadn't. Which meant that, as vivid as she'd seemed to me, the ghostly girl in the doorway must have been just a dream.

"Bram?"

"What time is it?" I asked, pushing the girl out of my mind. There was no point in questioning my mental health. I had no choice but to trust myself. I was the only person on earth I could truly depend on.

"Seven-thirty. I wouldn't have bothered you so early—I know you had a rough night—but you have a guest downstairs."

"How can I have a guest? I don't have any friends," I groused.

"Apparently you have a friend you didn't know about. She brought you breakfast. I let her in and sent her down to the kitchen."

I sat up in bed. "It's Maisie, isn't it?"

"How did you know?" Miriam asked.

"Wild guess." After she'd seen me with Nolan the previous day, I wasn't surprised that she'd hunted me down. If I was lucky, she'd brought more than breakfast. I was hoping Maisie had beans to spill.

I got dressed and hurried down to the kitchen. Maisie was wearing her black fur coat again, and the lipstick she'd chosen was too red for daytime. But somehow the effect seemed sweet rather than sexy—like an eight-year-old girl playing dress-up.

"Hey there!" she said, holding up a brown bag with a grease-stained bottom. "I brought croissants!"

I stood and stared at her, not quite sure if she might be an impostor. The chipper attitude was definitely phony. I preferred doom-and-gloom Maisie.

"Do you usually make croissant deliveries at the crack of dawn?"

"Sorry!" She clearly wasn't. "I just wanted to catch you before you went out."

"Out? This is Louth. Where would I go?" As far as I knew, I didn't have any social plans for the next few months.

Maisie smiled in response, and we experienced one of those weird psychic moments that girls sometimes share. I suddenly knew exactly why she was in my kitchen at seven-thirty in the morning. She wanted to catch me before I set out to find Nolan. She shook the bag of croissants she was carrying. "These go great with coffee. Mind if I make us some?"

Where were my manners? "Knock yourself out," I told her.

"Fabulous." She filled the kettle and lit the stove before she stripped off her coat and tossed it over the back of a chair. The body-hugging black jumpsuit she wore underneath would have turned heads down in town. I had a hunch she knew that better than anyone else. Maisie's wardrobe was a language all its own. Each outfit seemed chosen to send a message.

She pulled two plates from the cupboard and placed a

croissant on each. The perfectly browned crescents were still warm to the touch.

"Wait—did you *make* these?" I marveled.

"I'm sure I don't look like the kind of girl who knows her way around an oven," she said. "But I've got baking in my blood. There have been plenty of cooks in my family. A few of them even worked here at the manor." Maisie's eyes roamed the room. "You know, back in the day, a girl like me would spend her whole day slaving away in an underground kitchen. Only rich girls like you got to see the sun."

Rich girls like you. It wasn't exactly something I'd expected to hear from someone wearing what I would have bet was a two-thousand-dollar jumpsuit. I was pissed she'd assigned a stereotype to me, and I wondered how she would feel if I did the same to her. Had the girl in front of me been anyone else, I might have asked. Instead I chose to ignore the insult.

"So, you really grew up here in Louth?"

"Yep. My mom grew up here, too," she said as she rooted through the fridge in search of jam. She seemed perfectly at home in the manor's kitchen.

I found it hard to believe Maisie was related to anyone from Louth. "And your dad?"

She pulled her head out of the fridge. "I don't have a dad," she told me.

"Me either," I said.

Maisie stood there with her hand on the fridge handle, and another long look passed between us. We both knew just how much was being left unsaid. I let it go for the moment. There were a few other subjects I was eager to get to right away.

"What did you come here to talk about, Maisie?" I asked her. "How much you hate Nolan?"

I saw her smirk before she stuck her head back into the fridge. "'Hate' is *such* a strong word, don't you think?"

"Despise? Loathe? Fantasize about chopping into itty-bitty pieces?"

She was laughing when she turned around and set a jar of jam down on the table. I think she enjoyed the picture I'd drawn. "Okay, fine. I hate him."

"Why?" I smeared jam onto a piece of croissant and popped it into my mouth. It was a hundred times better than the one I'd bought at the bakery. "He seems relatively inoffensive for a guy our age."

"You don't know the Turners like I do," Maisie said. "They're womanizing assholes. Gavin's been married three times, and the last wife left him after she caught him messing with an intern. They think being rich gives them the right to treat women any way they want."

"Nolan, too?" I knew the type, but still, it didn't seem

fair to judge the son by his father. I'd been ready to dislike him, but I'd seen no evidence at all that Nolan might be a douchebag. "Did he do something to you?"

"God no." I saw Maisie shudder, and her disgust seemed sincere. "Nolan would never go for a girl like me, anyway. He prefers easier prey. Next time you see him, ask him about his last girlfriend."

I couldn't have cared less about Nolan's love life. I was far more interested in why Maisie was so eager to keep me away from him. "Then you're here to tell me I shouldn't get involved with Nolan."

"That's part of it."

I held her eye. "I don't think you should worry about that. I'm not interested in Nolan. What's the other part?"

"I'm concerned about your safety here in Louth."

"Why do I keep getting the feeling you're trying to scare me away?"

"I am," she said. "Bad things happen to girls in this house."

"I think I'm safe enough here at the moment," I said, though I wasn't sure I believed it. After the previous night, I wasn't sure about anything.

"They probably all thought that." Maisie's face bore no trace of the smirk it had worn when our conversation had begun. Her croissant sat untouched on her plate.

"They?"

"The three women who've died here."

I'd been so focused on Grace Louth that I'd forgotten about the mysterious third woman that Maisie had mentioned my first day in Louth. "I know about Dahlia and Grace. Who else died here?" I asked.

"A girl named April Hughes. She passed away in the 1980s. She was our age at the time. They say she bolted out of the manor in the middle of the night and froze to death in the woods. No one knows what she was running from. I heard the story a hundred times growing up. Here in Louth, it's one of the Dead Girl stories—"

I had to stop her. "One of the *Dead Girl* stories?" I felt like I'd heard the name somewhere before, but I had no idea what it meant. "What the hell are those?"

Maisie's smirk reappeared when she saw she'd managed to shock me. "You know—ghost stories. Kids tell them at sleepovers and on camping trips. There's Grace Louth, April Hughes, and a bunch of other girls who supposedly fell victim to the manor's curse. There's also a ghost girl named Matilda who hitchhikes from Hudson to her grave here in Louth—"

I stopped her again. "I get it, but why do you call them 'Dead Girl stories'?"

"I guess because around here all our best ghosts are girls. Aren't yours?"

I took a moment to consider the question. I'd heard

plenty of tales about men with hooks and maniacs hiding under the bed. But I couldn't recall a single story about a male ghost. Maisie was right. All the best ghosts *were* girls.

Maisie leaned across the table toward me. Her breath smelled like toothpaste and coffee. "I think you just experienced what they call an epiphany," she said. "Ghosts and girls go hand in hand. Why do you suppose that is?"

I could have offered a few theories. Instead I shrugged.

"It's because we're more likely to die in horrible ways. Take poor April Hughes, for example." Maisie sat back. "I always thought April's story was the scariest. A man out hunting in the woods catches sight of a teenage girl who appears to be lost in a snowstorm. He follows after her and stumbles across her frozen corpse, its mouth stretched wide in an eternal scream." Maisie paused to offer a hideous imitation. Her blood-red lipstick made it all the more gruesome. "That's not what really happened, of course. But April *was* a real person. Lark found out she was staying here at the manor when she died."

"Lark was researching April Hughes as well as Grace Louth?" I asked, and Maisie nodded.

"She was fascinated by the manor and the girls who died here. The last time I saw her, she told me that this house knew things."

My excitement was growing, but I tried not to show it. "Like what?"

Maisie shook her head. "She didn't elaborate."

"Did she ever mention a ghost here? In the manor?"

"No," Maisie said. "But she did tell me she heard strange things at night. That's why she started looking into the Dead Girls in the first place."

Lark had heard noises, too. What had she seen?

"And you're convinced Lark was perfectly sane?"

"Is anyone perfectly sane? All I know is that Lark didn't set the fire." Maisie leaned across the table as though she had a dangerous secret to share. "By the way, don't you think the *crazy girl burned down the house* excuse is getting a bit old? They've been recycling that shit since *Jane Eyre*. Ever noticed that the crazy ladies all die horrible deaths before we get to hear their side of the story? Pretty convenient, don't you think?"

I couldn't agree more. "Yes," I said. "And for the record, I don't think Lark set the fire."

That took her by surprise. "You don't?"

I took a leisurely bite of croissant while I savored her expression. "No. That's why I came here. To find out what really happened. And that's why I'm not going away."

It was the first time I'd ever said it out loud.

"What about the curse?" Maisie asked. She wasn't toying with me. She was serious. "Aren't you worried?"

"What if there's no curse?" I said. "What if there's a perfectly logical explanation for everything?"

Maisie seemed completely stunned—as if she'd never heard anyone put it that way.

"So, if you know anything that can help me, I'm happy to listen. But you're not going to scare me away with Dead Girl stories."

The sound of heavy footsteps on the stairs pulled Maisie's attention away before she could answer. Someone was coming down to the kitchen, and it wasn't Miriam. Maisie and I both kept our eyes trained on the entrance, and a hulking figure soon appeared in the doorway. Muddy jeans and a serious case of hat head didn't stop him from looking like Captain America.

"Sam," Maisie said as though she'd been expecting him.

"Maisie," he greeted her casually. "Bram."

Suddenly I was outnumbered. "What's going on?" I asked cautiously, wondering if they were about to gang up on me.

"I asked Sam to come," Maisie explained. "He knows I'm right. You may not be safe here. Curse or no curse, the manor is dangerous."

"It's true," Sam said.

My gaze moved back and forth between them. They weren't joking around. "I appreciate the warning," I told them. "But I think I've made it clear that I'm staying."

"Bram refuses to leave until she finds out what really happened to Lark," Maisie told him. "So maybe you should go ahead and show her where everything's at."

My heart began pounding so hard, I was sure they could hear it. "What do you mean, *where everything's at?*" I asked.

"Two women used to live here," Maisie said. "Haven't you wondered where all their stuff went?"

I'm ashamed to admit that it hadn't crossed my mind. I'd been in every unlocked room in the manor, and I'd seen no sign of Dahlia Bellinger or her daughter. It was as though they'd both vanished without a trace. "Wait, is it all still here?"

"I helped your uncle move their belongings to a storage room in the basement," Sam said. "He said he couldn't bear to look at his wife's things. But he wasn't allowed to get rid of anything, either."

"Why not?"

"None of it belongs to him. Dahlia left everything to Lark. Lark's father got a judge to order that it all be kept in storage until his daughter is well enough to claim it."

"You're saying Lark's belongings are still here in my house?"

Sam nodded. "All the things she left behind when she went to stay with her dad."

Maisie lifted two perfectly sculpted eyebrows. "Be careful, Bram Howland. This isn't *your* house. You belong to *it* now."

Thirteen

I'd explored every unlocked room in the rest of the manor, but, aside from the kitchen, I'd avoided whatever was belowground. Basements were where monsters lived and bodies were buried. Where furnaces leaked noxious fumes and murderous clowns lured their victims. But basements were also where secrets were hidden. I knew I couldn't stay away forever. I would have to see what the manor held.

The basement was a maze, and with every turn Sam and I took, I kept expecting to meet its monster. We passed the laundry, the furnace room, and a workshop that looked like Miss Havisham's parlor. Everything inside was buried beneath a layer of dust. Someone must have been in the middle of restoring a chaise longue when they'd abandoned the project. It was almost pathetic to see the poor thing sitting there with its stuffing exposed, like a Victorian lady caught with her skirts pulled up.

I twisted the knob of each door we passed. At least half a dozen didn't turn. The farther we went, the more jittery I felt. The hallway seemed to grow darker. The spiderwebs appeared larger and the creatures inside them more eager to bite. As I followed behind Sam, I kept a few feet between us and stayed alert for sudden movements.

"So, you're friends with Maisie," I said when I could no longer bear the silence.

"I've known her my entire life. I like her well enough, but I don't know if I'd call us friends." Sam didn't mince words. "I'm not sure Maisie wants *friends*. She's always been a bit of a loner."

"I heard that her home life isn't so great." That's what Nolan had told me. I was hoping Sam would elaborate, but despite what Nolan had told me, Sam wasn't the type to gossip.

He looked back at me and paused for a moment until I caught up. "Where'd you hear that?" His face gave nothing away.

"The coffee shop in town." Technically it was true.

"Yeah, well, I wouldn't believe everything you hear

around here. Maisie's had more to deal with than most, that's for sure," he said. "She hasn't let it drag her down. I admire her for that."

Sam came to a stop in front of an old wooden door. The others we'd passed looked as though they hadn't been altered since the house had been built. But this one had been updated with three modern locks.

"You can't tell anyone I let you into the storeroom," Sam warned me.

"I don't like to lie."

"I'm not asking you to *lie*," he said. "Just don't say anything if you can help it. James doesn't know that I copied his keys. I'm going to give them to Lark if I see her again. But for now, even my mother doesn't know that I have them. So, *please*—can we keep it between the two of us?"

"Fine," I reluctantly agreed.

"You'll need to be quiet while you're in there. Once you're inside, you'll see a rolled-up rug just to your right. Lay it down against the door so light won't seep out under the crack at the bottom."

"Am I hiding from James?" I asked. "Will he be mad if he finds me?" The locks had been installed for a reason. James obviously didn't want anyone rifling through his wife's and stepdaughter's belongings.

"I don't know," Sam admitted. "But there's no point in finding out, wouldn't you say?"

I couldn't have said it any better. Before he inserted the first key, Sam paused for a moment and seemed to listen. Then he unlocked all three locks and handed the keys to me.

"They're yours now," he said. "Keep the door locked while you're in there."

I turned the knob and stepped into the room. It was filled with brown boxes of every size. Half the boxes bore no markings at all, while the other half had the letter *L* neatly written in the top right corner, along with a label indicating the contents' origin—bureau, closet, bathroom, nightstand. A narrow path separated the marked boxes from the unmarked.

"I packed all of Lark's things myself," Sam said. "They're stacked on the right. I tried to label them the best I could so she'd know what was in them when she got home from the hospital. What do you want to look at first? Books and papers and stuff?"

I didn't trust myself to speak, so I nodded.

He squeezed down the path and began pulling out boxes labeled *L: Bookcase*.

"What's wrong?" he asked as he brought the first two boxes to the front of the room for me.

I couldn't answer. In my mind's eye I was watching moving men carrying my father's belongings out of my family home. I remembered sitting on my window seat and counting the boxes as they went down the stairs. Seventy-two boxes, none of them labeled. When boxes aren't labeled, you know someone won't be unpacking.

Sam took a step toward me. "Bram, are you okay?"

"After my dad died, they put all his stuff into boxes like these. They piled them into a truck and drove them away. I was young when it happened. I was afraid to ask where the truck was going. I still don't know where it went."

Once the movers had gone and the truck had disappeared, I'd searched the house. Even the basement. It was like he'd never been there at all. Like maybe I'd imagined him, too.

"How old were you when your dad passed away?" Sam asked gently.

"Twelve," I said.

"How did he die?"

"Carbon monoxide poisoning." I'd been asked what that meant so many times that I'd prepared an answer I could recite by heart. "Carbon monoxide is a colorless, odorless gas produced when any kind of carbon-based fuel is burned. If the gas isn't properly vented, it can fill a building and kill everyone inside. More than two thousand people die from carbon monoxide poisoning every year."

I watched surprise take over Sam's face as he put two and two together. "I know what carbon monoxide poisoning is. Isn't that how—" He stopped.

"Go ahead," I said.

"Isn't that how your uncle's first wife died, too?"

"Yes," I told him. "It is." I forced a smile. That was all I was going to say. "Thank you for bringing me here. If you see James, tell him I've gone out for the day. If I'm not at breakfast tomorrow morning, you can assume I've been eaten by spiders."

"I'll be sure to check in on you before that," Sam assured me. "I know Louth hasn't felt like the most welcoming place, but none of us want you to get eaten by spiders."

"What a relief," I told him.

Once he was gone, I locked the door and got down to work. I opened the first box of books, setting aside my own history as I dug into Lark's. I'd been fascinated by her for months, but I don't think she'd been real to me until that moment. The books shared secrets about her that the town gossips had never known. Several novels appeared to have been dunked in water, which puzzled me for a moment, until I realized Lark must have liked to read in the bathtub. She loved the Brontës and Wharton and du Maurier. Her copy of *Rebecca* was falling apart, and the tattered cover had been carefully taped together. The first page of every book bore an embossed stamp. *From the Library of Lark Bellinger,* it read in a fancy-script font. I ran my finger over the raised letters the way she would have. The embosser must have been a present from someone she loved. The style hardly fit the girl I'd seen in the photos. And yet Lark had used it religiously. She was sentimental.

When I'd finished with the two boxes that Sam had brought out, I went to grab more. I discovered four more boxes of books, two labeled *Stuff*, and a box marked only with the letter *X*. I pulled off the strip of tape that sealed it and found a stack of seven framed photographs inside. They had all been taken at the manor at various points in history. There were women in flapper dresses playing croquet on the lawn. A man in a tuxedo with ridiculously wide lapels was hosting a lavish party. Dahlia descending the renovated grand staircase in an evening dress. At the bottom of the box was a little leather book with a clasp. I thumbed through enough of the brittle, yellow pages filled with phone numbers and addresses to conclude that it couldn't have belonged to Lark—or anyone else from the twenty-first century.

I unpacked and repacked three more boxes before I hit pay dirt in the form of a black cardboard scrapbook. It was old, but not old enough to look interesting. Used, but not loved. It looked like something Lark might have found at a thrift store or a flea market. Anyone who'd seen it on a shelf would have left it there. From the outside, it seemed like a scrapbook meant to be filled and forgotten.

I opened it, and inside was a different story. I flipped

through the scrapbook, page by page. Brittle photos that looked a hundred years old and clippings that appeared to have been printed right off the internet were attached to black sheets that felt like preschool construction paper. Captions and notes written in white pencil accompanied many of the pictures. They weren't scribbled down. Lark had taken the time to write clearly. She'd known that the scrapbook wasn't just for her eyes. She had planned to share the stories she collected, but I don't think she'd finished. The book ended with a third of its pages empty.

I went back to the beginning and started going through it more carefully. The first dozen pictures Lark had carefully adhered to the pages were all of Grace Louth. Arranged chronologically, they followed Grace's development from a plump infant in frilly lace dresses to an impish child and later to a beautiful young woman with long blond hair worn in a single plait. In every picture, Grace stared fearlessly at the camera with such interest and intelligence that she seemed to be peering into a different world on the other side. This was not the girl I'd pictured as the heroine of the ghost stories I'd read online. I'd imagined a dainty doll with ringlets and ruffles. That girl had nothing in common with the real Grace Louth.

The final two images of Grace had been pasted side by side in the scrapbook. One was a photo, the other a newspaper illustration. The photo showed Grace at seventeen or eighteen. She was standing against a wall, her hair piled in a bun on top of her head and her arms crossed in front of her as she peered down at her photographer. She appeared thinner than she had in the earlier pictures, perhaps a bit paler. But the look in her eyes was the same as it had been—confident and determined. In a word, unafraid.

Beside the photo was a newspaper illustration that had accompanied a story about Grace Louth's tragic death. The drawing was a perfect copy of the photograph in all ways but one. The newspaper artist had altered Grace's eyes. Instead of peering out confidently at a photographer, they now gazed up toward the heavens. It changed everything. The girl they'd drawn looked like she was ready to throw herself into a river. The real girl in the photo looked far more likely to push someone in.

On the opposite page were Lark's notes in white pencil.

Grace was born in New York City 1872. Died 1890 in Louth.

She fell in love with someone in Manhattan. (Can't find a name.)

Must not have been rich enough. Daddy dearest was furious.

Legend says Grace and her lover were going to run away together.

The night they planned to elope, the dude was a no-show. (No proof this ever happened.)

Grace came here to Louth Manor to recover from a broken heart.

She refused to leave the house, so her father hired an artist to bring the outdoors to her.

The artist seems to have been a woman. (Can't find any more.)

A little while later, Grace discovered that her beloved had married someone else.

That night she put on a wedding dress she'd made in secret. (How do you make a wedding dress in secret?)

She ran out of the house. (How?) Two servants chased after her.

Before they could catch her, she leaped into the river and was carried away.

No one noticed the girl in the mural until a few days later.

The artist had vanished by that time. (How'd she know what was going to happen???)

Frederick Louth blamed himself for his daughter's death.

He died of a heart attack while trying to destroy the mural he'd commissioned.

Mrs. Louth never came back to the manor.

People say the house is cursed. It preys on the weak, and young women are its favorite victims. In Louth, they're called the Dead Girls.

I call bullshit.

What really happened to Grace?

I read Lark's notes over and over, lingering each time on the last three lines. I'd been right. Lark hadn't believed the official story. She'd been searching for the truth about Grace Louth—just as I was trying to figure out what had happened to Lark. She knew there had to be more to the story, and *that*, not mental illness, had been the reason for Lark's obsession. The discovery thrilled me. Still, I felt a twinge of jealousy. No one had ever bothered to look into *my* story.

I turned the page and discovered a picture of Grace's parents on their wedding day. Clara Louth, dressed in a white gown, sat on a plush chair with her husband standing guard behind it. Frederick was a short, stocky man with a mustache that probably hid most of his face for a reason. His willowy wife appeared decades younger, and I had a hunch Clara was sitting down to disguise the fact that she was taller than her husband. People didn't smile much in photos back then, but Clara looked ready to burst into tears. Even before I read Lark's notes, I knew it hadn't been a love match.

Frederick Louth and his happy bride, 1870.

Frederick grew up poor and made a killing in coal.

Literally a killing. Thousands of men died in his mines.

Clara was from a fancy New York family with a dwindling fortune.

Clara's family traded her in for big bucks. Frederick got respectability.

He was 45. She was 19.

The manor was her wedding present.

The people who worked here hated Frederick. People still talk about him in Louth.

He was cruel to his workers, and he didn't treat Clara much better.

They spent their first night together here at the manor.

Looks like she would have preferred to throw herself into the river.

The photos that followed showed Clara's wedding present being built. I found them fascinating. I'd come to think of the manor as an ancient part of the landscape. I couldn't have imagined the hill without it. Yet there it was, a bald patch of dirt, with every last trace of nature stripped away. Then, picture by picture, a skeletal frame emerged from the mud, and the mansion began to take form. Its white, perfectly stacked blocks looked awkward and out of place.

Lark had commented on only one of the photos, a picture of the completed manor as the gardens around it were being constructed. In the picture, gardeners were weaving strands of ivy through a massive metal trellis fixed to the front of the house.

Frederick must have decided his house looked a little too new.

He couldn't wait for the manor to age gracefully, so he cheated.

Seems ivy is perfect for social climbing.

The next photo showed the results of the gardeners' work. The transformation was remarkable. With its face covered in ivy, the brand-new house magically appeared at least a hundred years old. The photographer had captured a woman wandering through the manor's newly planted garden, a hand resting upon her swollen belly. The brim of her hat threw a shadow across her face, but I was certain the woman was Clara Louth, which meant the baby she was carrying would have been Grace.

The last picture of the manor had been taken eighteen years later, shortly after that baby died. It was published alongside an article in a New York newspaper following Grace's funeral. According to the story, you could see what many believed to be the ghost of Grace Louth lurking behind the rose room's windows. I'd already come across the photo online. There did appear to be a blurry, veiled figure standing in what was now my bedroom. But it could just as easily have been a trick of the light.

Then I turned to the next page of the scrapbook and gasped. Pasted to the paper was an enhanced close-up of the phantom's face. I don't know what digital witchcraft Lark had used, but the features were now clear enough to identify. I saw Grace Louth's piercing eyes staring out from behind the veil. The caption Lark had written below the picture was two words long. *That's her.* The girl who'd appeared to me had kept her face hidden. But the dress she'd been wearing had looked much the same.

I skipped over an old photo of the town of Louth and read through the obituaries for all three members of Grace's family. In 1916, Clara Louth was the last of the family to die. She'd moved to Europe following her husband's death at the hands of the rose room's mural. According to Lark's notes, she'd ordered that the painting be preserved, but she refused to return to the house. After she kicked the bucket, the house passed to a series of nephews, none of whom ever set foot in the manor—or touched the mural—for fear of the famous curse. Over the next seventy years, a series of rich New Yorkers rented the house to throw fabulous parties. Then, in 1986 the house was abruptly closed up, abandoned, and left to rot. Then the last Louth nephew expired, and the manor became the property of New York State. Shortly after that, my uncle James showed up and bought it.

Only four photos in Lark's scrapbook covered the years between 1916 and 1986. According to Lark, they were of young women in their late teens or early twenties who were rumored to have fallen victim to the manor's curse. The first photo was a black-and-white of a sultry girl with dark hair and a cupid's-bow mouth.

Violet Jennings stayed at the mansion in the summer of 1921. She's said to have jumped off a bridge the following winter.

If she did, it didn't kill her. According to her obituary, she lived to 96.

The second picture was a high school yearbook photo of a serious-looking young woman with chunky black glasses and a Peter Pan collar.

*Shirley Hill stayed at the mansion in the summer of
1940. She's supposed to have thrown herself into the
Hudson, Grace Louth–style.*

She drowned by accident in 1943—in California.

A sophisticated girl with bright red hair graced the third
photo.

*Ondine Connor stayed at the mansion in the summer of
1965. She lives in Dublin and thinks the rumors of her
death are hilarious.*

*She says she was bored out of her mind while she stayed at
Louth Manor.*

The last photo was of a gorgeous girl with long black
braids that cascaded over her shoulders.

*April Hughes CONFIRMED dead. She stayed at the
manor the winter of 1986, and her body was discovered
in the woods the next spring.*

WTF. I always thought this story was bullshit.

Pasted on the following pages were stories about April
Hughes from all the New York papers. She was spending
the week after Christmas at the manor with her parents

when she vanished without a trace on New Year's Eve. The police learned that, in the days before her disappearance, April had begged her parents to let her return to Manhattan. They had refused to allow her to go. For months, it was believed that April had run away—despite the fact that she hadn't taken any of her possessions with her.

The following spring, April's frozen body was discovered in the forest, still dressed in the nightgown she'd been wearing the night she'd disappeared. No one knew why she'd left the house—or how she'd managed to do so without being seen.

April's parents reported that their daughter had begun showing signs of paranoia shortly after the family's arrival in Louth. She'd claimed that someone was watching her inside the manor. Several nights in a row, she had pushed a dresser in front of her bedroom door. The morning she was discovered missing, it had required the strength of three men to push the door open. A psychiatrist interviewed by the *New York Times* suggested that April's behavior may have been evidence of a serious mental condition. Even he couldn't explain how she'd slipped past her own barricade. Confusing the matter even more was the note she'd left behind. There was a picture of it printed in the *New York Post*. Scribbled on ruled paper ripped out of a small three-hole binder, it said, *SOMEONE'S AT THE DOOR*.

Lark's last entry was a police photograph of April

Hughes's body. The girl had crawled under a spruce tree and curled into a ball. The freezing temperatures had preserved her perfectly. She was the most beautiful corpse I'd ever seen.

Alongside the photo were three lines written in Lark's handwriting. *G knows this house. G won't leave. G wants to hurt me.* I couldn't figure out what they were supposed to mean, though.

The rest of the scrapbook's pages remained tantalizingly blank. I sat for a while, staring at the last picture ever taken of April. If you believed the stories, three girls had gone mad in the manor. Grace Louth had drowned herself. April Hughes had run out into the night. And Lark Bellinger had jumped from a balcony. No wonder people thought the manor was cursed. Only the house knew for sure what had happened to the girls.

I closed the scrapbook and set it aside. I'd just begun rooting around in another box when I heard something outside in the hall. My eyes shot to the door, where the rug I should have used to hide the light was still propped up against the wall. There was no time to position the rug as Sam had told me, so I dove for the light instead. I flipped the switch, and the bare bulb that lit the room flickered out.

The darkness was absolute. I couldn't see my own hands in front of me. As the footsteps grew louder, I stood motionless, too terrified to move. I had no idea if the person had spotted the light beneath the door. I wondered if they could hear my lungs pulling in the dusty air, and prayed I wouldn't feel the urge to sneeze.

Hide, a voice whispered urgently inside my head. What scared me the most was that the voice wasn't my own. I turned and groped through the darkness until I found the narrow passage between the boxes. I followed it until I reached the space Sam had carved out when he'd removed the first boxes. Then I crawled in and curled up with my knees to my chest. I put my hands over my ears as I had when I was a kid, and counted until it was over.

Fourteen

In the dark, it made no difference if my eyes were open or shut. At some point, I must have fallen asleep, because I found myself back in Manhattan, standing at the front door of my uncle's old house on the day five years earlier when my life had changed forever. The memory was so clear, it was as if I'd traveled back in time. A winter storm had surprised the city, and school had let out early. The snow was piling up quickly, and though my walk had been short, my feet were frozen.

James and his wife lived two blocks from my school in what they called a town house—and what most people in New York would have recognized as a mansion. I'd been a regular visitor since the day they'd moved in. I adored my handsome, charming uncle and my beautiful, brilliant aunt. But that wasn't the only reason why I spent so much time at their house. Even back then, I seized any opportunity to avoid my mother. I'd known since I was little which adults were happy to have me around—and which wished I'd just go away. When I was with Sarah, my mother never called and asked me to come home.

While James focused on his business, Sarah and I grew even closer. By the time I was eleven, my uncle would leave town for weeks at a time. Sarah worked from home, and I sensed she was lonely, so I stopped by more often. She always seemed exhausted, as though James's professional troubles were taking a toll on both of them. He'd lost weight, and dark circles filled the hollows beneath his eyes. When he lost his temper, I barely recognized him at all. Sarah swore the situation was only temporary. James had promised her he would start spending less time at work.

Sarah had given me keys to their house, and I was allowed to come and go whenever I liked. On the day in question, I was paying my first visit in over a week. Sarah had just returned from a desert spa, and James was away on business, as usual. I rang the doorbell and waited. Most of the time Sarah or her housekeeper answered the door. But no one seemed to be home yet. So, I pulled out my keys and let myself in.

The house felt unnaturally still. Sarah's cat didn't greet

me in the entryway as she usually did. I don't recall a strange smell in the air. I just remember thinking that the house felt airless and stuffy. But I kept moving, as if on autopilot, toward the kitchen at the back of the house. I was passing the living room when my eyes landed on a shoe next to one of the sofas. It was a woman's high-heeled pump in a pale flesh tone. I stopped and stared at it. I didn't know why, but it unnerved me. Nothing else in the room seemed out of place. Just that single shoe, lying there by itself, as if abandoned by an absentminded Cinderella. *Strange,* I thought. Then I took a step forward and saw the foot.

Sarah had slumped forward on the sofa, her face buried in its cushions. One foot wore only stockings. The other had kept its heel. An arm dangled over the edge of the sofa. The sleeve of its blouse was pushed to the elbow, and the skin of her forearm bore fading purple blotches.

A few feet from my aunt, a man lay on his side on the floor. I couldn't see his face at first, but I knew the suit well. It was one of my father's favorites. He'd been wearing it that morning when he'd kissed me on the top of my head and wished me a good day at school. I walked over to wake him. His glasses had fallen off, and I reached down to pick them up. That's when I saw that his eyes weren't completely closed. They were staring blindly at the rug, and gravity had pulled his tongue halfway out of his mouth.

I was twelve years old. I'd never seen a dead body before.

I'd been trained to dial 911 since I was old enough to read numbers. But when I pulled the phone out of my pocket, I couldn't figure out who to call. Even I could tell there was nothing any doctor or ambulance driver could do. When I thought I heard someone else in the house, I was relieved. Help had arrived. I was no longer needed. I slipped through the kitchen, where my aunt's cat lay dead beside its water bowl, and left via the service entrance. Then I walked home through the snow, sat on my bed, and waited.

I wasn't going to tell anyone that I'd been there. I didn't want them to know what I'd seen. I was sure that if I didn't breathe a word, I could pretend none of it had ever happened. I wish I'd known then—that's not how it works.

Five hours later, the news finally arrived. I'd been sitting on the side of my bed, still wearing my winter coat, since eleven-thirty. It was dark when my mother came to my room to tell me my father and aunt Sarah had died. I remember her face was so pale that I wondered if she might be dying, too. Nothing she said made any sense. She told me that Sarah's maid had discovered the bodies when she'd arrived at work at three o'clock.

"Where is James?" I asked when she'd finished.

"He's flying back from Chicago," my mother told me.

"I'll wait here for him," I told her. James would know what was true.

I waited all night. James never came.

My therapist used to tell me that everyone responds to grief differently. Some people look to those they love for support. Other people push their loved ones away. And some people choose to run. I was told that all reactions to grief are valid and normal. When I was twelve, I didn't buy it.

I only saw James once in the days after my father and Sarah died. He was shaking hands with guests at Sarah's memorial. I was surprised to see him there. He hadn't joined my mother and me during the service. When I'd been told he was having trouble coming to terms with Sarah's death, I'd imagined him in bed with the curtains pulled. But there he was in a perfectly cut black suit, thanking the mourners who'd come to say goodbye to his wife. All the stress had whittled away at him. His cheeks were sunken and his body skeletal. He barely looked alive himself.

I was too timid to cut through the crowd. I decided to wait for the guests to leave. When I took a seat in one of the chairs that lined the walls, it felt as though I'd vanished from view. The mingling grown-ups didn't notice me.

"It was a carbon monoxide leak," I heard a woman whisper. I glanced up to see a classmate's mother.

"I know," said a lady standing beside her. "I swear to God, I had our boiler guy in our basement thirty minutes after I heard."

"I think we all did."

My classmate's mother lowered her voice. "They found him on top of her," she whispered. "They were both half-clothed."

The other woman gasped. "You're kidding!"

"Think about it—why else would he have been there at three on a weekday?"

"I wonder how long it had been going on," said the woman. "Oh my God, I feel so terrible for Jane. What a way to find out."

"Apparently, James is completely broken. I don't think anyone could love another human being as much as he loved Sarah."

It took me a minute to realize what was being said. I knew about sex, of course, but back then it wasn't the first place my mind took me. When I finally caught on, I was horrified. I didn't believe it for a moment. But I thought maybe that was why James was avoiding us. He must have heard the rumors, too. He thought my father had destroyed his life. I could lose James, too, unless I set the record straight and told the truth.

I searched the funeral home until I found my mother in the luxurious powder room touching up her makeup. I stood behind her and waited until her lips were perfectly painted and her cheeks tastefully rouged. The woman in the mirror was stunning. I could understand why my father had fallen into her trap. And I knew she took no pleasure in looking back at me. At the time, it seemed like I might never grow into my face. I had my father's bushy black eyebrows and untamable hair, along with a nose that seemed several sizes too large. And yet my mother and I both knew that, despite her great beauty, I was the reason my father had chosen to stay.

"Yes?" my mother said.

"I heard two women talking," I said. "They said Dad and Aunt Sarah were having sex."

"Oh dear." My mother's face softened. She was the picture of compassion when she turned and took my hand. "I was hoping you wouldn't hear the gossip until you were old enough to process it."

"I don't need to process anything," I told her. "What they said isn't true."

My mother sighed. "I'm afraid it is, sweetheart," she told me. She only called me "sweetheart" when she thought I was being childish or stupid.

"No, it's not," I insisted. "I was there before the maid. I saw them. They both had their clothes on, and Dad was lying on the floor a few feet from Sarah. They looked like they'd been talking before they died."

My mother recoiled and dropped my hand as if it were rotten or diseased. "Why would you make up something like that?" she asked.

I was confused. "I'm not making anything up," I insisted.

"That's what I saw. I thought you and James would want to know."

Her expressions shifted so quickly that I couldn't keep track. For a moment, though, I was sure she believed me. "Oh, darling," my mother said, bending down so we were eye to eye. "I think this tragedy has damaged you much more than I thought. Don't worry—we'll get you help. But for now, promise me, Bram. Keep all of this to yourself. Don't tell a soul. You're all I have left. I can't lose you, too."

And so began my long relationship with the mental health industry. Though I was only allowed to speak to my therapist, I continued to insist that I'd seen what I'd seen. I couldn't help it. The images never went away. My father's face, blue and lifeless. Sarah's toes, perfectly packaged in her Wolford hose. The cat dead by its water bowl. These pictures were always in the back of my mind, waiting for the moment when I let down my guard.

On my thirteenth birthday, I made one last attempt to convince my mother. I don't know what I was thinking. Maybe I hoped she'd believe me now that I was officially a teenager and no longer a child.

"Why do you insist on lying like this?" she snapped. "If they weren't having an affair, why would your father have been there when James wasn't home?"

Somewhere deep down inside, I knew the answer.

Back then, it was only a collection of sounds and feelings. I couldn't figure out how to interpret them. I couldn't put what I knew into words.

My therapist told me that sometimes we invent stories we'd like to be true. It's not *lying,* she said. It's called wishful thinking. *I must be pretty sick,* I thought, *to wish I'd seen the corpses of two people I loved.* So, I tried making up nicer stories. None of them were true, but my therapist was thrilled with my progress. I didn't dare tell her I still saw the bodies every hour of the day. A couple of years later, I discovered drugs that could turn off the slideshow inside my head. I raided my friends' medicine cabinets for painkillers. I checked their parents' nightstands for sleep aids. Before I went to bed at night, I'd pop a few painkillers and chug them down with wine from the bottle my mother always had open. And then I'd fall into a dark, dreamless oblivion as quiet and peaceful as a grave. The ghosts in my head never bothered me there.

Then one morning, a year before I arrived in Louth, I slept straight through my alarm. My mother's maid, sent to shut the damn thing off, found me unresponsive. When I regained consciousness three days later, I was in the hospital. By the end of that week, I'd been shipped off to rehab.

In the storeroom below the manor, I finally opened my eyes. I felt nothing, the way I had when I'd woken up all alone on a cot in an unfamiliar rehab facility. I saw nothing, just the darkness all around me. I figured I'd slipped back down to the bottom of my hole, and this time I planned to stay. I'd crawled out once before, but I didn't have the strength to do it again.

Then I heard something. Someone knocking on the storeroom door. Softly, but insistently. Whoever it was knew I was in there. Then I remembered where I was and how I'd gotten there. It had to be Sam, coming to check on me. I let the sound guide me to the door. When I opened it, there was no one standing outside. The knocking had been replaced by the patter of bare feet, and I caught a brief glimpse of a girl in a white satin dress running for the stairs.

Fifteen

I sprinted upstairs and came to a stop in the entrance hall, beneath the twinkling chandelier. I listened for footsteps but heard nothing. Outside the windows, the world had gone dark. Inside, the house looked deserted. But it wasn't. Someone was there with me. I just couldn't see her.

I didn't need to pinch myself. I knew I was awake. This time, I couldn't dismiss what I'd heard. It wasn't a dream. There were three options to choose from: prankster, ghost, or hallucination. I didn't like any of the choices, but the last scared me far more than the others.

"Who's there?" I whispered. I got silence for an answer.

"Grace? Is that you?" It was worth a try.

"April?" I tried. Nothing. "Dahlia?"

"Please!" I begged. "Someone talk to me! Tell me I'm not going crazy!"

Then the doorbell tolled. It was deep and solemn—like the sound of an old church calling people to prayer.

I spun around to face the door. I couldn't believe it. I'd called and she'd come. A Dead Girl could be waiting for me behind door number one. I glanced up at the stairs, half expecting Miriam or James to appear. Neither seemed to be home. I slid silently toward the door. The peephole was too high for me, and I had to lift myself up on my tiptoes. My eye was almost to the glass when the bell rang again. I stumbled backward, my heart beating wildly. It took so long for me to gather my wits that I was sure there would be no one there when I looked again. And yet, there was.

A tall figure stood with his back to the house, as though he was taking in the view from the manor's front door. But it was dark out there. There was nothing to see. His black hair and dark coat blended into the night, and I couldn't make out who it was. I watched until my feet ached from standing on tiptoe, but he didn't move an inch. He seemed perfectly content to wait.

I wasn't going to answer. I planned to slip away. Then, as I dropped down to my heels, the button on my jeans scraped against the door handle. It wasn't loud. I didn't think he could have heard. When I shot back up to my tiptoes to check, a face stared back at me from the other side. Under the blue outdoor lights, his skin appeared bloodless, and the fish-eye lens inside the peephole stretched the man's smile into a Joker's grin. I yelped and dropped down to my heels.

"Bram? That you?" Nolan called through the door.

I kept a hand pressed to my chest. It felt like my heart might burst right through my ribs.

"What are you doing here?" I demanded. "It's the middle of the night."

There was a pause, then laughter. "Middle of the night? Have you cracked the lock on the liquor cabinet? It's not even seven o'clock."

That threw me. I had to stop and repeat the last part to myself. I'd been certain it was the dead of night. "Show me your phone," I ordered.

It was his turn to be confused. "What?"

"Your phone—hold it up to the peephole so I can see the time."

"If you insist," he said as though indulging a child.

I rose to my tiptoes and saw a lovely photo of a frozen lake surrounded by snowy mountains. The time at the top of the screen was 6:58. My face flushed with embarrassment, I cracked open the door.

"What are you doing here?"

"Nice to see you, too." He seemed amused by my brusqueness, which annoyed me. I wondered if there was anything he didn't find funny. "Your uncle and my father had to drive down to Manhattan. I came by to see if you'd like to have dinner."

I opened the door wider. "Miriam probably has dinner waiting for me downstairs," I told him. "I don't want to be rude."

"Your housekeeper has tonight off," Nolan countered.

The hair stood up on the back of my neck. He'd come at a time when he'd known I'd be alone and I couldn't help but think of Maisie's warnings. "Who told you that?"

Nolan sighed wearily. "My father and your uncle work together, remember? Look, if you don't want to eat, that's okay by me."

My stomach chose that very moment to rumble loudly. I had no idea what food was in the house—and no clue if any shops or restaurants would be open in town. There was also the matter of the girl in the white satin dress. Whether she was a human, ghost, or hallucination, I wasn't sure I was ready to be all alone with her in the manor.

"Fine," I said, opening the door all the way. "Where do you want to go?"

"How 'bout my house?" Nolan said.

"You know how to cook?" I found that extremely hard to believe.

"You underestimate me, Miss Howland," Nolan replied. "I'm a man of many surprises."

He was kidding. I knew that. I also knew what nasty little truths often hid beneath jokes. "I don't like surprises. The last guy who surprised me spent the night in the hospital."

I kept my eyes trained on Nolan until his smile faded.

"Well, okay, then," he said, not sure what to make of my warning. "The truth is, I don't cook. Our housekeeper, Janna, had a pot of soup on the stove when I left."

My stomach rumbled again. "Your housekeeper is there?" That made the invitation much more appealing.

"Yes."

"What kind of soup is it?"

Nolan grinned. "I believe she said it was clam chowder."

"Manhattan or New England?" I demanded.

"Manhattan, of course. New England clam chowder is like eating hot yogurt."

I couldn't have agreed more. "Then we have a deal. Wait here for a second while I get my stuff."

I ran upstairs and grabbed my bag off the vanity chair. I checked to make sure everything I might need was inside. Wallet, phone, bear repellent, and box cutter. I hadn't been joking. Not even a little bit. I planned to be ready for anything.

As I came down the stairs, I realized that Nolan had entered the house. I also noticed that his expression had changed. He seemed nervous—perhaps even spooked.

"What?" I asked.

"I thought we were here alone."

I paused. "We are," I said, carefully.

"I just heard someone on the second floor walk into the north wing."

I swear, I could have hugged him at that moment. I wasn't going insane. Hallucinations don't make noises other people can hear.

I let out my breath. "I caught a glimpse of a girl just before you arrived," I told him, in a rush. "Maybe it was Maisie playing a prank on me?"

"No." Nolan shook his head. "Maisie's at home. I saw her just before I got in the car."

I tried to offer another rational explanation, but I couldn't seem to find one, so I shook my head.

"Holy shit, Bram. Does that mean I just heard the ghost of Grace Louth?" Nolan asked.

"Do you believe in ghosts?" I asked, watching him carefully.

"I guess I do now," Nolan said, eyes wide. "Aren't you scared?"

I thought about it for a moment and realized something I hadn't yet realized. "No," I told him. "I'm not."

The snow was coming down hard, as though the heavens were trying to bury the town. The clock on the SUV's dashboard confirmed it was early evening, yet Louth had already closed up shop for the night. The sidewalks were empty. Even the lights at JOE were off. It felt as if all the living had fled—and whatever had scared them away could be crouching around the next corner.

While Nolan steered the car down one of the narrow streets, I searched for signs of life. Then he slammed on the brakes, throwing me against the seat belt. A figure had stepped out in front of the car. She stood in the center of the road, less than two feet from our bumper, one hand to her face to shield her eyes from the glare. The headlights washed the color from her hair and drained the blood from her skin. A long white nightgown fluttered in the wind beneath an open bathrobe. Despite the snow, she wore only slippers on her feet. For a moment, I would have sworn on a stack of Bibles it was April Hughes.

"Good God," Nolan groaned. "Not again."

As she came closer, I could see it wasn't a dead girl, but a living woman. "There's something wrong with her," I said.

"Yeah, she's drunk," Nolan said.

"We need to get her inside," I said. "She'll freeze to death out here."

I went to open the door and was startled to see the woman right outside my window, her palms pressed against the glass. Then she began to pound with her fists. I didn't want to be scared, but I was. Mascara smudges ringed her eyes, and dried blood filled the deep cracks in her lips. "Get out!" she shrieked. Nolan stepped on the gas, and she jumped back.

I twisted in my seat to look for her. "What are you doing?" I demanded. "We can't just drive away! That woman needs help!"

"She won't let us help her," Nolan said. "Believe me. I've tried." He turned the corner and pulled to the side of the road, picked up his phone, and tapped out a message. I leaned over and could see what he was writing. *She's on the loose in town again.*

"Who did you text?" I asked when he pressed send.

"Her daughter."

Nolan's phone chimed as a response arrived. He held up the screen for me to see. *Fuck you and your whole fucking family.* It was from Maisie.

"That was Maisie's mom?" I thought of the beautiful girl with her bright lipstick and bold furs. She'd seemed so formidable. Now I'd found the chink in her armor. I wished I hadn't. I didn't think she would have wanted me to see it.

"*Fuck your whole family.* That's what you get for trying to help people around here," Nolan mused. Then he looked over at me. What he saw must have worried him. "Hey, Bram, don't look so terrified. Nora's going to be okay. This kind of thing happens all the time. She's had a pretty serious drinking problem for years."

He pulled out, and just as we turned onto the road that led along the river, a brand-new Mercedes raced past in the opposite direction, spraying Nolan's car with slush. The driver was wearing a red fur coat, her bird finger pressed against the window.

"You're welcome!" Nolan shouted at the speeding car. Then he turned to me with a sheepish expression. "Sorry," he said. "You said no surprises. I guess that wasn't a good way to start our evening."

"You do remember this isn't a date," I said flatly.

"Yes," he said, rolling his eyes. "You've made it perfectly clear. You don't date."

As we continued up the road, I got a good look at the three lovely old houses that sat perched over the Hudson River. The first still seemed to be closed up for the winter. The second belonged to Maisie and her mother. Its lights were blazing and the front door stood wide open. That meant the third house was Nolan's. He pulled up in the drive and clicked an app on his phone, and the porch lit up.

"Impressive," I said, admiring the stately building. They were probably only built a few decades apart, but his house and my uncle's belonged to different centuries.

On the way to the door, I noticed cameras tucked under the eaves. The three that I could see were positioned to cover the front lawn and the road that ran along the river. I assumed there were more hidden elsewhere around the house.

"What's up with all the security? I thought the country was supposed to be safe," I said.

"Nora used to wander over and pass out on our porch. My dad was worried we'd wake up one morning and find her frozen to death," Nolan explained. "Now whenever the cameras catch her heading our way, he just phones the police."

"The police?" I asked. "Isn't that overkill?"

Nolan stopped at the door and took out his keys. "You obviously haven't spent much time with Nora. Tonight you saw a damsel in distress. A few more drinks, and she turns into a demon. Last week she threw a vodka tonic at my father's head. Glass, ice cubes, and all."

He held the door open for me, so I went in. Inside, Nolan's house was beautiful and reeked of old money. I could smell the soup on the stove, but other than that, there was no sign of anyone else in the house.

"Where's your housekeeper?" I asked.

Nolan picked up a note that had been left on a table near the door.

"I guess she finished up and went home. She says that the soup should be ready whenever we want it."

I knew in my bones that I should ask him to take me back to the manor. His father might have been my uncle's business partner, but I didn't really know Nolan, and I didn't want to be alone with him in his house. The truth was, though, I was tired and hungry. So I let Nolan help me out of my coat.

The house was freezing. I felt myself shiver and wondered why no one had turned up the heat. Instinctively I kept my bag—and the weapons inside it—close.

"Sorry. It's a bit cold in here, isn't it?" Nolan observed. "My dad likes it to feel like a meat locker. Why don't we go into the library and I'll start a fire? It should get toasty in there pretty quickly."

I followed Nolan to the wood-paneled library, which felt less formal than the rest of the house. Book-filled shelves stretched from floor to ceiling, and a sofa upholstered in a dark-colored tartan waited in front of the fireplace. It was the perfect place for rich old men to sip scotch and scheme. I stopped in front of a collection of photos in silver frames and scanned the faces in the pictures. At least four generations of privileged Manhattanites looked back at me, the women sharp-eyed and stylish, their brothers and husbands rakishly handsome. I traced Nolan's Roman nose back through the decades to a barrel-chested, mustachioed man standing on the prow of a boat.

"That's my great-grandfather August." Nolan was looking over my shoulder. "He's the one who sailed up the Hudson and brought us all to Louth. He spent every minute he could on that boat." He pointed to another photo of a very old man with his arm around a teenage boy wearing a tuxedo. They appeared to be at a formal party. "That's him as well. He lived to be a hundred and three."

"Are you the kid in the picture?" I asked, though I knew he couldn't be. Everything about the photo screamed 1980s.

"It's my dad," Nolan said. "Before he lost his hair. And yes, I pray every day that the same fate doesn't await me."

I sat on the edge of one of the sofa cushions and watched Nolan stack wood in the fireplace and light the tinder that he'd wedged beneath. His strong, agile hands knew just what to do, and his dark hair fell forward as he worked. A distant part of me recognized how attractive he was, which made another part of me want to run.

Headlights swept along the library walls as a car pulled into the driveway next door. When the lights went out, I walked up to the window and watched Maisie help her mother into the house. Maisie walked slowly with her arm wrapped lovingly around her mother's waist. Their bodies leaned together like two grief-stricken guests at a funeral.

One wasn't sure she could make it. The other wouldn't let her give in.

"What happened to Maisie's mom?" I wondered out loud. I didn't really expect an answer.

"I'm sure Nora's had a rough life," Nolan said. "Growing up in Louth isn't easy. Apparently, she tried to get out at one point, but the town dragged her back. This place is like a black hole. It's hard for people here to escape."

"She must have been young when she had Maisie," I said.

Nolan shrugged. "Yeah," he said, as though the thought had never occurred to him. "But that's pretty common around here."

"Who's Maisie's father?"

"They say it was someone she met in the city. I guess she went down there to be a model or actress and ended up back in Louth with a baby. I've heard lots of rumors, but the only thing anyone knows is that the father had loads of money."

"Who do people think the father might be?" I dug.

"Ask around, and you'll hear people claim it's everyone from the Rock to Derek Jeter. But I try not to listen to the gossip," Nolan said. "Too much of it is all about me."

Sixteen

The clam chowder was delicious, though I was so famished, I would have eaten just about anything. I sipped my soup, trying to swallow my anxiety, as Nolan chatted away. All I wanted to do was eat and leave, even if it meant going home to the mysterious girl in white. But I couldn't waste an opportunity to pick his brain about Lark.

"The other day on our walk, you mentioned that Lark drove my uncle James crazy," I finally ventured. "What exactly was she doing? Do you know?"

Nolan nodded as he swallowed. "She told me she heard things at night in the manor. That's what got her interested in the legends. She used to stay up all night investigating the noises. I guess that's when Lark's mom got fed up and sent her to live with Ruben."

"So, it really was her mother's idea?" I asked. I remembered the sound of Ruben's shotgun cocking. What kind of mother would send her daughter to live with a man like that?

"That's what Lark told me. May I ask *you* a question now?"

"I guess," I said cautiously.

"Why do you act so freaked out when we're alone? Do you do that with every guy, or is it just me?"

"It has nothing to do with you," I told him.

"Are you sure the rumors haven't scared you?"

That piqued my interest. "What rumors?" I asked, watching him carefully.

"The name Ella Bristol doesn't ring a bell?" he asked.

"No," I said. I'd never heard the name before, but I had a hunch she was the girlfriend Maisie had briefly mentioned. "Who's that?"

"Wow. I'm surprised Maisie hasn't whispered it in your ear yet. Ella is a girl I went out with a few times the summer before last. She was great, but at the end of the summer, I had to go back to school. That fall, Ella ran away from home. According to social media, she's somewhere in Manhattan, and everyone here thinks I lured her there."

"Did you?" I demanded. I knew bad things could happen to trusting girls. But I also knew that gossip like that spread because it was scandalous—not because it was true.

Nolan screwed up his face as though the idea were ridiculous. "No! I was at school in Connecticut. And for the record, I've never *lured* anyone anywhere."

My eyes narrowed. I was sure he was holding something back. "Then why would they think that?"

"Because every Little Red Riding Hood tale needs a Big Bad Wolf, I guess. No one can imagine that maybe Ella skipped town because she was an interesting girl and Louth is the most boring place on earth. So." He cocked his head. "Are you sure that's not the reason you're so freaked out?"

I let the subject of Ella Bristol go for the moment. I could see I wasn't going to get anywhere, and there were plenty of other subjects that seemed more promising. "Like you, I know better than to believe every rumor I hear," I said. "There are a few floating around about me as well."

"Really?" He seemed a little too interested. "Do tell."

Before I could answer, Nolan's phone chimed and his expression instantly darkened.

"Hold on one second." He pulled the phone out of his pocket.

"What is it?" I asked.

Nolan's face was grim. "The perimeter of the property

is wired. Something just tripped the alarm." He tapped at his security system app. "Don't worry. Unless Nora's broken loose again, odds are it's a deer."

I leaned in and saw that multiple cameras were transmitting live video to Nolan's phone. He swiped through the feeds until movement in one overlooking the front yard caught our eyes. Three large figures in black were making their way across the grass toward the house. Ski masks concealed their faces, and though I couldn't tell what they were holding, I could see that their hands weren't empty.

"What the hell?" I gasped.

Nolan hit a button on the app, then grabbed me by the arm, dragged me down the hall, and pushed me into a windowless bathroom. "Lock the door and don't come out until help arrives," he ordered.

"What's happening?" I asked, panic surging in my chest. "What do they want? Can they get inside?"

The last question was answered by the sound of shattering glass. "Don't make a sound," Nolan said before he shut the bathroom door.

The instant I turned the lock, I realized I'd left my bag at the table. Without my weapons, I had no way to defend myself if the men got inside. But there was no going back. It sounded like a tornado had just hit the house.

"Nolan!" I shouted over the din. I couldn't understand why he wasn't hiding, too.

There was no shouting, no screaming. Just the sound of glass breaking and wood splintering. A minute later, the racket came to an abrupt halt. I sat on the floor, my back against the wall. I could feel cold air seeping under the bathroom door. I knew I needed to check on Nolan, but my hands were shaking so badly that I couldn't turn the knob. I heard the wail of sirens in the distance. They grew louder, almost deafening. Soon after, they were followed by the sound of boots on the porch and a banging on the front door. Then there were voices. I was relieved to hear Nolan's among them.

I got to my feet, unlocked the door, and opened it to see the living room covered in broken glass. The windows around me were all shattered. Only a few jagged teeth protruded from the panes. An icy wind swirled around the room, lifting the drapes and rustling the pages of a magazine on the coffee table. As I made my way to the sound of Nolan's voice, I hit something with the toe of my shoe, and a sharp pain shot up my foot. A brick was lying on the rug. It wasn't the only one. Strewn around the room were a dozen others just like it. They had to be heavy, and the arms that had thrown them must have been strong.

Nolan was standing, arms crossed, in the entryway facing a middle-aged woman and a younger man—both of whom were wearing brown hats and uniforms trimmed in gold. The sight of them jolted me. Suddenly I remembered that it might be best for me to avoid the law.

I was backing out of the room, when the female officer's eyes locked on me.

"It's okay, Bram. They're gone now," Nolan said. "This is Sheriff Lee."

"Who is *this*?" the sheriff barked as she flipped open a notepad. She did not seem happy to see me. "You didn't mention you had a guest. What's your name?" she asked me.

"Bram Howland," I told her.

"James Howland's niece?" she asked without looking up.

"Yes," I said. Then after a pause, I added, "Ma'am."

My attempt at politeness made zero impression.

"Is there anyone else in the house?"

"No," said Nolan. "My father is in the city tonight."

"And which city is that?" the sheriff asked flatly. "There's more than one. Albany? Buffalo?"

"He's in Manhattan." I could hear the frustration in Nolan's voice, and I understood why. He'd just been the victim of a serious crime. There was evidence lying all over the floor. And yet somehow Nolan was the one being questioned. The injustice of it made me furious.

"Shouldn't you be taking our statements?" I demanded. "Don't you want to know what we saw?"

The sheriff glanced up at me with the strangest expression.

"Mr. Turner has already provided all the information we need. I'll talk to the neighbors and examine the footage from his security cameras myself, but it sounds like the vandals did a pretty good job of concealing their identities."

"Vandals?" I repeated. "This wasn't a bunch of asshole kids knocking over tombstones. These guys were out to hurt us. Don't you want to check the footprints in the snow or examine these bricks for prints?"

"Please, miss," the deputy piped up. *"Language."*

The sheriff didn't seem to care. "It's snowing, Miss Howland. The footprints they left have been covered with new snow. As for fingerprints on the bricks, folks around here usually wear gloves when it's cold outside. The people on the security tapes don't appear to have been any different."

The lady wasn't stupid. She just wasn't interested in solving our crime.

"This is a small town," I said. "You must have *some* idea who'd be capable of doing this."

The sheriff stayed silent and let her deputy answer. "To be honest, miss, it could have been anyone."

I'd never heard anything so insane. "What does *that* mean?" I demanded.

"It's okay, Bram," Nolan assured me. "No one was hurt and the house is insured."

"You got lucky." The sheriff was looking at me when she

said it. "We'll keep an eye on the house tonight, but I think it's best if I take Miss Howland back to the manor."

"I agree," Nolan chimed in, before I had a chance to argue.

I looked up at him in surprise. "But what about you?" I asked, wishing we could have a moment to talk alone.

"I'll be fine. I have Louth's Finest looking out for me."

I was marched outside—one cop in front of me, another bringing up the rear—as if I might make a break for it at any moment.

"Hey! Is she okay?" a girl's voice called out. Maisie was stomping across the yard in her nightgown, her long, bare legs tucked into snow boots. I almost didn't recognize her. Without her lipstick, she looked like a kid. "Bram?"

"There was a disturbance at the Turner house, but Miss Howland wasn't harmed. I'm taking her back to the manor," the sheriff responded matter-of-factly. Then she turned to her deputy. "You stay here with Mr. Turner until I get back."

"Is Bram going to be okay up there all alone?" Maisie asked as the sheriff opened the door of her car for me.

I don't know why Maisie asked the sheriff, when I was right there in front of her.

"I'll be fine," I said. "But some guys just attacked Nolan's house. If I were you, I'd go back inside and lock all your doors."

Maisie didn't move. She just stood there and stared while I got into the cop car. She was still standing there when I was driven away.

Seventeen

Riding up to the manor with Sheriff Lee, I watched the darkness at the edge of the headlights, expecting to spot something. Strange figures standing among the trees. Ghosts in white dresses. Dead Girls in their nightgowns. Animals far too large to be pets. Men in black coats holding bricks in their fists.

I didn't see anything, but that didn't mean they weren't there.

We drove in silence until the sheriff pulled the cruiser to a stop at the top of the drive. The glare from its headlights reflected in the manor's ground-floor windows. Wrapped in its ivy coat, the house seemed ancient and deserted. I reached for the door handle, eager to make my escape. Then the sheriff switched off the headlights, and the world went dark.

"Sit tight. I'd like to talk for a moment." The sheriff reached up and turned on the cruiser's interior light, and I caught her gaze in the rearview mirror. I'd thought she'd been holding back from asking me questions on the drive, but all the while she'd been sorting through her thoughts and organizing her queries. "What's the nature of your relationship with Nolan Turner?" she asked.

I reluctantly settled back in my seat. I didn't like being trapped. "We're friends, I guess," I said, and she shot me a skeptical glance. Apparently, my answer hadn't satisfied her. "No, really. I'm serious. Just friends," I added.

"You're aware that he was friends with Lark Bellinger, too?"

My heart skipped a beat at the mention of Lark's name. "I am," I told her.

"Are you aware that Lark paid a visit to the Turner house the night of the fire?"

"What?" That was a surprise. "No. Nolan never mentioned that." Why hadn't he told me? "Do you think Nolan had something to do with the fire?" I asked.

"Footage from his security cameras showed Lark entering his house and leaving roughly two hours before the fire began. Nolan remained inside."

"Then he *wasn't* involved?" I didn't get what she was driving at.

"Nolan didn't start the fire," the sheriff agreed. "But I sure would love to know what the two of them talked about. When I spoke to Lark in the hospital, she had no recollection of the visit."

"What did Nolan say?" I asked.

"He said Lark told him she'd heard strange things at night. Has he ever mentioned any of this to you?"

"He told me about the noises."

"Have *you* heard anything since you've been here?"

I shifted in the seat. Things had gone far beyond unusual noises. I'd seen things I still couldn't explain. I didn't want to lie to the sheriff, but I didn't know what to tell her, either. "It's an old house," I said instead. "It's filled with strange noises."

The sheriff peered up at the empty manor. "Looks like your uncle's not home," she noted. "Will he be coming back tonight?"

"As far as I know. He's in Manhattan with Nolan's dad. That's why I went over to Nolan's for dinner."

"And where's Miriam Reinhart? Shouldn't she be here?"

"I guess it's her night off. She's probably out painting the town."

The sheriff didn't appreciate my sense of humor. "I'll call

her and have her come back. You shouldn't be alone in this house," she told me. I didn't argue. I wasn't exactly keen to spend the night alone, and I had a hunch Sheriff Lee knew something she wasn't sharing.

The sheriff pulled out her phone and dialed. Miriam must have answered on the first ring. Their conversation was short. I figured Miriam had already heard the news and was on her way. The sheriff ended the call and sat back in her seat and stared up at the manor. I tried to open the cruiser's door, but it was still locked.

"What's the rush?" the sheriff asked.

"Are we really going to sit here in the drive and wait for Miriam?" I asked, incredulous. "Why can't I go upstairs and get ready for bed?"

"You're right," the sheriff finally said. "I'll walk you inside."

The sheriff unlocked the doors, and I climbed out of the cruiser. She marched ahead of me all the way to the front door. Then she stepped aside to let me open all the locks. When I turned to say goodbye, she motioned for me to go inside. "I'll see you up to your room," she said. My discomfort grew, but I said nothing.

She took off her hat and hung it on a coat hook by the door. Without it she was a couple of inches shorter than me, and I noticed she wore her black hair in a large bun at the nape of her neck. She moved like she knew every muscle in her body. She unzipped her coat, but she didn't remove it. I wondered if she wanted access to the gun that sat holstered on her hip.

I took the lead and headed for the stairs. Every time I glanced back at the sheriff, her eyes were somewhere else. She was either taking it all in—or scanning the surroundings for intruders.

"I guess you've been here before?" I asked her.

"Many times," she replied.

When I stopped outside the rose room, I detected a flicker of surprise on the sheriff's face. "This is where you've been sleeping?" she asked. "Do you realize this was Lark Bellinger's bedroom?"

It felt strange living in a house everyone knew. The sheriff brushed past me and inspected the chamber. She opened the closet, stuck her head into the bathroom, and checked the balcony outside. Her search was thorough. There was no way there could have been another human being in that room with the two of us.

"How long will you be staying here with your uncle?" she asked when she'd finished.

"A few months at least," I told her.

"I know what happened to you in New York." She said it as though she were simply stating a fact. To my surprise, I didn't get the sense that she was judging me. "Why did you choose to come here, of all places?"

There were two answers to that question, both of them true. I went with the easiest option. "There was nowhere else for me to go. My mother doesn't want me, and James is my only relative. My father—" I saw the pity on her face, and I couldn't finish the sentence.

"I know about your father, too," she said. "It was a terrible tragedy."

I nodded.

"Lock your bedroom door tonight. If anyone knocks, don't let them in."

"Are you talking about Nolan?" I asked.

"Mr. Turner will be spending the evening with me going through security footage," said the sheriff.

"Then who do you mean?"

She cocked her head as if to say, *Stop playing around.* "I think I've been perfectly clear. No one comes into this room tonight. *No one.* You have a phone with you?"

I pulled out my cell phone and held it up for her to see. "You're really scaring me," I told her.

"Good," the sheriff said. "I want you that way. You'll be safer if you're scared."

The door opened downstairs before I could reply.

"Hello?" Miriam called up. "Bram?"

"Remember what I said," Sheriff Lee told me. "No one comes in here."

I nodded. The sheriff unbuttoned one of her breast

pockets, pulled out a card, and wrote down ten digits on the back. "This is my personal mobile number," she told me. "Don't share it with anyone. I don't usually give it out. Call me if you need anything. Don't bother going through 911."

"What am I supposed to be afraid of?" I asked.

"I don't know yet," she admitted.

Those were the four words that finally got to me. And when I looked into her eyes, I saw that she was scared, too—and that terrified me. "What do you mean?" I asked. "You're the sheriff. Why don't you know?"

"Something is going on in this town. In this *house*," she said. "I keep hearing that people who've stayed in this room have heard noises—and I don't believe in ghosts. I'd send you back to Manhattan if that were an option. Since it's not, I'll do my best to protect you. But you're going to have to work with me, Bram. Be careful. Don't take any more risks."

She left me standing there in my doorway with her card in my hand. Downstairs, I heard her greet Miriam. Then the two moved to another room, speaking softly so I couldn't eavesdrop. I quickly closed my door and turned the lock. After that, I pulled the chair out from the vanity and wedged it under the door handle.

I lay in bed with my legs tucked to my chest and my arms wrapped around them. That was what I'd done in rehab when the drugs had worn off and I couldn't make the memories go away. The pictures and audio were as clear as they had been when I was twelve—but I processed them with a seventeen-year-old brain. I saw things and heard things I hadn't noticed before. Every bit of it scared me, and I didn't understand what it meant. It was like watching a movie in which key scenes had been deleted. The only thing I knew for a fact was that the heroine of the film was completely screwed.

Sometimes, if I fell asleep with my own arms around me, I'd have the dream. If it went the way it was supposed to, nothing really happened. I didn't know where I was, or what we were doing, but I was with my father, and I felt safe. He seemed larger than life. There was nothing on earth that could ever get past him. While I was with him, no harm would come my way. In the morning, I'd keep my eyes closed, and the feeling would last a few precious minutes until the truth hit me and I knew that none of it had been real.

I woke the next morning to the sound of my phone ringing. I hadn't had the dream. My father hadn't come to me, but I hadn't been alone, either. Someone else had been there with me during the night.

I sat up and threw my legs over the side of the bed. I was starting to reach for my phone on the nightstand, when

I realized the nightstand was no longer beside me. I lifted my eyes, and my gaze fell on the door to the hall. The chair I'd wedged under the handle was still there. So was a bureau that had been on the other side of the room. I hadn't touched it. Someone else had pushed it in front of the door and stacked my nightstand on top. My phone was ringing from inside the drawer.

I should have been terrified. That would have been the normal reaction. While I'd been sound asleep in my bed, someone had moved all my furniture. But the sheriff herself had checked the whole room the previous night. There had been no one in there but me when she'd left. I knew that the girl in the white satin dress was responsible. She wasn't a hallucination. She was real, but now I knew I had nothing to fear from her. I could see she'd done her best to protect me.

Eighteen

I was sliding the bureau back across the room when my phone started ringing again. I grabbed it out of the nightstand drawer and accepted the call without looking at the screen. There was only one person it could be. I wasn't in the mood for a chat, but I knew she'd only keep calling if I didn't answer. It wasn't often that my mother felt like parenting, but when she did, there was no denying her.

"Mom," I said.

"Bram! Where have you been?" she demanded. "I've been calling all morning."

"It's not even nine o'clock yet, and you've only called twice," I corrected her. "The first time I was busy."

Nothing I ever said, no matter how minor, was ever accepted without scrutiny. "Doing *what?*"

I wasn't going to make something up just to suit her. Not anymore. "Moving my furniture back to where it should be. Someone rearranged my bedroom in the middle of the night."

There was silence on the other end of the line. Then, "Is this one of your jokes?"

The response was so utterly predictable that I didn't see any point in getting pissed off. "Think what you want, Mom," I told her. "You always do."

"What's going on up there? Have you started taking drugs again? Do I need to call your uncle?"

I'd planned to humor her, but my temper flared. "Go ahead and call him. Call a doctor. Call the sheriff. Call anyone you like. I'm one hundred percent clean and sober." Then I turned the tables. "By the way, I'm glad you phoned. There's a question I've been meaning to ask you. What did you do with Dad's belongings?"

"Your father's belongings?" She understood the question perfectly. She was just buying time. That made me even angrier. She must have known I'd ask at some point. She'd had five years to come up with an answer.

"After Dad died, seventy-two boxes were hauled away from our house. Where did they go? Did you put them in storage?"

I could imagine her sitting at the desk in her tasteful office where she spent her days talking to other rich women and swapping checks for their favorite charities. "The items of value were auctioned off. The rest was donated to worthy causes."

A full minute passed before I could speak. Everything was really gone. I think I'd always known it was. That's why I'd been afraid to ask. "Did it ever occur to you that I might want some of it?"

"Where is this all coming from, Bram?" my mother asked. "Why are you asking these things now?"

"Because I was twelve years old when my father died. I didn't know what to ask. And for the last five years the only people who would talk to me about any of this were the therapists you paid to listen. What do you think they'd say if they knew you erased every last trace of my father two days after he died?"

"What was I supposed to do?" she snapped. She wasn't used to being questioned. "Dwell on what happened? Let myself get mired in the past? I had to move on, Bram. I tried to help you move on, too. But you couldn't accept what your father had done. It drove you to drugs. It drove you to *crime*." She whispered the last word as if it were too shameful to say out loud.

"How did the leak in the basement start?" I asked. "No one ever told me."

"The leak?"

"You know what I'm talking about. How did carbon monoxide leak into Sarah and James's house? Answer the question!"

"Don't you dare speak to me like that," she hissed. "I'm not an engineer, Bram. I don't know exactly how it happened." She was desperate to get off the subject.

"Then tell me what you *do* know." I wasn't going to give in.

"There was something wrong with the furnace. Your uncle was supposed to have someone come take a look, but he hadn't gotten around to it. James and Sarah had both been out of town for days. The house was sealed up tight. Sarah left her cat with a neighbor and gave the maid the week off. While everyone was gone, the gas must have built up in the house. The police said the carbon monoxide detectors probably went off, but there was no one around to hear them. The batteries ran down before Sarah got home. At that point, the carbon monoxide had built up to lethal levels." She paused. "It's not that unusual. These things are a lot more common than you'd think, Bram."

Suddenly the air seemed to grow thicker. I couldn't draw enough of it into my lungs.

"I have to go, Mom," I said. "I'll call you back later."

I'd remembered something—the last thing my mother had said to James when she and I had paid our one and only visit to the manor together. *After everything that's happened, you really think you can run an inn?* she'd demanded. *How many guests will you kill with your negligence?*

At the time, it had seemed needlessly cruel. Now it felt like a warning.

I threw on some clothes and rushed downstairs. Miriam greeted me on the landing, but I raced right past her. My coat was still unbuttoned and my boots unlaced when I sprinted down the drive toward the hardware store in town. I got there fifteen minutes before it opened and paced the sidewalk in front of the shop. A few townsfolk bundled up in thick down coats waddled by, eyes narrowed. Cars slowed as they passed, as if I were an accident on the side of the road. I kept my head down and tried not to look back.

At ten to nine, the store's owner showed up and let me in. It must have been a bit odd to find a seventeen-year-old girl waiting in the cold to purchase carbon monoxide detectors. It probably seemed even weirder when he found out I'd forgotten to bring money.

"Everything okay up there at the manor?" The owner was a big, burly guy with a John Deere hat and a week's worth of stubble. I wasn't surprised that he knew who I was. I was shocked that he seemed to care.

"My uncle's worried there might be a leak," I said, praying James would never find out.

"Then don't worry about the money. I'll add these to the manor's account," the man said, putting the boxes into a thin plastic bag. "If one of those alarms goes off, you need to phone the fire department straightaway, all right? Carbon monoxide's no joke. And call me if you need anything else. I'll have one of the boys run it up to you."

"Okay," I said. I probably stood there for too long. He'd sounded just like my dad.

"Be careful up there, sweetie," he told me.

I felt my eyes starting to well up. "I'll try," I told him.

I left the hardware store and stopped to wipe my eyes. When I looked up, I saw the sheriff parked across the street. She rolled down the passenger-side window and beckoned to me. I took a moment to collect myself before I crossed over to speak to her.

"Morning, Miss Howland. I phoned your house a few minutes ago, and Miriam Reinhart said you'd flown out the door like a bat out of hell. Everything go okay last night?"

I almost confided in her. I should have told her everything. But I'd been called a liar for so long that I didn't trust anyone aside from myself. "Yep," I said. "Woke up safe and sound."

"What you got there?" she asked, pointing at the bag in my hand.

"Carbon monoxide detectors," I said.

The sheriff arched an eyebrow. "You woke up safe and sound this morning and decided to come down to purchase carbon monoxide detectors?"

"My father died from carbon monoxide poisoning."

"Yes, I know," she reminded me. "As did your aunt, I believe."

I nodded.

"Are you worried there might be a leak at the manor?" the sheriff asked carefully. She knew something was up.

"It's better to be safe than sorry, don't you think?" I wasn't ready to talk.

"I do," the sheriff agreed. "I'm glad you're starting to take your safety seriously. And I hope going forward, you'll be pickier about who you spend time with."

I assumed she was talking about Nolan. Though she hadn't come out and said so, the sheriff clearly thought that Lark going to Nolan's on the night of the fire meant something. The fact that Nolan had never mentioned Lark's visit made me suspect the sheriff was right. I just couldn't figure out what it might mean. Nolan had stayed at home when Lark had left. Had he said something that had inspired her to trek up to the manor in the middle of the night?

"You take care, Miss Howland," the sheriff said. "If you ever want to talk, you have my number."

Nineteen

As soon as the sheriff's cruiser disappeared around the corner, I made a beeline for Nolan's house. Despite the sheriff's vague warnings, I had to ask him about the night of the fire. Ten minutes later, I reached his drive and stopped to gape. The previous night, I hadn't gotten a true sense of the destruction. Every window had been shattered. Without them, Nolan's house was little more than a shell. Curtains fluttered in the wind while blinds banged against panes lined with jagged glass teeth. The house had seemed safe, but it had been an illusion. All it took was a few rocks to shatter it.

Two trucks were parked side by side in the drive, and

a team of construction workers was unloading gear. As I watched from the road, I saw one of the men punch a colleague in the arm and point toward the house next door.

Maisie was standing on her front porch in a silk nightgown and an emerald-green kimono, looking as out of place in Louth as a tropical bird perched atop an iceberg. When she waved me over, I heard whistles of approval from one of the construction workers.

"You're on camera, assholes," Maisie shouted at them. "How 'bout I send copies of the security tapes to your wives?"

When I glanced over my shoulder at the men, they'd all turned away to mind their own business.

"Nice work," I told Maisie once I'd made my way up the steps to her porch.

"Fuck them," she said. "If you're looking for Nolan, he hasn't been back to his house since last night. Come inside and have some coffee. You look like you're about to freeze to death."

I gratefully followed her into the house. I don't know what I'd been expecting, but the interior was Instagram-perfect. The walls were painted pale blue and trimmed with dark gray. An antique sofa upholstered in gold velvet sat in front of the living room windows, which framed a view of the icy Hudson. I felt like I'd stepped into a showroom. The furniture looked like it had never been touched.

"Your home is gorgeous," I said.

"Thanks," Maisie replied. "I'll be sure to pass along your praise to our decorator. My mom and I had nothing to do with it. The lady even chose which family pictures to frame."

She gestured to a photo on the living room wall. It was a typical studio portrait with a mottled gray background. A stunning girl with black braids sat on a fur rug, cradling an infant. The baby stared straight at the camera with such ferocity that I had no trouble identifying her. The mother seemed stunned to find a baby in her arms.

"Wow. Your mom was—" I glanced back at Maisie. The resemblance was remarkable.

"Young?" she offered.

"I was going to say 'gorgeous,'" I told her. "But, yeah. She looks really young, too."

"She wasn't even eighteen when that picture was taken. She was two months older than I am when she had me."

I didn't say anything.

"Were you with Nolan when he passed my mother in town last night?" she asked.

I nodded.

"So you saw her. Or what's left of her, anyway. They called her a whore when she was our age. Now she's the town drunk." Maisie looked back to the portrait and lifted her chin and clenched her jaw as if preparing to take a hit.

"I'm in no position to judge anyone," I said softly. "I can only imagine how hard it must be for you."

"Not as hard as it is for her," Maisie said. She took in a deep breath and forced a smile. "So—want a quick tour?"

I didn't, but I sensed there was something she wanted to show me. "Sure," I said.

I followed Maisie upstairs. There were four bedrooms on the second floor. Two looked as though they'd never been entered. I was certain the accent pillows in both were lying right where the decorator had tossed them. A layer of dust made the furnishings appear faintly fuzzy. Spiderwebs clung to the room's corners, and dead bugs littered the windowsills.

"We can't get a housekeeper," Maisie explained when she saw I'd noticed. "No one in Louth wants to work for us. I do all the housework myself, but there's no way I'm busting my ass in a bunch of rooms we don't use. Come on," she said, ushering me down the hall. "I'll show you where the magic happens."

Her room faced the river. The view was spectacular, but it was difficult to comment on the décor, since no trace of it could be seen. An enormous closet was literally overflowing. At least six rolling clothes racks crammed with formal wear were positioned around the room. Every piece of furniture had been loaded down with so many dresses, jumpsuits, jeans, and blouses that there was no way to tell what might once have been a desk or a chair. I spotted Chanel, Marni, and Prada labels.

"I don't know what I'd do without online shopping," Maisie said, sounding bored.

"Oh my God," was all I could offer in response.

"I know, right?" Maisie replied. "All dressed up and no place to go."

I'd visited plenty of rich girls over the years, but I'd never seen a collection of clothing like Maisie's. Just the items lying on the floor were worth tens of thousands of dollars. Where did she get all the money?

"And over here," I heard Maisie say, "is a glimpse of my future." She'd opened the door to the room next door. Her mother lay facedown on a king-sized bed, dressed in the same filthy nightgown she'd been wearing the previous night. "That's what happens to girls in Louth."

"Maisie, have you thought about getting your mother some help?" I asked gently.

"Sure. As a matter of fact, I'm working on the root of her problem right now." Her lips curled into something between a smile and a snarl. "But before I get started for the day, I need some coffee. Let's go back downstairs and have a cup."

I hadn't heard a question, so I didn't bother to answer. I just followed the girl in the emerald-green robe.

"It really is a lovely house," I said awkwardly as we headed to the kitchen.

"Meh," Maisie said. "I chose it for the location. Isn't that what they say? Location is everything?"

"*You* chose it?" I asked.

"Yep," Maisie said. "I did everything but sign the papers." Then she leaned toward me and whispered, "Actually, I did that, too."

The kitchen appeared to be where the two of them lived. A mound of dirty dishes rose from the sink, and we passed a trash can devoted entirely to bottles. Maisie grabbed a teacup off the kitchen counter, then guided me to a breakfast nook where a pot of coffee was already waiting. The nook's window looked out at Nolan's house next door. An army of workers was climbing its walls. It was amazing to think that such an enormous crew had been assembled in only a matter of hours.

"Why were you over there last night?" Maisie asked as she poured coffee into my cup.

"My uncle was out of town and the housekeeper was off. I was hungry and Nolan offered to feed me."

"Nolan works fast," Maisie droned.

"I'm not interested in Nolan," I said for what felt like the hundredth time. "It wasn't a date."

Maisie wasn't convinced. "You must like him," she pressed. "You walked all the way here to check up on him."

"Actually, I came to ask him about something the sheriff

mentioned. Did you know Lark was at his house the night of the fire?"

A sly smirk spread across Maisie's face. "Of course. Who do you think told the sheriff?" she asked. "I saw Lark go in, and I saw her leave in a rush a little while later."

"Why was she there, do you think?"

"That's a very good question, isn't it? If Nolan ever comes back to Louth, you should ask him."

"You think last night could have scared him away for good?" I asked.

"I was hoping it might," Maisie said. "But it doesn't seem to have rattled you."

"I'm different," I told her. "I have nowhere else to go." I didn't want Maisie's pity—and I couldn't imagine she wanted mine. After what I'd seen, I knew Maisie wouldn't judge me. She'd understand. That's why I told her.

"Doesn't your mother live in Manhattan?" Maisie asked.

"She won't let me come back." I'd never said it out loud, and I was surprised how brutal it sounded.

"And you don't have a dad?"

"I did," I said. "But he's dead. The official story is that he was fucking my aunt and they both died of carbon monoxide poisoning."

"Jesus." Maisie's tough-girl façade slipped for an instant. I quickly moved on to another subject before I lost my composure.

"Yeah, so after I got kicked out of Manhattan, this was the only place I could go."

"Why'd you get kicked out of Manhattan?" she asked. "Was it because you were addicted to drugs?"

It felt like a punch in the gut. "Where'd you hear that?" I asked.

"Your uncle told anyone who would listen about his good deed—inviting you to the inn to help you recover," Maisie replied.

I found myself at a loss for words. I wasn't shocked. I was disgusted. What kind of asshole humiliates his own niece to make himself look like a hero? Maisie waited patiently until I was able to respond.

"I've been clean for over a year. I got kicked out of town because I hit someone." It felt good to offer a simple, honest answer to a simple, honest question.

"That's it?" She didn't seem to think the punishment fit the crime.

"I punched him several times in the face," I added. "And when he fell down, I kicked him in the stomach. Too many times to count."

Maisie and I stared at each other across the table. We both knew that what came next would make all the difference.

"Did he deserve it?" she asked.

"Yes," I told her. "He did."

She didn't ask what he'd done, and I didn't need to say it out loud. I knew she believed me. Unlike the mother I'd known my whole life, this girl I'd just met had looked me in the eyes and known I was telling the truth.

"And you're the one who got sent away. Figures."

"He's very rich," I said. "And I'm what they call 'troubled.'"

"Me too," she replied.

"I know," I told her. "That's why I like you."

Of all the things I'd said, that was the one that rendered Maisie temporarily speechless. When she looked down at her cup, I think she was trying to keep it together.

"Then listen to me, Bram, and believe me this time when I tell you that Louth is a bad place."

"I believed you the first time," I told her. "And the second. I'm still staying. I need to find out what happened to Lark."

"You might be risking your life," she said. "Why is it so important to you to find out what happened to a girl you don't even know?"

I could have sidestepped the question. Instead I answered it. I suddenly wanted her to know everything. "Because Lark and I have a lot in common."

"Like what?" Maisie asked.

"We've both been called crazy," I told her. "And blamed for things we didn't do. Neither of our stories is as simple as it's been made out to be."

"So, what's your real story?" Maisie asked.

She was waiting for my answer when loud pounding on the front door made both of us jump. We sat in silence, our eyes focused on the same spot, hoping whoever it was would go away. The pounding began again, only this time louder.

"I'm really sorry. I have to get that." Maisie groaned as if she were faced with a terrible chore. "He'll wake my mom if I don't. Go out the back door. You shouldn't be here for this. I'll come find you later."

"Who is it?" I asked.

"The neighbor," she said. "I've been expecting him to turn up all morning."

"Nolan?" I asked.

"No, his father."

I didn't like the sound of that. "You're sure you don't want me to stay?"

"I'll be fine," she assured me. "Trust me—you don't want Gavin Turner to know that we're friends. It could make life difficult for you."

As she headed for the front door, I made a move for the rear exit. But I didn't leave. I wasn't going to abandon her to face a grown man on her own.

"Hello, Mr. Turner," I heard her say in a voice that was dripping with sarcasm.

"May I speak to your mother?" Gavin replied coldly. He obviously didn't have any desire to talk to Maisie.

"She's asleep," Maisie announced. "How may I help you?"

"I came to ask if either of you know anything about the incident last night."

"I know it woke me up," Maisie said. "Sounded like quite a party."

"Do you have any idea who might have been responsible?" Gavin asked.

"Goodness." I imagined Maisie batting her eyelashes theatrically as she said it. "It could have been half the people in town. I'm not sure if you know this, but your son doesn't have many friends."

An awkward pause followed. I would have given anything to see Gavin Turner's face at that moment. "The security footage showed three young men. If I had to guess, I'd say they were your age."

"And you're implying what? That I used my womanly wiles to have them trash your house?" Maisie sneered.

"I'm not implying anything of the sort," he spat. "I'm trying to protect my son. There was a young woman there last night as well. She could have been injured."

"Yes, but fortunately someone threw rocks at your house before anything happened."

"Miss Wilson, I'm not sure what you have against my son, but—"

Maisie cut him off with a bitter laugh. "Stop right there. You've got to be out of your mind. You do realize who you're talking to, don't you?"

"Yes," Gavin said. "Do you realize who *I* am?"

"If you think I'm scared of your money like everyone else in this town, you've got another thing coming. You don't belong here. It's time for you and your family to pack your bags. In the meantime, get the fuck off my porch," Maisie said. "Before I have my 'boyfriends' come back and drag you off."

As soon as I heard the front door slam, I slipped out the back.

Twenty

I slunk away from the house, careful not to be seen. I was disappointed in Maisie and ashamed of myself. I'd assumed she was like me—an ordinary person trapped in a terrible tale. But after eavesdropping on her conversation, I was no longer sure who she was. She obviously knew more about the incident at Nolan's than she'd let on. I'd been willing to tell her what had happened to me in New York, but she'd kept her own cards close to her chest. I ran back through everything I'd said, wondering just how much I'd revealed.

Even if most of my secrets were safe, it scared me how eager I'd been to share them with a stranger. I don't think it had ever occurred to me just how lonely I was—how desperately I'd longed for someone who would listen. I should have known better than anyone else that *who* you tell is just as important as *what* you tell them. There was only one person I could trust with my story. That's how I ended up in the cemetery, on a bench by Grace Louth's empty grave.

I'd read in Grace's obituary that her parents had built her a marble mausoleum in the style of a Roman temple. There was only one like it in Louth's graveyard. Peering between the columns, I could see the statue of a girl inside. She was kneeling at the far end of the tomb, her head bowed in sorrow or shame and her face hidden in her hands. The statue was meant to be Grace—but a much younger version. Grace had been eighteen years old when she'd died, but the statue was of a little girl.

I was struck by her outfit—a pinafore dress. It reminded me of the school uniform I'd worn when I was younger—the same uniform I'd been wearing when I'd discovered my father's dead body. The uniform I had on when I walked past the scene of his death twice a day, five days a week, for four whole years.

Tears welled up in my eyes as I thought about the little girl that I'd been. No one had seen that I was trapped in the worst day of my life. I lived it over and over and over again. If I'd been an adult, I could have escaped from the city and left it all behind. But I was twelve years old. I had nowhere to go. My father had left my mother a fortune to add to the one she already possessed. She had all the money in the world, but she refused to move. A therapist once suggested that it might be better for me if we bought a house on a different street. My mother kept the house and bought a new therapist instead.

Back then, I had the same dream every night. I dreamed about the building where my father had died. As I walked past on my way to school, it would start sinking. Within seconds, the hole would swallow everything around, and I would be standing on the edge of an abyss. I'd look for the bottom, only to realize there wasn't one. Anything that fell into the hole would keep falling. Then the hole would swallow me, too.

During the day, I was tortured by images I couldn't bear to describe. They came without warning, and I was powerless to stop them. Then, when I was fifteen, a friend showed up at school with a bottle of pain pills that she'd stolen from her grandmother. A bunch of us swallowed them and went to the park. I didn't even notice a huge difference at first. The other girls seemed high. I just felt free. That evening, I walked right past the house where my father had died. I didn't even realize I'd done it until I was at my front door. I'd spent an entire afternoon in the present. Death hadn't followed me around that day.

The next morning, I woke up back in the past. That

was when my quest for the pills began. I had no idea how hooked I became. Over the course of a year, I lied and stole and did things I later regretted. If pills hadn't been easy to come by in Manhattan prep schools, there's no telling how far I might have gone. Until the very end, no one suspected a thing. My grades remained reasonable, but everything else went to hell. I stopped talking to my friends. I only showered when my mother yelled at me. Still, no one ever guessed I was doing drugs until the day I popped a few pills too many and almost died. And still, my mom kept insisting it wasn't an overdose. If an EMT with a syringe of naloxone and a healthy disrespect for authority hadn't chosen to ignore her, my body would be buried next to my father's.

I spent my sixteenth birthday in rehab. There, the images returned with a vengeance. All the pictures I'd tried so hard to erase played nonstop in my mind. At first, I still didn't understand what I saw. Then a bubbling, boiling rage began building inside me. It was toxic waste, and I had no idea where to store it. I didn't even know what it was.

I passed the following summer in a lovely psychiatric facility in Virginia. I'd been off drugs for months at that point, but my mother thought it was best to keep me under twenty-four-hour surveillance. Eventually the people at the psychiatric facility told her I had to leave. When my mom picked me up in August, she informed me I'd soon be going back to school. Not the same school, of course. After all the drama, she just couldn't face the old teachers and parents. So she'd enrolled me in a different school on the other side of Central Park. As if that were far enough away to start a whole new life.

It wasn't. Everyone knew. It was as though my "condition" had been announced over the loudspeaker on the first day of school. No one was terrible to me. I was a curiosity—like a goat with two heads or a kid with a face tattoo. Most did their best not to stare, but I could always feel eyes on me when I turned around. My mother said they all stared because I'd finally gotten pretty. It was such a backhanded compliment that I figured it might be partly true. Still, "pretty" didn't explain why people seemed to find the back of my head so damn *gorgeous*.

Then one day my life suddenly changed. It was noon on a Monday, and I was eating a sandwich all by myself when suddenly the king of the whole damn school sat down beside me. I thought Daniel was handsome and charming, but I wasn't interested in a boyfriend. I was focused on my schoolwork. I'd had tutors at rehab, so I wasn't that far behind. Still, I couldn't screw things up again. College was my only escape plan. My mother insisted I stay in the city and go to Columbia, which was fine with me. I knew she'd never deign to set foot in Morningside Heights.

I tried to keep Daniel at bay, but he refused to give up. He sat with me at lunch every day. He brought me iced coffees in the afternoon and walked me across the park. He said he was happy to just be friends. Everyone else at school took their lead from him. People began to say hello to me in the halls. I don't think I knew how much I'd missed all of that. I stopped resisting. I jumped right in. I took Daniel's persistence as a sign of sincerity. It never even occurred to me that it might be a game.

We'd been hanging out for a few months when he announced he was throwing a party. His parents would be out of town, but they'd given their permission. I'd bought a dress for the occasion and thrilled my mother by finally having my brows done. I remember looking in the mirror before I left and actually understanding why someone might find me appealing.

There were at least fifty people from school at the party, and they all had their phones out. I'd bet thousands of photos were taken that night. Everyone was drinking out of camping mugs to disguise the liquor inside them. When Daniel handed me a mug, I took it for the worst reasons. I didn't want to disappoint him.

I took a couple of sips just for show and then dumped the rest into a plant as soon as no one was watching. When I put the mug down, Daniel invited me out to the terrace that wrapped around his apartment on the eighteenth floor and overlooked Central Park. He'd told his guests that the outdoors was off-limits, which made perfect sense. The last thing anyone needed was a drunk teenager plunging eighteen floors to her death. When he opened the door, I understood the rule was just an excuse to keep the balcony empty. He'd saved the space just for us.

I remember standing at the railing with Daniel, looking out over Central Park. The windows and glass doors must have been soundproofed. I couldn't hear the party raging inside. When Daniel leaned down to kiss me, I felt my legs wobble. I thought maybe I was just overwhelmed. Then my knees buckled, and Daniel caught me before I fell. It seemed sweet for a moment—until I tried to thank him and realized I could barely talk.

There were fifty people on the other side of the windows, but it was dark outside and they were all having fun. I caught a glimpse of my reflection in the glass and saw myself hanging limply over Daniel's shoulder. A group of girls were posing on the other side. There were multiple cameras aimed right at me. Someone must have seen something.

Daniel carried me to the far end of the terrace, away from the party and back into the apartment through one of the rooms that had been declared off-limits. I was dumped down on a bed in what I now know was his parents' bedroom. I'd had my little Chanel purse strapped across my chest. I remember feeling one of the chains pop as he yanked it off. Then he pulled down my underwear and pushed up my dress. He probably assumed I'd chugged the whole drink.

If I had, I would have been catatonic. My head was swimming, but I was still capable of thought. And I was thinking about fucking killing him.

I'd spent years swallowing rage. When it rose to the surface, I'd gulp it back down. A molten lake had been growing inside me. The pressure was building. Cracks and fissures were forming. That night it broke through and I finally erupted.

I lurched upward and shoved Daniel off me. He flew backward and landed with a crash, hitting his head on the edge of a bureau. The element of surprise had made it possible, but when I rose to my feet, I felt power coursing through me. I walked over to where he lay with his head in his hands, and I kicked him. It felt so good that I did it again. And again. And again.

There are plenty of pictures of me emerging from the bedroom, looking like a crazed junkie. I froze when I saw everyone. I'd forgotten where I was. There are big parts of that evening that are still a blur. I can't remember what happened next, but there's video of the entire incident. Daniel limped out of the bedroom with my purse in his hand. Both sides of his face were badly bruised. I stood there, panting like a rabid beast and swaying drunkenly in my heels as Daniel handed me my purse and planted a sad little kiss on my cheek. Then he asked two of the guys there to escort me downstairs and told the rest of the crowd that he needed an ambulance.

I don't recall getting home, but somehow I managed to take off my dress and crawl into my bed. The next thing I knew, my mother was shaking me awake. The police were there to see me. Inside my bag they found a bottle of pills with his dad's name on the label.

Daniel had told the police that I'd left him on the balcony to use the restroom. When I'd taken too long, he'd gone to look for me. He'd found me in his parents' room rifling through their things. It was clear I was high, and I'd raided the medicine cabinet. When he tried to help me, I attacked him.

By the time the cops arrived at my apartment, the story had already made the rounds. There were twenty texts from my new friends on my phone, offering their support in my time of need. *Addiction is a disease,* one of them said. There was one from Daniel as well. *We're all here to help you get better.*

No one had to get hurt. That's what Daniel was telling me. *Play nice, and everything can go right back to the way it was.* I threw the phone at the wall. When it didn't break, I took the heel of a shoe and smashed the screen. Then I put on some clothes and went to the police station to answer questions.

With my mother at my side, I told the officers the truth. Daniel had slipped something into my drink and then attempted to rape me. I heard my mother gasp when she heard the word "rape." "Bram!" she snapped, as if I'd uttered the most ridiculous lie. I guess everyone knows that good-looking boys from rich families don't "need" to rape anyone. Especially not friendless junkies like me.

One cop took notes. The other asked all the questions. They showed the video someone had taken of when I'd come out of the bedroom. My mother was shocked. She said out loud that I barely looked human.

"You told us that your daughter has had substance abuse issues in the past," a cop said to my mother. "Did she ever steal medications to support her habit?"

And that was it. There was never a trial, but I was found guilty.

I wasn't going to let him get away with it. The following Monday, I went to school. People I barely knew stopped me to offer their best wishes. My friends acted like I was fighting cancer. They were just so *supportive*. Until lunch. With everyone in the school watching, I made my big announcement. I told them all exactly what I'd told the cops. The looks of pity quickly turned cold. Knowing he'd won, Daniel approached me, his arms open wide as if to show them that all the crazy girl needed was a hug. I punched him in the face, and when he dropped to his knees, I kicked him. By the end of the day, I'd been expelled from school and the entire world had turned against me.

No one gave a damn about the pills I'd supposedly stolen. I was being punished for the worst sin of all. I'd refused to keep my mouth shut.

That's how I got kicked out of Manhattan. I was an embarrassment to my mother and a liability for her fundraising. Daniel's parents could have made sure that her beloved charity never received another dime. Heaven forbid the pets of America were made to suffer on my behalf.

While I was under house arrest and my mom was researching boarding schools for troubled girls, I caught up on my reading. My mother had briefly mentioned the fire at the manor. Somehow she'd failed to mention that James's wife had died. And imagine my surprise when I discovered that there was another mad girl in the family. This one had started a fire that destroyed her house and killed her own mother. At least that was what everyone had been told.

The story had everything people crave—scandal, death, and damsels in distress. In terms of made-for-TV awesomeness, it was right up there with "woman seduces brother-in-law and dies in his arms." Or "fatherless girl turns to drugs and crime." Or how about "abandoned at the altar, girl drowns herself in the Hudson."

After Daniel, I knew better than to believe everything I was told. I knew that everyone lies. There wasn't much I could do to salvage my own reputation, but Lark Bellinger didn't seem like such a lost cause. So I decided to help her. I needed to prove that the truth still mattered. Because—if it didn't—there wouldn't be any reason to go on.

I'd been sitting in the cold by Grace Louth's grave for so long that my entire body had gone numb. I needed to get somewhere warm, but I had a call to make first. I pulled out my phone and looked up the number for Hastings—the mental hospital where Lark had been taken after the fire. I knew the chances were slim that I'd be able to speak to her, but I was desperate enough to give it a shot. By that point, there were a million questions I wanted to ask.

I dialed and waited as it rang.

"Hastings Psychiatric," said a chipper voice at the other end of the line.

I sat up straight. I hadn't expected anyone to answer so quickly. "Hello," I said. "I need to speak to one of the patients at your hospital. Would it be possible to see if she has phone access?"

"Give me the name and I'll check," the woman said.

"Lark Bellinger."

"I'm sorry," she said without a pause. She didn't need to check her computer. I suspected I wasn't the first person to call. "We've been instructed to direct all inquiries to her father, Ruben Bellinger."

"Have there been other inquiries?" I asked.

"Sorry," the receptionist answered. "I'm afraid that counts as an inquiry as well."

"Do you have visiting hours at Hastings?" I asked, reaching, I knew.

"Yes, we do, but if you would like to visit Lark Bellinger, you must speak with her father. I'm afraid I can't help you with that."

"Thanks," I said.

"You are welcome." She sounded so relieved to get off the phone. "Have a wonderful day."

Twenty-One

The only route home from the graveyard took me back through Louth. I would have preferred to avoid town altogether. After listening to Maisie's conversation with Gavin Turner, I didn't trust anyone. Everyone knew everyone in Louth, and I knew nothing. I was an outsider and I always would be.

I was halfway down Grace Street when I felt someone watching. Back in the city, I'd gotten so used to being the object of unwanted attention that sometimes I could actually sense the eyes on me. I looked behind me. There was no one else on the street. The person had to be watching me from inside one of the shops, but the glare from the snow on the ground was blinding, and I couldn't see through the windows. I felt like I was back in the interrogation room, staring into the one-way mirror, wondering who was studying me on the other side.

Then I heard a door open and the crunch of heavy boots on snow.

"Hey there!" a guy called out. His voice was deep but young. There was nothing sinister in what he said. If I hadn't known better, I would have thought he sounded friendly. "Hold up for a second. We want to say hi."

I tried not to turn around. I knew I shouldn't give them the satisfaction. But I couldn't resist stealing a quick peek over my shoulder. There were two of them about half a block behind me on the opposite side of the road. Both of the guys were my age, and they were wearing the Louth uniform—down coats and wool hats. One coat was navy. The other a deep burgundy. In the dark, the coats might have been mistaken for black.

It was broad daylight, of course. There were other people out on the sidewalks. I'd been in far more dangerous situations. But the pair scared me. There was something urgent in the way they scaled the snowbank on their side of the street and hurried across the salt-covered road. I hadn't brought my bear repellent or my box cutter into town. All I had to defend myself was a plastic bag filled with carbon monoxide detectors.

I kept going. The hardware store sat at the end of the

block. I pictured the kind man I'd met earlier that morning, and figured I'd be safe with him if I could just reach his shop. But the path was icy, and there was only so fast I could go. My stalkers caught up with me before I could get my hand on the door handle.

I spun around to face the two of them. "What do you want?" I demanded.

"Whoa," one said, putting his hand out as if to fend off a beast that might charge. "Calm down. I know you have to act tough in the city, but do we look like bad guys to you?"

I had no idea what bad guys were supposed to look like. Before Daniel, I suppose I'd had a picture in my head. It wouldn't have resembled either of the people who were standing before me. The silent one was cute and dopey. The one talking had a face from the 1950s, complete with a smattering of freckles across his nose.

"I asked you what you wanted."

Freckles glanced over at his friend. "We saw you down by the river earlier, and we just wanted to say hi. That's Brian. I'm Mike. And you are?"

I didn't want to give them any of my names—real or fake.

"It's all right." This time there was an edge to Mike's voice, but he kept his smile. The people in Louth were good at that. Back in Manhattan, no one tried quite as hard. "You don't have to answer. We know who you are, Bram How-land. Your uncle owns the manor."

"How do you know that?" I asked.

"This is a small town. Word gets around fast, especially if you hang out with people like Nolan."

"You should be careful," Brian blurted out, sounding about as dumb as he looked.

"Why?" I shot back. "Are you going to break all *my* windows next?"

I heard the delicate tinkle of the bell over the hardware store door.

"Hey." It was Sam's voice. "Everything okay?"

I felt light-headed with relief. "These two were just welcoming me to town," I informed him. But when I looked back at Sam, I could see he hadn't been talking to me. There were three bags in his hands—two from the hardware store and a third filled, oddly, with lemons. His eyes were locked on Mike's. I don't know what kind of telepathy those two were using, but there was no doubt that information was being exchanged.

"We were just—" Brian started.

"It's okay." Sam cut him off. "You guys should go."

I didn't say anything. I just let my eyes pass over them. Three tall, strapping guys in down coats. One navy. One burgundy. One black. In the dark, on a surveillance camera, their coats would have seemed the same color.

The standoff lasted for a few seconds. Then Brian gave Sam a curt nod. "All right, then. See you around," he said. I couldn't tell if he was talking to me.

I stood next to Sam and watched them go. Brian took the lead. The snowblowers hadn't cleared enough sidewalk for two broad-shouldered boys to walk side by side.

"Your uncle's been looking for you all morning. You headed up to the manor?" Sam asked as soon as they were out of earshot.

I nodded.

"I'm on my way back, too. I'll walk with you. There's another storm coming. We should get you home before it hits."

I turned my eyes to the sky. A few minutes earlier, the sun had been shining. Now I saw nothing but clouds. I felt like I was stuck in a game on survival mode. The world kept changing without warning, and all I could do was race to adapt.

Sam began lumbering down the sidewalk, but I wasn't ready to follow. "Hey!" I called out. "How do you know those two? Are they friends of yours?"

I could tell he had no idea how scared I'd been. Mike and Brian hadn't had weapons. They weren't wearing masks. A six-foot-three quarterback like Sam couldn't understand how two guys his size might intimidate someone like me. I wondered when he'd last had to fear for his safety. He probably had no idea that some girls fear for theirs every day.

"I wouldn't call us buddies, but I've known them since preschool. They were both on the football team when I was captain. They're regular guys."

Regular guys who chase girls they don't know down sidewalks. "They told me to be careful."

A car driving by slowed down as it passed us. The passenger was so bundled up, I couldn't tell if it was a male or a female. Sam raised a hand in silent greeting, and the person did the same. Then Sam looked back down at me. "If I remember correctly, I once told you to be careful, too. I heard you were at Nolan's last night. I guess you didn't listen."

I was on the verge of asking Sam who'd attacked Nolan's house, when I heard the tinkle of the hardware store bell, and a group of men emerged, all wearing down coats in dark colors.

That's when it hit me. It really could have been anyone.

"So are we going?" Sam asked.

"Why didn't you come back to the storeroom to check on me yesterday like you promised?" I asked.

"I did come back," he said. "Just as you were climbing into Nolan's car. Don't worry. I won't stop looking out for you, even if you have terrible taste in men. Now if you don't mind, these bags are getting heavy."

I could see the contents of Sam's plastic hardware bags. Inside one was a large screwdriver.

"Here, let me take that for you," I offered, knowing a screwdriver would make a suitable weapon in a pinch.

I relaxed a little when he handed me the bag, but the feeling didn't last long. Once we were on the road to the manor, the two of us were alone. The word "alone" had a different meaning in Louth. There weren't any cars passing by, and the forest on either side of us was dense enough to conceal any crime. All sound seemed muffled, as if I'd crammed cotton into my ears. If something happened, there would be no hope of rescue.

It started to snow when we were halfway up the hill. The first lazy flakes floated down through the tree branches and settled in my hair. I'd been in such a hurry to leave the house that morning that I'd forgotten to grab a hat. For a while, it was easy to shake them off. Then the wind picked up and the flakes fell faster. I could feel them accumulating along the part in my hair.

"Here." Sam took off his wool hat and held it out to me as he pulled up the hood of his coat. It was the first thing either of us had said. It was enough to convince me that he wasn't planning to kill me. At least not right away.

"Thanks," I told him.

"I know you've got a phone," Sam observed. "Don't you use it to check the weather?"

"I didn't realize I'd moved to the arctic circle," I replied. "Does the snow ever get a chance to melt around here?" I gestured at the waist-high snowbanks along the road that were beginning to grow once again.

"Not this year, I guess," Sam said. "By the end of March the snowbanks will be taller than both of us. They'll find some interesting stuff when it all starts to thaw."

"Like what?" I wondered what he knew.

I saw him glance at me out of the corner of his eye.

"Dropped phones. Dead deer. Lost dogs. Things like that."

"People?" I asked pointedly.

"Once," he replied. "Did Maisie tell you about April Hughes?"

I nodded. "Yeah. I guess you heard the story when you were growing up?"

Sam snorted. "At least a thousand times. Every time I went camping, someone would claim they'd seen her ghost wandering through the forest in her nightgown. Guys liked to make jokes about it. Every time you left the tent to take a leak, some douchebag would say you'd—" He grimaced at the memory. "Never mind."

"What?" I asked. "Tell me."

"They'd say you'd gone for a quickie with April Hughes."

I felt him glance over at me. I didn't look back. I turned my head toward the woods on the opposite side of the road.

A girl had died out there all alone. She was wearing a single slipper when they found her—along with a nightgown and a terry-cloth robe. I remembered the police photo that Lark had pasted into her scrapbook. In her final moments, April had crawled under the boughs of a spruce tree and curled herself into a ball. Just imagining the terror she must have felt made me want to cry.

"Sorry," Sam said softly.

"Why do people around here think April left the manor in the middle of the night?"

Sam seemed relieved that I was still speaking to him. "There are plenty of theories. The authorities were convinced she was suffering from some kind of mental disorder that had gone undiagnosed. I don't know how many people around here ever bought into that one. Most think April either arranged to meet someone in the woods—or ran away from the ghost of Grace Louth. Then there's my mom's theory."

"Your mom has her own theory?" For some reason, that surprised me.

"She met April the night she died. Believe it or not, they were around the same age in 1986."

I did the math in my head. He was right. I tried picturing April as a middle-aged woman, but all I could see was Maisie's mom. "How did they meet?"

"Back then rich New York types used to rent the manor for events, and people from Louth would be hired as staff.

April Hughes and her parents were here for a weeklong New Year's Eve celebration. My mom's family had always worked at the manor, so she got a job as one of the servers."

"She talked to April the night she disappeared?"

"Yeah," Sam said. "It's a weird story. On New Year's Eve, my mom's boss sent her downstairs to get some supplies, and she found April half-frozen in the cold storage locker."

That got my attention. "How'd she get in there?"

"April claimed she'd been exploring the manor and had taken a peek in the locker. She said she didn't know how to open the door from the inside and got trapped when it closed behind her. My mom didn't believe it. She thought April had been hiding."

"From who—or from what?" I asked.

"April wouldn't say, and Mom never found out," Sam said. "After April disappeared, Mom told the police what had happened, and they thought it was proof that April was suffering from some kind of illness. But Mom didn't think April was delusional, and she still doesn't. She thinks she was scared. April left a note—"

"The one that said *someone's at the door.*"

"Yeah. Mom thought the note looked like it had been ripped out of some kind of diary. But nobody ever found the rest."

We crested the hill and saw the manor's lawn stretched before us, perfectly white and pristine. The snow was falling furiously, and I was glad to see the topiary monstrosities disappearing again, under the cover of snow. I stopped for a moment to gaze at the manor.

"If the house isn't cursed, how do you explain all the terrible things that have happened here?" I said, not really expecting an answer.

"Lark once told me the manor is the key, not the cause," Sam said.

"What do you think she meant?" I asked.

"I'm not sure. She used to talk in riddles sometimes. But I don't care what people say. Lark was perfectly sane. She knew something. She just didn't get a chance to tell anyone before the fire."

That was exactly what I suspected as well. "Any idea what it was she knew?"

He shook his head. "I wish I knew."

We stood side by side, watching the manor as if it might show us its secrets. But it sat there sullenly, wrapped in its blanket of ice and ivy.

"I tried to call Lark today," I told Sam.

"They didn't let you through, did they? We've tried, too."

"The woman on the phone told me I'd have to speak to Lark's dad. I thought maybe I'd try."

"Ruben's not talking to anyone these days," Sam said. "If you try to go see him, there's a good chance you'll get shot."

"So he really is—?" I didn't want to say it.

"Ruben did two tours in Afghanistan as a medic. Lark said he saw things no one should ever have to see. Now his ex-wife is dead and his daughter is ill. I'd say he has every reason to be angry. Life hasn't been kind to him."

I was impressed by Sam's compassion. Most people show either pity or fear when they talk about people like me or Ruben. Few ever try to understand.

"Sam, there's something I need to ask you about. The other day when we were out here, I know I saw someone standing on the balcony of my room. It was a girl in white, and I've seen her since. Do you think it could have been Grace Louth?"

"No," he said firmly. "I don't. I don't believe in ghosts, Bram."

"Lark told people she heard things at night. Do you think she was lying?" I pressed.

Sam shook his head. "No. I just don't believe she heard a ghost."

I was getting frustrated. I couldn't understand why he was being so stubborn.

"Well, thanks for walking with me this far," I said, done with the pointless conversation. I handed him the bag I'd been carrying for him. I hated myself for feeling so disappointed. "I'll be fine on my own from here," I said, and left Sam standing at the top of the hill.

Twenty-Two

I let myself into the manor and snuck up the stairs toward the rose room. I made it as far as the landing of the grand staircase before James called out from behind me.

"There you are! Where have you been? I've been looking all over for you this morning."

I turned to face him, and I was surprised by how bad he looked. There were stains on his shirt, and his fly was half-down. Everything about him looked rumpled. Either he'd slept in his clothing or he hadn't slept at all.

"I went down to the village to get a coffee," I answered vaguely.

"What's in the bag?" James asked as he started up the stairs toward me. "Doesn't look like coffee."

I glanced down at the bag in my hand. The white plastic was so thin, it was almost translucent. He could see exactly what was inside it.

"Bram!" a voice called out from the front door. "Sorry! I must have handed you the wrong shopping bag."

Sam was standing below in the entryway, holding up a bag filled with lemons.

"You two were together just now?" James's gaze passed back and forth between us.

"We bumped into each other outside the hardware store," Sam said as he bounded up the stairs past my uncle. "Bram kept me company while we walked up the hill."

"Those for the manor?" James asked casually, nodding at the carbon monoxide detectors in the bag I'd been carrying.

"Nope, for our farm," Sam answered before I could open my mouth to speak. "Mom got a new generator after the last big storm, but she's worried it might leak gas into the house."

"And I had no idea you were such a fan of lemons," James told me.

"I mix the juice with salt and make a scrub for my face," I said, relieved that a lie had come so easily. "The dry heat in the manor has been murder on my skin."

James didn't look like he bought it, but what could he say?

"See you later, Bram," Sam announced, and headed back to the door. "Goodbye, Mr. Howland."

James didn't say a word. He kept his eyes on me the whole time.

"You certainly seem to have enchanted the young men of Louth," he said once the door had closed behind Sam.

I felt myself blushing against my will. "Excuse me?" I asked. I didn't know how else to respond.

"I'm sorry," James said. "I didn't intend to embarrass you. I'm just surprised that you're already putting yourself out there."

I stared at him blankly. I couldn't understand what he was doing.

"I heard you witnessed some trouble at the Turner house last night," he said. "You weren't injured, were you?"

"No," I confirmed.

"I thought you told me you weren't interested in Nolan."

"I'm not," I said. I was getting really tired of talking about Nolan.

"So how did you end up spending the evening with him?"

Where was this bizarre interrogation coming from? "He knocked on the door around seven o'clock and said you and his dad were out of town," I said. "Miriam wasn't here, and he invited me over for dinner."

"He cooks, does he?" I realized that I couldn't tell if my

uncle was smiling or sneering. It was difficult to believe I was talking to the same person I'd known when I was little. That Uncle James had always been laughing. He'd acted like he didn't have a care in the world, and when I was with him, my cares vanished, too.

But that James had disappeared long ago. The expectations of others had been too much to bear, and business burdens had squeezed the life right out of him. The man left behind was hard and bitter.

"I believe someone else did the cooking," I told him evenly.

"Well, you should probably let Miriam make your dinners from now on," James said. "I hear the Turners received some unexpected guests last night. I didn't mention the incident when I spoke to your mother earlier, but I'm not sure I can neglect to inform her the next time something happens."

I suddenly felt cold. "You spoke with my mother?" Had she told him I'd asked about the gas leak?

"Yes. She called shortly after you ran out of the manor this morning. She wanted me to check my medicine cabinets. She said you'd been talking nonsense on the phone, and she was worried you may have suffered a relapse. I informed her that all medications are currently under lock and key and I'd seen no evidence of drug use on your part."

"Thank you," I said cautiously.

"You are clean, are you not?" he asked.

"I am," I assured him.

"There's no need to schedule a blood test, is there?"

"No." I could feel myself shrinking.

"Good," James replied with a smile. "Because if your mother suspects you're using drugs again, do you know what she'll do?"

I assumed the question was rhetorical, so I didn't answer.

"What will she do, Bram?" James pressed.

"She'll send me back to rehab," I said.

"That's right. Which would be a real shame. I know you've only been here a few days, but you seem to be getting along so splendidly. You're happy in Louth, aren't you?"

"Yes," I said, trying my best to smile.

"Excellent." He pulled me into a hug that didn't feel reassuring. "What on earth did you say to your mother that made her think you might have relapsed?" he asked.

Tears gathered at the corners of my eyes. "I don't know," I told him.

He let go of me and took me by the shoulders, smiling. "Well, let's let bygones be bygones. What do you say?"

I nodded silently and turned to go up the stairs.

"Oh. And, Bram?"

I stopped. "Yes?"

"It's probably best if you stay away from Nolan Turner. I know it's crazy, but his father thinks you might be a bad influence."

I would have been mortified if I'd thought it was true. But I had a hunch that it wasn't, and that felt even worse. I'd come to expect low blows from my mother. I hadn't thought they were James's style. It hurt even more to be caught off guard.

An hour later, there was a knock at my door. When I opened it, I found Miriam standing in the hall with a tray of food.

"I thought you might be hungry," she said. "May I leave this on the vanity?"

"Sure." I had no interest in eating. I crawled back into bed.

She set the tray down and then walked over to where I sat. She stood over me for a moment. There seemed to be something she wanted to say.

"May I show you something?" she asked at last.

"Sure," I said.

Miriam gestured for me to get up. Then she carefully pushed the bed away from the wall. Plugged into an outlet was a small beige device with a green light. I knew what it was the moment I saw it.

"I have carbon monoxide detectors hidden all over the house," Miriam said. "I put them where no one can see them. Your uncle can be quite prickly when it comes to such things. But I promise you'll hear the alarms if there's a leak."

I didn't know what to say. Sam had known how James would react when he saw the detectors. He and his mother were savvier than they were letting on.

"I chose this brand because it's electric, with backup batteries in case the power goes out," Miriam continued. "I wouldn't sleep in the manor without them." She pushed the bed back against the wall, concealing the carbon monoxide detector from view. "Now," she said. "May I please have my lemons? I can't make a lemon tart without them."

Twenty-Three

I woke up that night to find a girl standing by my bed, wearing a white dress and veil. I wasn't scared when I saw her. More than anything else in the world, I wished she would stay. Real or not, she was on my side. I don't know how I knew, but I did.

Still half-asleep, I slowly pushed myself up and glanced at the clock. It was three in the morning, and I'd left the curtains open again. The moon was a sliver short of full, and I could see my room clearly. When I turned back, the girl was gone, but my bedroom door, which I'd been careful to lock, was ajar. That's when I knew for sure that I wasn't dreaming. I slid out of bed with my phone in my hand. I could hear someone in the hall.

I tiptoed to the door and peeked outside my bedroom. When I saw the figure at the far end of the hall, I almost ducked back inside. Her tattered gown glowed faintly in the moonlight. The fabric seemed to be satin, but it was no longer pure white. The hem and sleeves were black with soot, and the train of the dress left a trail of dampness on the floorboards.

I lifted my phone, but I didn't dare take a picture. I knew that the girl didn't want to be seen. She slouched toward the north wing, her back hunched with her eyes on the floor. Her head swiveled slowly from side to side, the movement as regular as a pendulum keeping time. The floorboards creaked and groaned with each step she took. I wondered if I was hearing the same sounds Lark used to hear.

I followed her, doing my best to remain hidden in the shadows. That night, I was the one haunting her. We entered the burnt-out north wing of the manor. Every room I passed through was colder and darker than the last. And with each room, the girl's search seemed to grow more urgent. She examined the walls and scoured the floor, but she never looked behind her. I could tell she was searching for something—something she never managed to find.

I thought of all the stories I'd read about poor, lost souls forced to relive the same terrible moments for all of eternity. The jilted lover would always jump off the same cliff. The condemned woman would flee down a hall. The murdered hitchhiker sought nightly rides back to town. I'd always wondered if it was some kind of cosmic punishment. But maybe they kept going because they hoped the next time would be different—that the universe would eventually let their story end happily.

I followed the girl through the blackened chambers until we reached the room with plywood boards nailed to the wall. The balcony from which Lark had jumped lay on the other side. There, the girl came to a stop. A cold breeze squeezed through the boards and ruffled her tattered veil. I watched her head slowly tilt until her ear was up in the air. She was listening to something. Then I heard the sound through the cracks in the boards covering the windows— heavy footsteps in the snow outside the manor, making their way to the front door. There wasn't much light in the north wing. When the girl turned around, I couldn't make out a face behind the veil. There was no way to know if she was looking my way. I stayed perfectly still, hoping I'd blend into the shadows. Downstairs, there was someone at the door.

"Run!" she whispered.

And I did.

I raced back through the north wing, my arms stretched out in front of me, my hands treading the darkness. I was sure that I'd touch something—or that something would reach out and grab me. When I finally emerged from the north wing, the moon came out from behind the clouds, and I could see my bedroom door open ahead. I'd almost made it to safety when I heard a loud bang in the entryway.

I ran to the stairway banister and looked down. The front door stood open and snow was blowing inside. My uncle lay sprawled out on the floor below. A bottle still clutched in his hand was leaking what little was left of its contents. As I stood watching, his body began to convulse. Then a low moan rose from his throat. When it was over, he began to sob.

"What's going on?" Miriam stood outside a room down the hall, wearing her plaid flannel robe. She raced right past me when I didn't answer, the robe floating behind her as she took two stairs at a time and dropped to her knees by the body. "James," she said as she rolled my uncle over onto his back. "James, can you speak?"

I'd never seen a living person look so dead. His face was a chalky white, and his lips and the tip of his nose were blue. His hair remained frozen, its stiff silvery tendrils reaching out in every direction.

"She's gone," he wailed pitifully.

Miriam looked up and saw me still standing at the top of the stairs, with my fingers clenched in terror on the banister.

"It's okay, Bram," she said. "You can go back to bed. Your uncle will be fine. He's just very drunk."

I didn't need her to tell me that. I was no stranger to booze. Plus, I'd recognized the bottle in his hand. It had been my father's favorite whisky—a rare Orkney scotch. I'd ordered a bottle just like it and had it sent to James on the day of his second wedding. My mother screamed bloody murder when her assistant flagged the eight-thousand-dollar charge on her credit card. But I didn't give a damn. I'd wanted James to know that, even though I couldn't be at his wedding, he was still on my mind. I knew he'd agree—it was the thought that counted.

"Where was he just now?" I asked.

"Dahlia's mausoleum," Miriam said. "He doesn't sleep much. He goes there at night to be with her."

"So he really loved her," I said.

"Yes," Miriam told me. "I think he really did."

I went back to the rose room and closed the door, but I didn't lock it. I curled up under the covers with my knees tucked to my chest and my arms wrapped around my shins.

Twenty-Four

The next time I woke up, the sun was rising. I hadn't closed the curtains, and the wind had blown one of the balcony doors open. The room wasn't frigid yet, though it was well on its way. I crawled out of bed to close the door. Just as the latch clicked into place, I caught a glimpse of a figure moving toward the edge of the woods, and I pressed my forehead to the glass. She was dressed in white, which made it difficult to see her against the snow. But it was the same girl. There was no doubt about it. I threw on my boots and coat and went after her.

I wasn't hallucinating, but I wasn't thinking straight, either. I was so fed up with mysteries that I was willing to risk everything for a clue. By the time I reached the tree line, the girl was nowhere to be seen. Still, I plunged into the forest, deeper and deeper until I couldn't tell where I was. I wandered until sheer exhaustion finally brought me to a halt. I stopped under a tree to catch my breath, and I felt the cold overtake me. My limbs were numb, and my mind began to drift, but I was too tired to move. I slumped down against the tree trunk, my knees tucked against my chest. Time passed, and then something seemed to ignite inside me, and warmth spread throughout my body. My mind left the forest, and I found myself back in my bedroom in Manhattan, getting ready for Daniel's party. Everything seemed right in the world. For the first time since the incident, I felt at peace. I could have stayed in the moment forever.

The next thing I knew, I was staring up at a moldy ceiling. I felt no fear at first, just a crushing sadness. I knew, the moment I opened my eyes, that I hadn't died and gone to heaven, though I wasn't so sure about hell. I was hot—too hot, and I was lying on a ratty old sofa. A fire was crackling somewhere nearby, and the room reeked of animal hair and old grease.

I tried to sit up, and discovered I could barely move. I was wrapped in blankets, my arms pinned to my sides. The panic set in, and I flailed like a fish in a net, arching my back and kicking my legs to break free.

"Don't struggle. You'll hurt yourself," a man ordered, and I froze. I didn't recognize the voice. It was deep and emotionless—classic serial killer. For a few unpleasant seconds, I imagined the worst. I waited to hear the rev of a chain saw or the whetting of a knife.

Then I felt him lift my shoulders from behind and push me up into a sitting position, and I almost wet myself in terror when I got a good look at the house. There was no way any normal person could possibly live like that. The wood-paneled walls were lined with teetering towers of books, and at least one of the stacks had fallen, scattering books across the floor. At the far end of the room, on a table made from two sawhorses and an old door, the head of a dead buck sat facing me, two dark holes where its eyes should have been. Dirty dishes were stacked up beside the head, and several cases' worth of beer cans had been tossed into the nearest corner. Aside from the worktable, everything in the room was covered with a layer of soot, and the floorboards were black with grime.

"They're clearing the drive to the house right now so the ambulance can get through," the man said.

I latched on to the word "ambulance" like it was a life preserver. I was so relieved that he wasn't going to kill me that it took a few moments to realize that I might be hurt.

"Why do I need an ambulance?" I managed to croak as he walked around the sofa.

"You don't, as far as I can tell, but I figured I'd let the EMTs make that call." He sat down across from me in one of those leather recliners you see on old TV shows. I suppose at some point in the past he'd been handsome. But it looked like it had been a while since he'd showered or shaved. The bags under his eyes suggested he hadn't been sleeping much, and the state of his work pants told me that laundry wasn't exactly a priority, either. But he didn't look homicidal. He didn't even seem dangerous. If I'd had to pick one word to describe the man, I probably would have said he looked haunted.

"Are you Ruben Bellinger?" I guessed.

"I am indeed, and you must be Miss Howland," he replied politely. Then Lark's father glanced over his shoulder. "I apologize. I should have thrown a sheet over my workbench. Taxidermy isn't for everyone."

The voice that had terrified me now sounded tired. And as my eyes passed over the books all around us, I picked up a few of the titles. There were a few taxidermy manuals mixed in, but there didn't seem to be a subject that wasn't of interest to Ruben. If he'd gotten through even a third of his library, there was no doubt he was the best-read man in town. I'm sure the Unabomber's cabin had a few interesting titles, too, but it's hard to be frightened of someone with a Budweiser, a bag of Cheetos, and a copy of *The Life of the Buddha* on their coffee table.

There was something else there. A black hair tie. Nothing fancy—just a rubber band that you'd use to put your hair into a ponytail. It must have been Lark's. I had no idea how long it had been sitting there, but the sight of it made my heart ache. I could only imagine how bad things must have been if Dahlia had been willing to force Lark to live here.

"How do you know who I am?" I asked Lark's father.

"It's a small town," he told me. "Everyone knows everyone."

By then I was thoroughly sick of that answer, and Ruben Bellinger didn't strike me as the kind of guy who dabbled in small-town gossip. I remembered Nolan saying that my uncle thought Ruben used to watch the manor at night. I wondered if it could be true—and if my host might still enjoy peeking in windows.

"How did I get here?"

"I carried you. I found you halfway between this place and the manor. I don't know how you got as far as you did without snowshoes. Might ask your uncle to buy you a pair. And next time you take a walk in the woods, consider wearing a hat and changing out of your pajamas."

"What were *you* doing out in the woods?" I asked.

Ruben laughed. "Funny, I was looking forward to asking you the very same thing," he said. "I woke up hungry and went out to do a little hunting. Lucky for you that I left the house when I did. A few more minutes in the snow would have turned you into a Popsicle."

"You really saved me?"

Ruben's eyes were a bright, almost unnatural blue, and when he stared, it felt like he was reading my mind. "You sound like you find that hard to believe."

"I walked by your house with a friend the other day, and I heard you in the woods. You must have been watching us. I know you had a gun."

I can't believe I had the guts to say it. I knew nothing for certain—until Ruben confirmed it. "I always have my gun with me in the woods," he said. "And if your friend Nolan Turner had stepped one toe over my property line, there's a good chance I'd have used it."

"Do you think Nolan had something to do with what happened to Lark?"

"Not necessarily," Ruben said with a shrug. "I just never cared all that much for his family. Bunch of parasites, if you ask me. People like them have been feeding on this town for over a century."

"Did you know Nolan was friends with Lark?"

"My daughter is allowed to make her own friends," Ruben said.

"I wish I could talk to her about the night of the fire. Is there any way I could visit Lark—or maybe call her on the phone?"

I shouldn't have asked. The moment I did, Ruben Bellinger lost interest in humoring me. "No, Nancy Drew," he said. "Lark doesn't want to talk to anyone."

"Are you sure?" I wasn't quite ready to give up. "I swear I'm not trying to be difficult. It's just that I spent a few months in a mental health facility last year. It was a pretty lonely place. I would have killed for a phone call."

Most people would go on alert the moment they heard that I'd been locked away. I'd seen their spines stiffen and their muscles tense—like they were preparing to defend themselves or make a run for the hills. A lot of the time the shift was subtle. I'm sure they didn't even know what they'd done. But if you're on the receiving end often enough, you learn to pick up on the signs.

Ruben had the opposite reaction—he relaxed. My confession seemed to render me less of a threat. "Miss Howland, even if Lark did want to talk, she wouldn't be able to answer your questions," he said softly, as if he were sorry to break the bad news. "She suffered a brain injury the night of the fire. She doesn't remember much about all of that anymore. Now, if you'll please excuse me."

He rose from his chair and walked out of view. I could hear him shuffling around in what I assumed was the kitchen, but I was wrapped up too tightly to turn around for a look.

"Mr. Bellinger, would you mind loosening some of these blankets?" I called out to him.

"I think it's best you sit tight until help arrives," he replied. "But you'll be glad to know I can hear the snowplow. I don't think we'll have the pleasure of each other's company much longer. And in the future, Miss Howland, please stay out of my woods. It would be a real shame if I mistook you for a deer."

I lay back on the sofa and waited for the EMTs to arrive.

Turned out Ruben Bellinger had done a bang-up job of bringing me back from the dead. The doctor who examined me knew the Bellingers well (because everyone in Louth . . . blah, blah, blah). She confirmed what Sam had told me—Ruben had been a medic in Afghanistan. He'd been stationed in the mountains, where cold-related injuries and amputations were as common as bullet holes. I understood why he'd want to keep to himself after that. I knew what it was like to see things that you can't unsee.

It took about ten minutes for the doctor to draw my blood, watch me wiggle all of my digits, and give me a clean bill of health. After that, I had a nice long chat with the hospital's psychiatrist, who informed me that it wasn't entirely normal to be found in your pajamas in the middle of the woods. I told her something close to the truth—that I saw a girl run into the forest and I thought she might need some help. I didn't mention that the girl in question could very well be dead. I could tell that the shrink didn't buy a word of my story, but she didn't seem to think I was suicidal, either. She said she'd be paying close attention to the results of my blood test, and I heartily encouraged her to do so.

After that, I was free to sit in the hospital waiting room, though I wasn't allowed to leave. An adult needed to check me out, but the plows hadn't yet reached the manor, and James was still snowed in—and likely nursing the mother of all hangovers.

Just before noon, I was flipping through a four-year-old copy of *Modern Maturity* in the waiting room when Miriam and Sam charged through the door. They bustled right past me on their way to the reception desk. Judging by the stricken looks on their faces, you'd have thought they were on their way to my deathbed. Sam was wearing sweatpants tucked into his snow boots, and Miriam clutched a manila envelope in one hand. I shuddered when I imagined what forms were inside it. As they leaned over the desk to speak to the woman seated behind it, I considered sneaking out of the hospital. I was halfway out of my chair when the Reinharts both swiveled in my direction. In the gap between them, I saw the hospital's receptionist pointing directly at me.

Twenty-Five

"They gave me a drug test!" I announced, shrinking back into my chair as the Reinharts approached me. "You can ask the doctor! I'm clean!"

Miriam and her son shared a confused look. "What?" Sam asked.

I gestured at the envelope in Miriam's hand. I was sure it contained the paperwork needed to send me away. "The rehab center won't take me if I haven't been using. It doesn't matter what forms my mother signed."

Miriam pulled a chair across from mine and sat down. Sam did the same. "This isn't about rehab," Miriam said in a low voice. "I don't need to see any drug tests."

Having known my mother for seventeen years, I assumed

the worst. "She's having me committed to a mental hospital?"

Sam shook his head vigorously as Miriam reached out and put a hand on my knee. "No, Bram! You're not going anywhere! Your mother doesn't even know what happened this morning, and your uncle was still sleeping when we left. I wrote him a note, but I doubt he's read it."

"Then what's going on?" I asked. "What's in the envelope?"

Miriam took in a deep breath as if to steel herself. "I'm going to show you," she said. "But first I need you to be completely honest with me. The hospital told me you followed a girl into the woods. Is that true?"

"Yes," I admitted.

"Do you know who it was?" She seemed to be holding her breath as she awaited the answer.

"It was a girl who looked just like Grace Louth," I told her. "She was in the north wing last night—right before James showed up drunk. I saw her again this morning going into the woods, and I tried to follow her to see where she was going."

Miriam's eyes darted toward her son. "You saw her in the house last night?"

"Yes. She seemed to be looking for something."

"Looking for something?" Miriam's face was ashen. "Are you sure?"

I lost my patience at that point. "Of course I'm sure! I'm not crazy! Sam's seen her, too." I looked right at Sam. "Haven't you? Tell your mom about the girl on the balcony!"

"Calm down," Sam whispered. "No one thinks you're crazy. We both know you're telling the truth."

"There's something we need to share with you." Miriam unsealed the envelope and pulled out an old black-and-white photograph, which she promptly handed to me.

The photo showed two elderly ladies standing in front of Louth Manor. Judging by the style of their dresses, the photo had been taken in the 1940s or 1950s. The two of them were grinning at the camera as if they'd just pulled off the biggest heist in history. I couldn't understand why they were supposed to interest me. I turned my attention to the manor instead, and scanned its windows for signs of ghosts.

"I don't get it," I finally admitted. "What am I supposed to be looking at? Who are these people?"

Miriam reached over and tapped one of the figures. "That's my great-great-grandmother Edna. She was a maid at the manor when she was young." Then Miriam slid her finger over to the second woman. "And that is her friend Grace Louth."

I couldn't wrap my head around it. "No," I insisted.

"Yes," Miriam countered. "Although, by that point, she'd been living under the name Flora Davis for most of her life."

I studied the photo more closely, recalling the photo of

Grace Louth that Lark had pasted into her scrapbook. I could see that girl in the old woman's eyes. She was the same badass she'd always been.

"This photo was taken on Grace's first visit to the manor in the sixty-two years since her father's death," Miriam told me. "She was eighty years old at the time. She'd waited until she knew that no one in town would recognize her."

"So Grace didn't drown when she was eighteen?" I asked.

"No," Miriam said. "The night she jumped into the river, she simply stopped being Grace Louth."

I thought of the girl in the mural. For over a century, everyone had assumed the portrait showed Grace running to meet her death. I remembered the first moment I saw her—the morning after I'd arrived at the manor. To me, she'd looked fierce and free. Before I'd heard the stories, I'd gotten a glimpse of who Grace really was.

As I learned from Miriam, there was some truth to the legend of Grace Louth—one little grain around which a grotesque pearl had formed. Grace had indeed fallen for someone her father considered unsuitable. Frederick had intercepted a letter which had made it clear that the two were intending to run away. When confronted, Grace refused to reveal the identity of the letter's author. All that mattered to Frederick was that his daughter was in love with someone he hadn't chosen. Girls like Grace didn't get to pick for themselves.

And yes, Grace was sent to the family's country home. But it wasn't to recover from a broken heart. When she'd refused to end her affair, she was imprisoned by her father. Men could do things like that back in those days. If a daughter vanished, her father's explanation was almost always accepted.

As soon as Grace arrived at the manor, she was locked in the rose room. The servant tasked with looking after her night and day was a twenty-year-old girl who would one day become Miriam Reinhart's great-great-grandmother. She was Grace Louth's keeper as well as her cellmate.

According to the tale passed down in Miriam's family, Frederick Louth considered Grace's romance nothing more than a temporary nuisance. He'd broken Grace's mother. He didn't anticipate any trouble breaking their daughter as well. He assumed that a lover who was out of sight would soon be forgotten. But that wasn't what happened. Grace spent her first week of captivity scheming to escape and the second week raging at her lack of success. By her third week in Louth, she had fallen into a funk. After a full month in the manor, she was a mere shadow of herself. Locked away day and night, her skin lost its color and Edna began to worry that Grace would disappear completely.

Having spent countless hours together, the servant and the prisoner had grown fond of each other. One came from wealth, while the other's family was desperately poor. But neither girl had a dime of her own. One was imprisoned, and the other remained technically free. But as young women, neither could control her own destiny. Edna wanted more than anything else to help the fiery girl whose light was dimming. Grace refused to allow her. If she escaped, her father would hold Edna responsible. And what men were able to do to their daughters paled in comparison to the cruelties they could inflict on their female servants.

Edna prayed for an answer, and when she heard that Grace's mother was coming to town, she was sure her prayers had been answered. Then she laid eyes on the woman, and her hopes drained away. Clara was tall, with a face that resembled her beautiful daughter's. But though she wasn't quite forty, everything about Clara Louth was gray. Her skin had turned sallow and her eyes were lifeless. She moved with painstaking caution, as if she were trying not to make ripples in the world around her. Her eyes trailed the ground and she rarely spoke. Marriage to Frederick Louth had left Clara little more than a wraith.

Still, Edna knew she had to try. She begged to speak with Clara Louth concerning her daughter's health. When she was granted an audience, Edna didn't mince words. She informed the girl's mother that Grace would not survive being locked away from the world. Clara said nothing, and Edna left with her spirits crushed. There was no way for her to know that Clara had immediately written to her husband who'd returned to Manhattan for business. She knew she'd never convince him to release their daughter, so she appealed to his common sense instead. A missing daughter was one thing, she wrote him. A dead daughter would be much harder to explain. She asked permission to hire a new servant to help keep Grace alive. A few days later, a young woman arrived at the manor's door. She was an artist, she informed the staff. She'd been hired to bring the world to Grace's bedroom.

Frederick Louth had issued a strict order that his daughter was to see no one but Edna, so Grace left the rose room every morning when the artist arrived to paint. The young woman worked tirelessly, and within a few days, she'd begun to cover the walls of the room with a mural of the manor's surroundings. Edna found the artist's choice of subject bewildering. The artist could have transported Grace to exotic places or legendary lands. Instead she'd chosen to duplicate the world right outside the window. The first thing she'd painted was a wooden boat on the river.

Edna may have thought it all very strange, but Grace was utterly captivated. Every evening when she returned to

255

her bedroom, Grace would gleefully tour the chamber with a candle in her hand, studying the latest additions to the mural. It seemed as if the painting had worked some kind of magic. Grace's color returned. She ate what the cooks made for her. She asked Edna to bring her books from the manor's grand library on the movement of the stars and the currents of the Hudson River.

At the beginning of June, the mural was complete and the artist vanished from Louth. On her last day in the house, she painted Grace into the picture. Given the fact that the two young women had never met, Edna thought it a remarkable likeness. After the artist was gone, Grace's mood changed once more. She started chewing her nails to the quick and pacing the floorboards. At night she whispered to herself in the darkness. She seemed to have lost the desire to sleep.

By midmonth, Grace had grown so frantic that Edna worried she might do herself harm. She begged Grace to say what had upset her so badly. Finally Grace confessed that she planned to escape the following night. She said the signs and stars in the mural had told her that was when it needed to be done. To Edna, it all sounded like the ravings of a madwoman. Grace was seeing things in the painting that couldn't possibly be there.

Then Grace pulled a book from her shelf and showed Edna a constellation that matched the one in the mural's nighttime sky. It was always over Louth in the month of June. Then she handed Edna a magnifying glass, dragged her to the mural, and pointed to a small sign in the window of the town's general store. RIVER FESTIVAL JUNE 15. The clock outside the Louth town hall was stuck at two. And finally Grace tapped on the little boat—the first thing the artist had painted. Edna bent down with the magnifying glass and examined the small wooden vessel floating on the water. Painted on its side was the name of the boat. *Patience.*

Everything in the mural had convinced Grace that a vessel would be on the river at two in the morning on June fifteenth, waiting to ferry her to freedom. But the only way out of the manor was to jump from her bedroom's balcony, and it was unlikely she'd survive such a fall uninjured. Anything Grace might have used to make a rope had been confiscated, and the rose room was searched twice every day. There were too many locked doors and too many servants between Grace's room and the boat on the river. The two girls agreed—escape seemed impossible.

That evening, a servant delivered a package from Grace's mother. The contents had been thoroughly inspected by Frederick Louth's men. He didn't trust his wife more than any other female. But there was nothing inside the box other than a collection of family photographs, a book in which to glue them, and a handwritten note from Clara Louth.

Dearest Grace,

I hope you don't mind if I borrow your girl this evening. My own maid has come down with a fever, and I'm feeling poorly as well. I feel terrible taking your one source of solace, so I've enclosed a diversion. I know this has been a difficult time for you, darling. You must have patience, and everything will work out well in the end.

Love, Mother

Grace was beaming when she read the last line of the letter aloud. *You must have patience.* Edna knew that *Patience* was the name of the boat in the mural, but the servant girl found it hard to believe that Clara Louth could know that. When she left Grace alone that evening, she feared the worst. The girl had pinned all her hopes on escaping. What would happen when those dreams were crushed?

That night, Edna was asleep on the floor beside Clara Louth's bed when one of Frederick Louth's men burst into the chamber with an urgent message. Word had come from the town that Grace had broken free and run down to the river. She wasn't wearing a wedding dress—just a long, white nightgown. But the story of her cruel romantic abandonment had been the talk of Louth, and the three people who witnessed her run through the town saw what they expected to see. When one of her shoes was discovered at the end of a dock, everyone assumed she'd jumped in and drowned. No one ever stopped to consider if Grace Louth knew how to swim.

Edna's whereabouts that night were well known. Clara Louth herself vouched for the servant girl's innocence. The truth was, Edna had no idea how Grace had escaped. But when news of Grace's death reached Frederick Louth, Edna still bore the brunt of his wrath. Despite Clara's best efforts to protect her, the girl was beaten mercilessly—and demoted to scullery maid. Leaving the manor was never an option. Her mother was crippled and depended on Edna's earnings to survive. The other servants were just as helpless in the face of Frederick Louth's cruelty. There were no other jobs in Louth.

As Edna spent the next day on her knees, scrubbing the manor floors, she began to hear whispers about the mural. Another maid had spotted the image of Grace running down the hill. The servants all agreed that the mural was either haunted or bewitched, and they refused to step foot in the rose room. Edna didn't tell anyone that Grace had believed the painting was a message—and she remained silent when she began to hear about the ghost.

While the entire town of Louth was gathered at the graveyard for Grace's funeral, a newspaper photographer snuck onto the grounds and snapped a picture of the manor.

Though the house was empty, the image showed what many believed was a girl dressed in a white gown and veil standing behind the rose room's windows. The servants agreed that the hazy figure was Grace's ghost. But Frederick Louth was a rational man with no time for supernatural nonsense. He insisted the photograph was a hoax and ordered the servants to be on the lookout for trespassers.

Yet the sightings continued. A maid passing by the open door of the rose room one evening saw a girl in white on the balcony. When the maid returned with backup, the girl had vanished. Others swore they saw the ghost on the grounds of the manor or in the warren of dark rooms in the basement. All the indoor sightings took place when the mansion was sealed tight. There was no way a flesh-and-blood girl could have gotten inside.

Then, one night, the entire household was awakened by unearthly screams in the rose room. The cries weren't those of a female, living or dead. When the servants gathered outside the room, they found the door locked. The keys to the rose room were nowhere to be found. Neither was the master of the house, and it quickly became clear that the person in the room was Frederick Louth.

Three of the burliest servants hurled themselves at the thick wooden door. It had been reinforced when Frederick Louth had turned the room into a prison, and fifteen minutes passed before the servants heard the first crack. By that time, the cries from within had already ceased.

They found Frederick Louth on the floor of his dead daughter's bedroom, his face purple and one hand clutched to his chest. In the other was a hammer he'd been using to pry plaster off the walls. There was no one else in the room, but the balcony doors stood wide open. One of the servants went to close them and saw a girl in white running down the hill.

Miriam paused, and I waited eagerly while she reached back into the manila envelope and retrieved a yellowing sheet of paper, which she passed to me.

"The evening after Frederick Louth died, my great-great-grandmother discovered this note under her pillow."

I unfolded the paper. On it were a few short lines scribbled in a hurried hand.

I'm sorry you suffered. He won't hurt any of us again. Your loyalty will be rewarded. You have our eternal gratitude.

I looked up from the letter. "And?"

"The next day, Clara Louth gave my great-great-grandmother five hundred dollars. That was a fortune in those days. Edna used it to purchase the land I now live on. When Clara said goodbye to Louth, she left my great-great-grandmother in charge of the manor. Edna never saw her again. It wasn't until sixty years later that she heard from Grace. For all those years, Edna never breathed a word of what had happened to anyone but her own daughter. That daughter passed the truth along to her own daughter. And then my mother told the story to me."

"So Clara Louth was in on it all?" I asked. "She helped Grace escape?"

"She must have. She hired the artist, and she was responsible for my great-great-grandmother's alibi."

"Does this mean Grace killed her own father?"

"I don't know," Miriam admitted. "Edna never asked. She said she liked to believe that he died of fright."

"But Grace *was* inside the rose room with him the night he died?"

"Edna was sure of it," Miriam said. "But no one saw Grace come out. They just saw her running down the hill after they broke through the door."

"If she was in the rose room, how did she escape?" I asked.

"That's another mystery," Miriam said. "My great-great-grandmother examined every photo in the box Clara Louth had delivered to Grace on the night of June fifteenth. Edna was convinced Clara had slipped secret instructions inside, but she was never able to find them."

The three of us sat there in the hospital waiting room while I let it all sink in.

"Grace lived a wonderful life," Miriam said. "Her mother was right. Patience was all she needed."

I shook my head. "I don't get it."

"'Patience' wasn't the name of the boat. It was the signature of the artist. Grace knew it was the name of the person who was coming to rescue her."

I had to laugh at my foolishness. "That's amazing!" I said, finally understanding. I'd been fed so many cookie-cutter romances that I'd managed to listen to Grace's story without ever considering that her beloved might have been another girl.

"So, do you see, Bram? There is no curse and there is no ghost. Grace died a happy woman."

"Then who's the girl in white?" I asked. "I swear I've seen her with my own eyes."

Sam cleared his throat. "It's not Grace Louth. We think it's Lark. And we think we know what she's trying to find."

Twenty-Six

In the moments that followed, I ran through all the encounters I'd had with the girl in white. The night she'd appeared after I'd woken up screaming. The furniture she'd stacked against the door of my room after the sheriff had warned me. Her moonlight search of the mansion's north wing. After so many strange happenings, a ghost had started to seem like the only explanation. The manor was always locked up too tightly for a flesh-and-blood girl to sneak in at night. Now I realized that Lark must have discovered Grace Louth's secret escape route.

"You told us you thought the girl was looking for something." Miriam fished around in her handbag and produced a mobile phone. She passed it to me. "I found it shortly after

I came to work at the manor. It had fallen into a heating vent. It must have happened the night of the fire."

"Is this Lark's phone?" I asked as I clicked the home button.

The answer appeared on the screen in front of me. Her wallpaper was a close-up of Grace Louth's face as portrayed in the mural. I switched the phone off immediately and looked around to make sure no one else could have seen it.

"Oh my God!" I whispered. "Why didn't you give this to the police?"

"You think Louth's sheriff's department has the resources to crack an iPhone password?" Sam asked. "Besides, the fire department determined that there wasn't a crime. So the phone isn't technically evidence. I drove up to Hastings to give it to Lark, but the hospital wouldn't let me see her. They wouldn't even deliver the phone to her room."

"That's when we started to wonder if Lark was still there," Miriam said. "Now we're convinced that she's not. We think she's here in Louth, and she's been sneaking back into the manor to look for this."

"But I don't understand. Why all the secrecy?" I asked. "It's her phone. Why doesn't she just ask if anyone's found it?"

"Remember when I told you I thought Lark had discovered something while she was researching the manor?" Sam asked. "Whatever it is, I think it's stored on this phone."

I knew he was right, and the phone in my hand suddenly felt a lot heavier.

"We want you to give the phone back to her," Miriam said. "But you can't let anyone else know that you have it."

"Not Maisie, not Nolan, and definitely not James," Sam warned me.

"Why don't you trust James?" I wanted to hear them say it out loud.

"He claims Lark inherited mental illness from her father—and that it began to surface after she moved into the manor." Sam looked over at his mother. "But Ruben suffers from PTSD. He got it serving our country. It's not something you can pass down to your children."

"I believe Sam told you that I was working at the manor the night April Hughes went missing?" Miriam asked, and I nodded. "People claimed she lost her mind and ran into the woods. I knew in my heart that what they said about her wasn't true. I did what I could back then, but I've always wished I'd done more. I've lived with the guilt for thirty-five years. I wasn't going to sit by and let the same thing happen to another girl."

"Especially after what Lark said when they found her that night," Sam added.

"James told me Lark was raving about the Dead Girls," I said.

"No," Sam said. "A friend of mine's dad is a fireman. He told me Lark was only talking about one Dead Girl that night. She kept saying she'd seen April Hughes."

The hospital emergency room's glass doors slid open, and the three of us went silent as two young men in down coats entered.

"What the hell are they doing here?" I whispered. It was Mike and Brian.

The two of them stopped a few feet inside and scanned the waiting room. I knew they were looking for me. Someone must have told them I'd be there. When they finally saw me sitting with the Reinharts, Mike gave Sam a curt nod.

"I need to go have a word with those guys." Sam rose from his seat. "Mom, why don't you drive Bram back up to the manor."

Miriam picked up her manila envelope and slipped the photograph and note back into it. "Come on," she said. "Let's get you home."

Out in the parking lot, Miriam guided me to a pickup truck. She opened the passenger door first, and took a moment to brush off the seat, which had been covered in a fine layer of dirt.

"Sorry for the mess," she said. "I had to take a fresh load of soil to one of my greenhouses before the snow started again yesterday."

"You have a farm?" I asked.

"My husband and I grow organic vegetables. Of course, he's been doing it all himself these past few months."

I was confused. "Why did you take a job at the manor if you have your own farm?"

"Hop in," she said, and I figured I wasn't going to get an answer. But after I climbed into the truck, Miriam was still standing there. "My husband thinks I've lost it. But a woman I liked died at the manor, and I wasn't satisfied with the explanation that was given. I don't know how this will all turn out, but the worst thing in life is regret, and I knew I couldn't live with doing nothing. And now that you're there, I'm not going anywhere."

She closed my door, and I watched as she walked around to the other side. At that moment, I envied Sam more than anyone else in the world. I would have given anything for a mother like his—someone I knew in my heart I could trust.

"Miriam," I said once she'd settled in behind the wheel. "Do you know those two guys Sam went to speak with?"

"Mike and Brian," she replied. "They were on Sam's football team last year."

"They've been following me all over town," I said.

"Following you?" When Miriam looked over at me, she must have seen I was serious. "I'll tell Sam to make it stop. If they continue, we'll have a chat with Sheriff Lee."

"Do you think they might be dangerous?" I asked.

I expected her to say no, but Miriam thought for a moment. "I can't say for sure," she admitted. "Most people can be dangerous under the wrong circumstances. I'll give you the same advice I'd give my own daughter. Don't trust what anyone tells you. A girl should always go with her gut."

The drive home ended too quickly. I'd hoped for a little more time to prepare. Before I knew it, we'd passed between the hedges on either side of the drive, and the manor had come into view. I could see that someone was waiting. The pickup rolled to a stop in front of the entrance, where my uncle stood in the doorway.

James hardly resembled the wild man I'd seen the previous night. A cashmere robe covered crisp blue pajamas, and his hair had been tamed by a comb. From a distance, he could have been mistaken for Mr. Rogers. I got out of the car, unsure what to make of the transformation, though as I got closer, I could see the red veins in his bloodshot eyes and patches of gray stubble that had escaped his razor.

"Bram!" When James threw his arms around me in a smothering embrace, I could hear his heart racing and smell the scotch seeping out of his pores. "What happened? I've been frantic! I woke up to a note that said you were in the hospital!"

"Your niece decided to take a walk through the woods this morning and ended up getting lost," I heard Miriam say. She managed to make the incident sound more annoying than life-threatening. "Ruben Bellinger found her half-frozen and called an ambulance."

When James released me, I saw real terror on his face. "That man was here? In the woods around the manor?"

"I believe Bram had wandered onto Ruben's property," Miriam said.

"Oh my God." James held my shoulders while he scanned my body as if searching for bloody wounds. "Are you okay? Did he hurt you?"

"No," I said. "He saved my life. Why do you think he would hurt me?"

James's expression twisted. He looked at me as though I'd sided with Satan. "Do you have any idea how lucky you are?" he asked, his voice rising. "That man is a lunatic. When Dahlia was alive, he used to sneak through the woods to watch the manor at night. I could hear him trying all the doors and windows. I had to install new locks just to keep him out. I don't even want to think about what he would have done to us if he'd ever gotten inside."

I could tell my uncle wasn't purposely lying, but I didn't believe he was right. "You heard Ruben Bellinger trying to break into the house?"

"Every night!" James exclaimed. "He couldn't accept the

fact that Dahlia had moved on and remarried. He would have done anything to get her back. I can't even tell you how often I had to stay up until dawn to protect my family from that hillbilly head case."

"If Ruben's so crazy, why did you let Lark go live with him?" I blurted.

James's expression turned dark. "I had no say in the matter," he answered. "It was her mother's decision. Dahlia had a soft spot for Ruben. She never believed that he might be dangerous. I warned her against letting Lark leave the manor, but she wouldn't listen. I think we all know how that turned out, don't we?"

"How *did* it turn out?" I pressed. I wasn't trying to be difficult. I truly didn't understand what he was trying to say. Did he think Lark's father had put her up to starting a fire?

James shook his head as if the answer should have been clear.

"What were you doing out in the woods, anyway?" he demanded.

"Taking a walk," I replied, realizing the moment I said it that I should have come up with a better excuse. "I've been down to Louth a hundred times. I got bored. I wanted to see something new."

"You went for a walk in your pajamas?"

"I didn't expect to run into anyone in the woods."

"The forest isn't safe this time of year," James said. "A

girl froze to death out there a while back. You know what your mother would think if she heard about this."

My life was stuck on a loop. No matter where a conversation started, the subject always returned to drugs. "They tested me at the hospital. I'm completely clean."

"I'm not sure a drug test would convince your mother you're well. Teenage girls don't usually set out to explore the woods in their pajamas first thing in the morning. It's a little unusual, wouldn't you agree? Do you really want to give your mother the excuse she's been looking for?"

And there it was. James had just confirmed what I'd long suspected. My mother wanted nothing more than to dump me into a cardboard box with no label and send me away. "No," I said. "Do you?"

"Of course I don't, sweetheart," he answered, his voice lowering. "I'm on your side. But you haven't lived in Louth long enough to realize what kind of trouble your misadventure will cause. By the end of the day, every single person in town is going to know about your visit to the hospital this morning. And they're all going to be talking about how another girl lost her mind at the manor."

He was annoyed because his reputation was at stake. He was my mother's brother, after all.

"I'll make sure everyone knows the truth," Miriam said. I'd almost forgotten she was there. I was grateful she hadn't left me to face him alone.

James glared at her. "You and I both know that no one in this town gives a damn about the truth. Look at what they say about Lark. The girl has a long family history of mental health problems, and they make her out to be the victim of an ancient curse." He turned back to me. "I'm trying to open an inn, Bram. The last thing I need are more stories about girls who've gone nuts here because of the curse. I invited you here because I thought we would be good for each other. I thought the two of us could prove all the rumors wrong."

That's why he'd invited me to stay. Maisie had told me that James had gone around town talking about the troubled girl he'd taken in. He'd used me to look like a good guy—and to prove that his inn wasn't cursed. "I'm sorry," I said. Sorry that I had such a selfish asshole for an uncle.

"And I forgive you," James responded graciously. "But I'll be keeping a closer eye on you until I'm convinced that you're responsible enough to make your own decisions. So no more walks in the woods for a while."

"There you are!" a voice called out. I turned to see Nolan hiking up the drive. "Hello, Mr. Howland, Ms. Reinhart," he greeted the others.

"Nolan!" I was almost relieved to see him. Neither of the others seemed thrilled.

"I just got back to Louth, and Jeb at the coffee shop said

you were in the hospital this morning." He gave me a once-over. "You okay?"

I glanced at my uncle, who was glowering. Nolan followed my eyes and saw it, too.

"I'm sorry," he said uncomfortably. "Am I interrupting something? Should I come back later?"

"We're having a family discussion," James informed him. "But, please—stay for a moment. My niece seems to keep finding herself in life-threatening situations. First she's in a house that's attacked by a band of thugs. Then she almost freezes to death in the woods. I know you were involved in the first incident. What did you have to do with the second?"

Nolan opened his mouth but appeared too stunned to answer.

"Nolan wasn't even in Louth this morning," I said in his defense.

"I couldn't sleep at our house last night, so I drove down to Manhattan," Nolan added. "But our windows should be repaired by this evening."

"Ah, yes, the broken windows," James replied. "Any progress identifying the culprits? How many enemies could anyone have in a town as small as this?"

There was a subtle shift in Nolan's expression. "As you know, my father's investment in the manor seems to have stirred up some resentment in town."

"Of course," James said. "The fact that they hate you couldn't have anything to do with the disappearance of a young woman named Ella Bristol."

Nolan's expression remained unchanged. "I think you've been misinformed, sir," he said. "Ella has not disappeared. She posts regularly on her accounts. I know there's lots of gossip going around town, but the truth is, Ella wasn't happy in Louth."

"You seem to be drawn to troubled girls. Ella. Bram," James said. "You were friends with my stepdaughter as well, were you not?"

"I never thought of Lark as troubled," Nolan argued. "I haven't seen one shred of evidence that Bram is, either." I felt my eyes widen. Nolan hadn't backed down. No one had ever stuck their neck out for me like that.

"Are you aware that my niece suffers from a drug addiction?" I gasped when James said it. He waited, eyebrow raised, for an answer.

Of course Nolan knew. James had told the whole town. But saying it in front of me added insult to injury, and both Nolan and Miriam could see it.

Nolan directed his answer to me. He seemed embarrassed that he knew. "I've heard that Bram is in recovery. Addiction is a disease, and I don't judge people by their ailments. I think it's amazing that she's done so well. I wish I were half as brave."

I could tell that James was getting frustrated that his revelations were having no impact. "Perhaps you're unaware that Bram narrowly avoided being charged with grand larceny after she stole pills from her last boyfriend's parents?"

I felt my face buring with anger and shame.

Nolan glanced at me again before he answered. "Yes, I have heard about it, and I'm afraid I find it all very hard to believe." I could hear the disgust in Nolan's voice. "If I were her uncle, I think I'd take a closer look at her accuser."

I don't know how I managed to keep my jaw off the ground. Someone actually seemed to believe I was innocent.

"My niece is an addict. Facts are facts." James shook his head as though the suggestion was ridiculous. "And the facts have led me to the conclusion that it is not in Bram's best interests to spend any time with you going forward. Will you please let your father know that if my niece disappears for any reason, I will hold your family responsible?"

After everything he'd said, I still couldn't believe that he'd gone there. "James!" I shouted, and my uncle turned on me.

"Stay out of this!" he roared.

"I'll pass along the message," Nolan said, perfectly calm. "I'm sure he'll find it quite interesting."

"I'm sure he will," James sneered. "Have him give me a call if he has any questions."

Nolan looked at me. "If you need anything—anything at all—come and find me."

"Thank you for your concern, Nolan," James said. "Now please, just go home."

Nolan kept his head held high as he turned and walked away.

James waited until Nolan was out of sight to speak again. "You are not to leave your room for the rest of the day," he told me. Then he turned to Miriam, who appeared utterly shell-shocked. "Escort my niece upstairs, please."

"I don't need an escort," I said. I touched Lark's phone, which I'd shoved into the back pocket of my jeans. I hadn't planned to leave my room anyway.

Twenty-Seven

Until then, James had kept his cruel side hidden. Now I knew who he was—and I knew what he thought of me. I couldn't stay at the manor much longer. If not for Lark, I would have marched out the door right then. But I had to finish what I'd come to do. Miriam had given me the phone Lark had been looking for. I was sure something important was stored on it. Whatever it was, Lark wouldn't be safe or satisfied until she had it. I had to find a way to return it to her.

I lay on my bed in the rose room and ran my thumb across the screen. Grace Louth appeared. She seemed so determined—and now I knew why. Had Lark looked at the mural and seen what I'd seen? How much had she discovered about Grace's escape? And why had April Hughes been the one on her mind on the night of the fire?

I ran through April's strange tale in my mind. A curse hadn't killed her. I knew that much for certain. And Miriam was convinced that the girl she'd met had been scared—not insane. But it couldn't have been a ghost that had scared her.

I pulled out my own phone and Googled "April Hughes." The top stories were the ones Lark had printed out and added to her scrapbook. It was on the third page of the Google search results that I found something that she hadn't included—perhaps because it wasn't about April. The article, from the college newspaper the *Columbia Daily Spectator*, focused on April's mother and had been written months before tragedy had struck. The first thing I saw was a picture of the Hughes family standing by the waterfront in Louth.

Bernice Hughes, a professor of maritime history at Columbia, had been chosen to curate a new museum to be built near the Hudson River in upstate New York. That's why she and her family had been in Louth. I enlarged the picture. April's parents looked like college professors. Her little sister had a grin like a Cheshire cat. And despite her terrifying 1980s outfit, April appeared perfectly ordinary. What could have happened to a girl like her?

I knew that the six-digit passcode on Lark's phone might

be all that stood between me and the answer. But I didn't dare have a go at guessing. I had no idea how many attempts I could make before the phone locked for good. Instead I tucked the phone under my pillow, closed my eyes, and tried to get a few hours of sleep. That night, I planned to finally meet Lark.

I opened my eyes to pitch black. I lay still for a moment and listened to the house. The clock said it was a quarter past one, and everything was quiet. I couldn't help smiling as I climbed out of bed. I slid Lark's phone into the pocket of my robe and imagined the two of us coming face to face. I couldn't wait to learn what had happened on the night of the fire—or to find out what she knew about April. Together, we could go to the sheriff with our discoveries. And I hoped, more than anything else, it would be my last day in Louth. I didn't know where I'd go, but in my daydream, Lark was welcome to join me. We'd live by our wits until I turned eighteen and my mother could no longer have me committed.

I continued to fantasize as I walked through the manor. Then I entered the empty black rooms of the north wing, where the wind whistled as it forced its way between the boards that covered the windows. Shards of glass and fallen plaster crunched beneath my shoes, and I felt my excitement draining away. This was the place where Lark's mother had died, and the girl I was searching for was still trapped there, reliving the very worst day of her life.

When I didn't find her upstairs, I summoned the courage to go down to the basement. Afraid I might scare Lark away if I turned on the lights, I navigated using the dim glow from her phone. The basement felt vast in the dark, like one wrong turn might leave me lost forever. I could only see a few feet ahead of me, and I trailed my fingers against the wall. I walked without knowing what might be waiting for me up ahead. I could sense that someone else was down there, and the farther I went, the more certain I grew that it wasn't Lark.

I turned and hurried back the way I'd come. I'd made it as far as the kitchen when the heavy thud of footsteps on the stairs stopped me in my tracks. As they came closer, I heard a man's breathing, and a surge of terror freed a memory I'd kept locked away for a very long time.

Hide! urged a desperate voice in my head. It wasn't mine, but I knew it as well as my own, though its owner had been dead for five years.

I opened a narrow door to my right and ducked into a pantry.

Hide, and don't come out until I get you! the voice whispered, and I did just as I was told. The cold doorknob felt familiar. So did the darkness that surrounded me when the door softly clicked shut.

I found myself transported to a night five years earlier. My aunt Sarah and I had come home from a day of shopping and movies. My uncle was away on a business trip, and Sarah and I were alone together in their massive town house. Stuffed and exhausted, I'd fallen asleep on her bed.

At some point in the early hours, Sarah shook me out of a deep sleep and told me to hide in the hall closet. Disoriented from sleep, I did as she'd directed. I burrowed between coats and shawls until I could crouch against the back wall. I breathed in the scent of my aunt's perfume on the scarf she'd worn to the movies earlier that evening. I could hear the muffled sound of someone large coming up the stairs and stomping past my hiding place. A monster was going to murder me and my aunt, I thought. Then I heard him growl, "Where is he?"

It was James. Relief washed over me, and I slid down the back wall of the closet until I landed on my butt. We weren't going to die. Still, I stayed in my hiding place, just like Sarah had told me. I didn't enjoy being around James anymore. Sometimes he frightened me. And though she wouldn't admit it, I knew he scared Sarah, too.

The man Sarah married had been charming and carefree. Over the years he'd gone cold. I knew from my mother that James's business was on the brink of collapse. And I knew from experience that a fiery temper bubbled below his icy surface. I'd heard him shouting at employees over the phone. Once he flung his laptop out of a third-story window. When he was in one of his moods, Sarah did her best to make sure everyone kept their distance. Only she was able to calm him down.

I woke up the following morning under Sarah's down coat. When I emerged, my aunt pretended she'd been looking all over for me. She claimed I must have been sleepwalking when I lay down in the closet. But Sarah was a terrible liar, and I wasn't a sleepwalker. Downstairs I saw James's crumpled-up airplane ticket on the kitchen counter, and I knew I hadn't imagined his voice. He'd come home. I looked up at my aunt, who didn't appear to have slept the previous night. There was a bruise on her forearm that hadn't been there when we'd gone to the movies. I had no idea what it all meant.

"Promise me, Bram," she said. "Don't tell anyone."

But I did. I told my dad.

I stood in the kitchen pantry with tears streaming down my face, too terrified to move an inch. The footsteps passed by my hiding space. Only two inches of wood stood between me and my monster.

"Sarah told you to sleep in a closet?" my father had asked after I'd told him about my bizarre experience.

We were riding down the West Side Highway in the backseat of his Mercedes. As his driver slipped through afternoon traffic, I looked out the window at the patches of ice floating down the Hudson River. Five years later, I could still hear my father's voice. He'd sounded more amused than concerned.

"Why on earth would she do that?" he'd asked. Now that I was older, I knew he'd kept his questions lighthearted on purpose. He'd been trying not to scare me.

"I don't know," I'd told him. But was that really true? Had I not figured it out? I may have been twelve, but I wasn't a fool. Neither was my father. He knew there was only one reason why Sarah would put me in a closet when she heard James come home. She'd been terrified of what her own husband might do.

"Sounds like Sarah may need a day to herself," my dad said, giving me a pat on the knee. "Why don't you go straight home after school today. I'll stop by her house later and make sure everything is okay."

"She won't be there," I told him. "She decided to go to a spa. She said she'll be back in a week."

"Great!" I remember he sounded so relieved. "That's probably just what she needs. I'll pop in and say hi to her as soon as she's back."

Twenty-Eight

"Bram? What's happened?" my mother croaked.

"Nothing's happened," I lied. "I just want to talk."

I heard her roll over in bed to check the clock on her nightstand. "It's seven o'clock in the morning. I don't talk until eight."

"No," I said before she could hang up. I'd already been waiting for hours. "I want to talk now."

"Excuse me?"

"I need to ask you a question about Dad."

"Oh my God. This again? What is it?" she asked.

"Before they died, did you ever suspect that Dad and Sarah were having an affair?"

"I am not going to discuss this with you, Bram. You're a child."

"I'll be an adult in five months. Answer my question, please."

"I never suspected a thing," my mother said. "James told me he thought Sarah was having an affair, but I didn't believe it. He'd been working himself half to death for months, and he was burnt out and tired. I told him his mind was playing tricks on him. As it turned out, James was right, and I was an idiot."

"What exactly did James say? Did he have any proof?"

She didn't want to tell me. It was almost as if she had to force the words out. "He said he'd seen signs that another man had been in the house. He even put up new security cameras to catch them, but he never did. He told me that meant that Sarah's lover had to be someone who knew the house as well as he did. As you may recall, your father's architecture firm designed the pool in James and Sarah's basement."

"So, James never had evidence of anything."

"Bram, your father and Sarah were practically nude when the housekeeper found them."

"Who told you that?" I asked.

"The police!"

"Let's say for argument's sake that they were wrong. Can you think of any other reason why Dad might have gone to see Sarah that day?"

"Good God. Where is this all going?" my mother demanded.

"I remembered something new."

"You're remembering new things from five years ago? I'm sorry, Bram, but I find that very hard to swallow."

"Don't you want to know what it is?"

"Quite frankly, I have no interest in revisiting the most painful period of my life. I'm not quite sure why you've chosen to spend the past five years torturing me."

"Torturing you?" It wasn't funny, but I almost laughed. "Do you want to know what's torture? Being forced to walk by the house where you found your father's dead body. Having your mother call you a liar when you tell her about the horrible things you've seen. And being convinced, deep down inside, that you were responsible."

There was silence on the other end of the line. "What are you talking about, Bram? You were twelve years old when your father died. Why would you think you were responsible?"

"I thought you didn't want to know," I said. Then I hung up the phone.

I was pulling on my coat in the entryway when Miriam made her way down the stairs.

"Any news?" she asked hopefully.

"No," I told her. I hadn't heard a peep from Lark. "Is he up?"

"Not yet," she said softly. "He had another late night."

"I'm going out. I'll be back in a bit."

Miriam's eyes widened. "James will be furious. Are you sure it's a good idea?" she whispered.

"It's the only idea I have," I replied.

"Where are you going?" she asked.

"You don't want to know," I told her.

Twenty minutes later, I was standing at the end of Ruben Bellinger's drive. The warning signs he'd posted screamed through the snow-covered trees. Ruben himself had told me not to come back. Sam had warned me not to go see him. My uncle swore Lark's father was dangerous. And I knew for a fact that Ruben kept animal heads on his dining room table. But none of that was going to stop me. I had to find Lark and give her the phone. However she was getting in, it was far too dangerous for her to keep coming back to the manor.

I took a step onto the Bellinger property. Then I waited and listened. I heard branches cracking in the distance. There was a caw of a crow from the canopy overhead. Another answered from a nearby tree. The woods looked empty, but they were filled with creatures and their noises. It was the ones who knew how to stay silent that worried me most. I cautiously took another step forward—the second on a journey that would probably take thousands. The Bellinger house lay deep in the woods. I pulled in a long breath and kept walking down the snowy drive.

I didn't even see Ruben when I passed him.

"Miss Howland." I spun around and immediately questioned the wisdom of coming. Ruben was wearing head-to-toe winter-white camouflage and holding a hunting rifle in his hands. It wasn't pointed at me, but I knew it could be in a split second. He reached up and removed the white ski mask that had concealed his face. "I thought I told you to stay off my property."

"Hello, Mr. Bellinger." I tried not to stammer. If I was wrong about Ruben, what I was about to say might get me killed. "I'm looking for Lark. I know that she's here."

Ruben snorted. "You don't know anything, Miss Howland. Now please, go on back up the road before I call the sheriff to come get you."

"If you call Sheriff Lee, I'll have to tell her that Lark's in Louth."

"Knock yourself out," Ruben said with a snort, and I realized that meant the sheriff already knew.

"Does she know that Lark's been breaking into my house at night?"

Ruben cocked his head and looked at me quizzically. "You're from the city, Miss Howland, so let me give you a few tips about how things work around here. You are on posted property, and you are speaking to a man who is holding a gun. You are not in a very good position to be asking questions. Get off my property before something bad happens."

"Lark lost her phone the night of the fire," I said. "That's why she keeps coming back to the manor, isn't it? She needs it to fill in the gaps in her memory."

Ruben didn't respond. He just turned around and headed off toward his cabin.

"If you don't let me help her, she might get worse," I called after him.

Ruben stopped and looked over his shoulder. "My daughter is not crazy, if that's what you're thinking. She hit her head. Her memory's a bit fuzzy. That's all."

We'd arrived at a subject on which I was an expert. "I know what it's like to have gaps in your memory. They're like sinkholes, Mr. Bellinger. If you don't fill them, they can swallow the rest of your life."

I could tell how much he loved Lark. I knew he only wanted what was best for his daughter, and he just wasn't sure what that was. Keeping people away from his home had been easy enough. But saving his daughter would require a leap of faith. My uncle owned the house where Ruben's ex-wife had died and his daughter had been injured. There was no reason for him to trust me with the life of the person he loved most in the world.

Ruben nodded as if he'd reached an agreement with himself. I waited when he walked away, and after a minute, he stopped. "You coming or not?" he demanded.

I jogged down the icy drive and caught up with him just as he unlocked the door of the cabin. He stepped to the side to pull off his snow boots while I stood on the threshold in shock. Ruben was working on a new taxidermy project, and the skins of two tiny lapdogs were laid out flat on his workbench.

Ruben followed my gaze. "Yeah, I know," he said. "It's gruesome as hell, isn't it? Not the way I'd choose to remember my pets, but the old man who owned them can't bear to be parted from Fifi and Fluffy. And to be perfectly honest, I need the money."

I stepped inside.

"Take off your boots, if you don't mind," Ruben said. "My daughter always yells at me for tracking mud and snow through the place."

I reluctantly pulled off my boots. If something happened, I wouldn't be able to run. "Can I see her?"

Ruben shook his head. "I wasn't lying to you, Miss Howland. She's not here at the house. She's been gone since yesterday, when she brought you to me half-dead."

I couldn't believe I'd gotten so close to her. "Lark was the one who saved me when I got lost in the woods?"

"She dragged you a good part of the way. As soon as

I heard her calling, I came out and took over. I wasn't too happy about it, as you can imagine. Truth is, you've been a massive pain in the ass. Before you got to Louth, Lark went to the manor a couple of times a week. That was bad enough, considering how your uncle feels about her. Now, thanks to you, she's up there almost every day. I hardly ever see her."

"She's been going to the manor because of me?" The second surprise hit me even harder than the first.

"Bad things have happened in that house over the years. Lark doesn't want you getting hurt."

"Who does she think might hurt me?" I asked.

Ruben shrugged. Even if she'd told him, he wasn't going to say.

"It's pretty clear that the biggest danger to you is yourself," he said instead. "You would have frozen to death yesterday if she hadn't come to your rescue."

He was right, of course, but there was still one thing I didn't get. "If Lark wants to help me, why doesn't she talk to me?" I took a seat on the sofa across from him.

"No one knows that Lark's back in town, and the sheriff wants us to keep it that way. She's worried someone might have it in for my daughter—and you happen to be related to one of the people she's been keeping an eye on."

"James."

"I hope you don't mind me saying so, but your uncle's a strange one," Ruben said.

"True. Though in his defense, he says the same about you."

Ruben started laughing. "You sure are blunt for a kid your age. You and my daughter have that in common."

"What do you think is so strange about my uncle?" I was determined to keep digging. It was a relief to be sitting across from someone who was willing to answer my questions—and seemed to be telling the truth.

"Well, for starters, he got it into his head that I was creeping around his house late at night."

"You heard about that?" I asked.

"Dahlia called and told me. She said she didn't believe it, but she had to ask."

"And was it true?"

"Hell, no." Ruben cocked his head toward the taxidermy table. "I don't go anywhere at night. That's when I do my best work. Dahlia knew that. We stopped being married a long time ago, but we were still good friends."

I wasn't sure peeling the skin off dead animals in the middle of the night was the kind of alibi that would convince a jury, but it made sense to me.

"So, you and Dahlia were close?"

"I know people find that hard to believe, but we were

always fond of each other. It drove your uncle nuts, from what I hear. That's why Dahlia and I didn't talk much toward the end. He even accused Lark of being my spy."

"What?"

"Yeah, he thought Lark was spying on him. Got real touchy about it. Otherwise Dahlia never would have sent Lark to live with me." Ruben gestured to the chaos all around him. "I love my daughter, but as you can see, I'm not much of a homemaker. After I got back from the army, I just couldn't bring myself to keep things tidy anymore. Lark doesn't like my bad habits any more than her mother did."

"How long had Lark been living with you at the time of the fire?"

"About a month. As far as I know, that night was the first time she'd been up to the manor since she'd moved into my house."

"Do you know why she went there?"

Ruben shook his head. "I suppose that's the million-dollar question, isn't it? All I know is, she told me she was going out to visit a friend. After the fire, your uncle pointed his finger at me. He tried to convince people that I'd put Lark up to setting the fire. I found the whole thing pretty ironic."

"Why?"

"'Cause at the time, everyone thought *he* was the one who'd burned the place down. Folks in town were sure it was all an insurance scam. They thought James must have murdered Dahlia for money."

"You don't believe that?"

"Not for a second. Your uncle's a strange bird, but he loved Dahlia. I'm convinced of it. And he didn't make a dime off Dahlia's death. Fact is, the fire nearly ruined him. Never thought it was a good idea renovating that house in the first place. Curse or no curse, it's got some seriously bad juju, that's for sure."

"But Lark didn't believe in the curse, did she?" I asked.

"No. She was scared, though. Her mother was, too. Dahlia never said anything, but I could tell she didn't like it up there."

"Lark told a friend she heard noises at night," I said. "Any idea what they might have been?"

"No, but that's what got her interested in researching those Dead Girls. The one who died in the woods was all Lark could talk about after her fall. That's why the hospital recommended I take her to Hastings for an evaluation."

"What was she saying?" I asked.

"Not much. Just that she'd seen April Hughes. Problem was, she kept saying it over and over again. A lot of people assume that if there's something wrong with your brain, you should be doped up or locked away. But the doctors at Hastings didn't agree. They said Lark would recover eventually. She still has a way to go, but she's getting there."

"How did you manage to keep everyone in town from finding out Lark had been released from the hospital?"

"Sheriff Lee spoke to the people at Hastings," Ruben said. "She asked them not to confirm or deny that Lark was a patient. She thought Lark would be safer if no one knew she was home. But I'd appreciate it if you didn't tell the sheriff that Lark's been visiting the manor. The sheriff would be angry with me if she found out Lark hasn't been staying home and recuperating."

"Why *do* you let Lark come and go whenever she likes?"

"My daughter says that what she's doing is important, Miss Howland. And I've never known her to lie. Lark is practically a grown woman now. Why would I try to stop her?"

Ruben's faith in his daughter was touching. I hoped my dad would have shown the same faith in me.

"I just have one more question," I said, aware I was in danger of wearing out my welcome. "Do you have any idea how Lark's getting into the manor? My uncle changed all the locks after the fire. The place is a fortress."

Ruben's brow furrowed. "No idea," he admitted. "All I can tell you is that after all her research, Lark probably knows that house better than anyone else."

"Thank you, Mr. Bellinger," I said. "I'm grateful for everything you and your daughter have done for me. If you see Lark before I do, please tell her to find me as soon as possible."

Twenty-Nine

I was right at the edge of town when the sound of crickets chirping took me by surprise. After a moment, I realized it was a ringtone. I pulled Lark's phone out of my bag and stared at it. It was just a number on the screen with no contact name. But there was a chance it might be Lark, and I couldn't let the opportunity slip away.

"Hello?" I answered cautiously. My heart was beating loudly in my ear.

"Don't freak out, Bram. It's Sam. I don't have your phone number, so I thought I'd try Lark's. Sorry if I scared you."

"It's fine," I said. I wasn't scared. I was disappointed. "What's up?"

"Your uncle is on his way down to Louth. He's coming

to find you, and he's in a nasty mood. Mom thinks it might be best for you to hide out for a while until he cools off."

"Is it really that bad?" I asked.

"Yeah," Sam confirmed. "When he's like this, things can get ugly. Trust me, you don't want to see his Mr. Hyde side."

"Okay, but where should I go?" I didn't know Louth well enough to hide. It wasn't even nine o'clock yet. Nothing but the café would be open at this hour, and I knew JOE would be the first place James would look. Then I saw a black Mercedes SUV approaching. "Never mind," I told Sam. "I've got it under control."

I ended the call as the SUV slowed to a stop beside me and the window lowered. "Need a ride back to the manor?" Nolan asked.

"I need a ride to anywhere *but* the manor," I told him. "I snuck out of the house this morning, and now my uncle's on the warpath. Any chance you can help me kill an hour or two?"

"It would be my pleasure," Nolan said. "Hop inside."

I walked around the vehicle and climbed in.

"If you're a fugitive on the run, you should probably stay low," Nolan said like a character in an action film. "This whole town is filled with spies."

"Whatever you say, Mr. Bond." I slid down in my seat until the top of my head couldn't be seen through the window. Nolan hit the gas.

"Since we have the time, want to see something special?" he asked.

"Sure." All I really wanted to do was escape.

We drove in silence for a few minutes, but as Nolan negotiated the car around a hairpin turn, I started to get nervous. I hadn't been on any winding roads in Louth. I had no idea where we were going, and I hadn't expected to leave town.

"All right," Nolan said, "you can sit up. We're all alone now."

I sat up in my seat and saw we were on a dirt road headed uphill. The snow piled on the shoulder was black with kicked-up gravel, but otherwise everything was white. There was nothing around to indicate where we were. The tree limbs knitted together above us, dimming the sun and hiding the sky. We were *very* alone.

"Where are we going?" I asked nervously.

He flashed me a smile. "My favorite place," he said. "It's where I go when I need to get away. You're going to love it."

I silently cursed myself. I'd made a mistake getting into the car. All I had to defend myself was the box cutter I'd shoved into my coat pocket that morning. After Sam had called to warn me about James, I'd been so relieved to see Nolan that I'd forgotten I still had one giant, lingering question where he was concerned.

"Hey, there's something I've been meaning to ask you,"

I said, hoping I sounded casual and calm. "The sheriff told me Lark went to your house the night of the fire."

"Yep," he replied, and I relaxed a little. He hadn't lied.

"Why didn't you tell me about her visit?"

Nolan shrugged. "I guess because there wasn't anything to tell. Lark and I talked for a little while. Then she left. She seemed totally normal, like she always did."

"Nothing about her visit seemed weird to you?" I pressed. "The sheriff told me the fire started a couple of hours after she left your house, so it must have been pretty late when she showed up to see you."

"It was probably about ten-thirty or so, but it was summertime," Nolan said. "There was no reason to go to bed early."

"But why did she want to see you at ten-thirty at night?"

"She told me she wanted to get out of the house because her dad was working on something smelly. He's a taxidermist, you know."

"You're saying she just came to hang out?" I paused when Nolan glanced over at me. "Sorry—I know I'm asking a lot of questions."

"No problem." He didn't seem annoyed at all. "Yeah, we hung out and talked for an hour or so."

"What did you talk about?"

"She told me about the noises she'd heard in the house, and we talked a little about Grace Louth, but other than that, it wasn't very interesting."

"*Nothing* strange happened?" I couldn't wrap my head around it. How could Lark go to his house, have an ordinary conversation, and then wind up trapped in a fire two hours later?

"Well, there was *one* little thing. She asked if she could take a picture of me before she left."

"That's it?" I wasn't sure that qualified as weird. "Why did she want a picture?"

"Your guess is as good as mine. At the time, I figured she just thought I was cute," he joked.

"Did she tell you she was planning to go up to the manor later that night?"

"No," he replied. "In fact, I distinctly recall that when she left, she said she was going to bed." He looked over at me again. "See what I mean? Nothing to tell."

What had happened to Lark after that? The answer to everything seemed to lie in the two-hour space between her leaving Nolan's house and her leaping from the second floor of the manor.

Before I could ask any more questions, the car started to slow and Nolan pulled to the side of the road and turned off the engine. I couldn't see anything worth stopping for—the world around us was a white blur.

"Come on." He winked at me and opened his door. "This is going to be a treat."

I sat for a second after his door slammed, watching Nolan

trudge toward the forest. At the tree line he stopped and gestured for me to follow him. I wasn't thrilled by the idea.

I opened my door a crack and felt the icy air slip inside. Nolan had already disappeared into the trees. The world was frozen and still. I had two choices, I realized—neither of them good. I could follow Nolan into the woods, or I could stay in the car, all alone in the middle of nowhere. I looked down the desolate mountain road and imagined a truck pulling up next to Nolan's car. Mike and Brian might be inside. Or the three men who'd scared me on my first day in Louth. Nolan had taken the car keys. Without them, I was a sitting duck. The box cutter in my pocket might help me escape from one man, but I knew I'd never stand a chance against two or more. I would have been a fool to trust Nolan completely, but there were men in Louth who scared me much more. The odds of locals showing up might have been low, but they weren't zero. I figured I would be safer with the devil I knew, so I slid out of the car and hurried to catch up with Nolan.

I was far enough into the woods to have lost sight of the car when I finally spotted him. He was standing motionlessly with his back to me. Just beyond where he stood, the woods appeared to end. His black-clad figure was framed by the slate-gray winter sky.

When I reached his side, I saw that he'd come to a stop

at the edge of an enormous lake, its windswept surface covered in ice. There were no houses here. No sign of mankind at all. Trees crowded the banks, trying to hide the water from view—as though only the gods were allowed to see it. Nolan was right. It was absolutely magical.

"Listen," Nolan said. He seemed to find the silence glorious.

"How did you find this place?" I asked. It seemed like the sort of spot only locals would know about.

"A friend of mine brought me here once, and I keep coming back." He held out a hand. "Let me show you."

"Where are we going?" I asked.

"Out there." Nolan pointed straight ahead toward the trees on the other side of the frozen expanse.

My heart picked up. "Across the ice? Is it dangerous?"

"It's the middle of February. The ice here is probably ten feet thick."

"You're sure?"

He walked out onto the ice and hopped up and down to show me how solid it was. "Trust me, Bram," Nolan said. "It isn't the first time I've done this. You're okay with me."

The ice took me back to the winter my father died. To looking out at the Hudson River as I rode down the highway on the west side of Manhattan. I wanted so badly to see the river freeze over. If it did, I could make a run for the opposite shore. Any map would have told me that the magical land on the other side was only New Jersey. But I was convinced that I'd be free. My ghosts wouldn't follow me there.

Standing at the edge of the frozen lake, it almost felt like that wish had been granted. Nolan held out a hand, and I took it, stepping onto the lake. I listened for the sound of cracks forming beneath me. All I could hear was the whistling of wind. Away from the shore, with no trees to shelter us, a strong gust sent me skidding across the slick surface. I was terrified—and exhilarated.

Nolan walked farther out across the lake, my hand still tucked in his. The shore was barely visible when we came across a circular hole cut into the ice. The black water inside looked like a portal to another world.

"What is that?" I asked.

Nolan kept walking, pulling me along. "It's an ice-fishing hole. The locals cut them into the ice and put tents up over them. Then they sit for hours, drinking beer and pulling fish out of the water."

"That's what people do for fun here in Louth?"

"Don't knock it." Nolan continued across the lake. "It's the only thing about them I understand."

When we finally came to a stop, it felt as if we were miles from land. The trees waved from the distant shoreline, and snow devils swirled around us.

"Look at this!" Nolan gazed up at the heavens. "Isn't this wonderful? You'll never see anything like this in Manhattan."

He was right about that. At that moment, it was hard to believe New York City existed. I felt free.

"The girl who brought me here told me it was the one place in Louth where she ever found peace. I know what she meant. In town I feel like I'm under a magnifying glass. Here, no one's watching. I don't have to be anyone but myself." He faced me. "I hope you feel like you can be yourself, too."

"What do you mean?" I asked, suddenly uncomfortable with where the conversation was heading.

"You want to tell me why you were at the hospital yesterday—and why your uncle has you under house arrest?"

Had he brought me out to the lake to question me?

"I got lost in the woods and nearly froze to death," I answered honestly.

"Why were you in the woods?" Nolan asked.

"Just seeing what was there." Technically it was true.

"You've got to be careful. I don't know if you've heard, but a girl died out there a while back."

"April Hughes," I said. "Did Lark tell you about her?"

"No," Nolan said. "I heard the story ages ago. I don't even remember who told me. April Hughes is pretty famous around here."

An idea was slowly taking form in my head. "When

Lark came to see you the night of the fire, did you guys talk about April?"

"Nope," Nolan said. "I don't remember ever discussing April with Lark, actually."

If Nolan was to be believed, Lark hadn't mentioned April Hughes when she'd visited his house—and yet a few hours later, when the fire department had discovered Lark wandering the grounds of the manor, April Hughes had been the only thing she'd wanted to talk about. Whatever had driven Lark to the manor that night had something to do with April. I was sure of it.

"So," Nolan said. "Ready to continue our adventure?"

I studied his face and wished I could read his mind. There was no way to know if Nolan had told me the truth about Lark or anything else. Maybe he was a womanizer, as Maisie had warned me. And there was always a chance that he'd convinced Ella Bristol to run away from home. But I'd seen no proof to support either claim, while I knew for a fact that the person standing in front of me had done one good thing.

"In a second." There was something I needed to get off my chest first. "Thank you for sticking up for me yesterday. No one's ever done that before."

"You're welcome," Nolan said. "Your uncle had no right to say those things about you—especially not to someone like me. My dad says he has a terrible temper, but that was the first time I'd seen it."

"You should know—most of what James said was true," I admitted. "I'm not ashamed of it, and I'm done running away from the past. I started using drugs a couple of years after my father died. I've been clean for a year."

"That's impressive," Nolan said, and it looked like he meant it, though I hadn't been fishing for compliments.

"You told James that you didn't believe that I'd stolen anything. You said that if you were my uncle, you'd take a closer look at my accuser. Why?"

He shrugged. "I just have a hunch you got blamed for something you didn't do."

My face flushed, and the frigid air could do nothing to cool it. "How do you know?"

His eyes dropped to his boots. "Okay, so I did a little cyberstalking," he admitted. "I read what the people at your school were saying about you and Daniel Lane. I know plenty of guys like that, and I know how they operate. I weighed what I'd read online against what I know about you. It seemed pretty clear that his story didn't ring true. Of course, it doesn't hurt that I know what it's like to be wrongly accused."

What he was saying sounded too good to be true. "When did you do all of this detective work?"

"A couple of days ago."

"Why didn't you say anything?"

"You obviously weren't planning to have all that crap follow you here to Louth. I figured you'd tell me if you wanted me to know. It's your story."

In the distance, from the road that ran along the shore came the sound of wheels on gravel. I caught a glint of metal and saw a truck speed past a break in the trees. Then the tires slowed to a crawl and stopped. The engine shut off and two car doors slammed. Someone had parked next to our car. I'd made the right choice to follow Nolan.

Nolan and I stood facing the shore, waiting for what might come next. There was no doubt it meant trouble. "Damn it," Nolan muttered. "I'm so sick of these people."

"Should we get back to the car?" I asked, wrapping my fingers around the box cutter in my pocket. I wasn't sure what other choice we had.

"Yeah," Nolan said. "We'll be fine. Just don't let them see that you're scared. We haven't done anything wrong."

As we walked across the ice, a bear on its hind legs appeared at the edge of the lake. I was relieved to realize it was Boris, the cabdriver, wearing his massive fur coat. A person of normal dimensions soon joined him. Next to Boris the man looked shrunken and small. The two of them stood there as we walked toward shore, their lips moving and arms gesturing. I couldn't hear a word of their conversation, but there was no mistaking the smaller man's anger.

As we neared, he stepped out onto the ice. He was bundled up for fishing, with only a strip of his face exposed. Ignoring me, he went straight for Nolan. Judging by the deep-set wrinkles that fanned out around his eyes, he had to be at least sixty. "How the hell do you know about this place?" he demanded.

"Google maps," Nolan replied calmly.

I glanced back and forth between them. It was a strange way to start a fight. I wondered if we'd been trespassing.

"That's a damn lie," the man growled. "Who brought you here?" His voice didn't rise, but it simmered with rage.

Nolan stared back at the man. "I'm sorry," he said politely. "Isn't this public property?"

"This lake belongs to the people of Louth," snarled the local.

"I *am* one of the people of Louth," Nolan pointed out. "My family contributes its fair share to the town's tax revenue."

"You don't contribute anything," the man sneered. "People like you and your father are killing this town. You're a bunch of goddamned bloodsuckers, and you always have been. You think you can come here and take whatever you want. Our homes, our businesses, our daughters—"

That's when Boris joined the conversation. He put both hands on his friend's shoulders and began to pull him back. The short, angry man tried to shrug him off, and I saw Boris's grip tighten until it must have been painful.

"Come away, Henry," Boris ordered his friend.

"Henry," Nolan repeated. His face had gone dark. "Henry Bristol. Ella's grandfather. I've heard about you. You're exactly the sort of man I expected you'd be."

"You know, one of these days," Henry Bristol growled, "I'm going to catch you up here on your own."

"And I look forward to that day," Nolan assured the smaller man.

"When it happens, I'm going to make you regret the day your fucking family sailed up the Hudson."

"You can save your energy," Nolan said. "I already do."

"You need to get your friend out of here, Miss Howland," Boris told me. "And if you're smart, you'll hop on a train right now and go home."

Nolan and I didn't speak until we were halfway down the mountain. To be honest, my mind had returned to New

York for a tour of all the places where I'd been harassed and threatened before I fled. Sidewalks, subways, dressing rooms. Until I'd left for Louth, there'd always been someone around to let me know that I wasn't welcome. I knew exactly how Nolan felt.

"I'm sorry that happened," Nolan finally said.

"You have to be more careful." It was my turn to warn him. "What would those guys have done if I hadn't been there? They could have shoved you into one of those ice-fishing holes, and no one would have ever known. You need to go back to the city right away."

"And leave you here with a bunch of scary rednecks and a crazy uncle? I'd never forgive myself." I felt his eyes turn to me. "Why don't we go back to the city together?"

After the kindness he'd shown to me, I didn't want to hurt his feelings. "Together?"

I was surprised to see him smile in response. "I promise you—I'm not looking for a girlfriend. When my dad told me you were coming to live with James, I thought I'd better keep an eye on you. Louth can be a pretty rough place, and from what I'd heard about James, I knew he might not be up for the job."

"So you thought you'd be my knight in shining armor?" I snorted.

"I know you're not a damsel in distress, and I know you

don't need to be saved. But you remind me a lot of Lark, and I don't want anything to happen to you. So how about it? Want to go down to the city with me?"

There was nothing I wanted more than to get the hell out of Louth. "Yes, but New York is the last place I need to be right now. I can't go anywhere else, either. I don't have any money or friends. I don't even have any family aside from James. I'm stuck here for now."

Nolan went quiet. Then he said, "Can I tell you a secret?"

"Why not." I shrugged. "You seem to know all of mine."

"No, I'm serious," he said. "This one could get me into a lot of trouble."

"Okay." He had my full attention. I couldn't help but wonder if I was about to hear a confession.

He rubbed his lips together as if he still wasn't sure he should speak. Then he appeared to throw caution to the wind. "That girl—Ella Bristol? The one everyone in town thinks I convinced to run away?"

I felt my smile fade. "Yeah?"

"I didn't convince her. But I did give her the money she needed."

"You did?" I asked cautiously. I wasn't sure what it all meant.

"She was desperate to get out of Louth. She said her family had her under surveillance every hour of the day. Henry back there was the worst of the bunch. I could see it was starting to take a real toll on her. So I gave Ella an envelope full of cash and promised to help any way that I could."

"Wow." I had to admit, I was impressed.

"I'd be happy to do the same for you," Nolan said. "Are you ready to disappear?"

I summoned my willpower because I knew this was going to be hard. "Not yet," I told him. "I still have work to do."

Thirty

Nolan dropped me off at the base of the hill, and I hiked up the drive to the manor. I had no idea what kind of situation I might be walking into when I opened the door, and I hoped enough time had passed for James to cool down.

I stepped inside and braced myself, but no one was there, so I made my way up the stairs. My relief was short-lived. As I approached the rose room, I could hear voices inside. When I reached the door, I saw Miriam rooting through my sock drawer. James stood behind her, issuing orders. The bureau's other drawers had all been emptied, and the clothes from my closet had been dumped onto a chair. My bed was stripped, and the sheets and covers lay in a pile on the floor. James and Miriam had inspected everything I owned, short of what I had on me.

Fortunately, the only thing worth finding—Lark's phone—was inside my coat pocket.

"Looking for something?" I asked, tamping down my anger.

Miriam's expression was pained—I knew she wasn't there willingly—but James didn't flinch. His nostrils flared and he held his chin high. He was convinced that his mission was righteous. "Yes, we are," he said. "Your mother insisted. She said she had a conversation with you this morning that made her question your mental health."

I calmly took a seat in the chair by the vanity. "Well, if you tell me what you're looking for, I might be able to help you," I said.

"Drugs," he announced. "Or anything else that might be contributing to your questionable behavior."

"Like what?" I asked, genuinely curious what that might be.

"Don't get smart," he snapped. "You've been missing all morning, even though I ordered you to stay in your room. No one knew where you were. Your mother thinks you've gone completely insane, and you haven't been answering any of her calls."

I pulled out my phone. I'd turned the ringer off, knowing she'd call back after our conversation that morning. There were thirty-one missed calls, all from her. And *I* was the one they all thought was crazy.

"May I have that, please?" James demanded.

"What?" I asked, looking up.

"Your phone." He was holding out his hand impatiently.

I rose from the chair. "You're kidding. There are no drugs on my phone."

"Give it to me right now," he ordered. "Or I'll have your mother switch off the service."

I was shocked that the situation had deteriorated so quickly. I passed him my phone, hoping he wouldn't frisk me and find Lark's phone still tucked away in my pocket.

"Now sit back down," he ordered.

I sat and watched him open apps and scroll through texts, photos, and emails. Former addicts with meddling mothers quickly learn not to keep sensitive information on their phones. I knew he'd find nothing, but I still couldn't believe it was happening. He seemed to grow angrier and more frustrated with every moment that passed. He'd been so sure I was guilty of something, and being proved wrong had enraged him.

"What exactly are you looking for?" I asked, again.

"I'll know it when I see it," he muttered, furiously scrolling.

"James?" Miriam asked, her voice gentle.

"What?" His hands trembled violently as he ransacked my digital life.

"James, we've looked everywhere. I don't think there's anything here in the room."

He looked up from my phone, his chest heaving and his teeth grinding. It hit me then. I couldn't believe I hadn't recognized it before. *James* was on drugs. Stimulants, from the look of it. I thought of all the veiled threats he'd made since I'd arrived at the manor—all the times I'd been warned that I could be sent back to rehab. He'd been as high as a kite the whole time.

I was furious and heartbroken all at once. For years, I'd prayed that my uncle James would come save me. His brief visits had been the highlights of my childhood. That man and this one had little in common. I'd never been able to understand his transformation. Now it made sense to me. Drugs had destroyed the uncle I'd loved. My only question was—when had it started?

He shook my phone in my face. "You're not getting this back unless your mother calls. Do not leave this room again without my permission." James stomped toward the hall. "Lock the door when you leave," he ordered Miriam.

"James!" Miriam called out to him. "I can't lock her in!"

He spun around, his face burning red. "Do it!" he roared. "Or get the hell out of my house and find yourself another job."

I put a hand on Miriam's arm. "I'll be fine," I promised. I needed her there. The last thing I wanted was to be left alone in the manor with James.

Miriam studied my face and saw I was serious. "Okay," she agreed, reluctantly. "I'll bring some food up to you later."

"Miriam," James growled.

"Don't worry about me," I assured her. "All I want to do right now is take a bath and get the chill out of my bones."

Miriam seemed utterly bewildered by how unruffled I was. It surprised me, too. But then, I finally knew what I was dealing with. The ground beneath my feet was feeling firmer than it had in years.

As soon as I was alone in the rose room, I filled the tub with steaming hot water. When I slipped in and closed my eyes, the first face that appeared in my mind belonged to a kid named Kevin. I didn't really know him, but we'd been in group therapy together, and I'd heard him tell his story. To be honest, I hadn't taken him all that seriously at first. There were kids in rehab who'd been addicted to heroin or meth. I preferred painkillers. Kevin had stuck to the tiny orange pills that had been prescribed for his little brother.

The way he told it, Kevin's parents expected nothing short of academic excellence, and Kevin was a B student at best. When he discovered that his brother's pills could help him cheat sleep and focus, he started popping them whenever he had an exam. After he got caught stealing the meds, he began buying them from dealers. Within a few months, he was taking six times the safe daily dosage. Not long after that, he started hearing voices.

Kevin was convinced the voices belonged to demons. They whispered horrifying things in his ears. His mother and father were trying to murder him. That's why they forced him to study all hours of the day. Once he died of exhaustion, they would bury him in the backyard and give his belongings to their beloved youngest son.

Kevin didn't tell anyone about the voices, even when they got louder and increasingly violent. He had to kill his parents, they insisted. He had to get his mother and father before they could get him. The cops would know it was self-defense.

Kevin began to interpret every action as suspicious. If his mother picked up a knife to chop carrots, he would imagine the blade lodged in his chest. When his father drove him to school, Kevin noticed if he wasn't asked to strap on his seat belt. *Kill them!* the voices screamed. Finally he had to take action. Rather than give in to the demons, Kevin decided to jump off a bridge.

Kevin had two broken legs when he came to rehab, and his body was emaciated. Like with James, the drugs had destroyed Kevin's appetite. He and my uncle also shared the delusions and paranoia that are symptoms of amphetamine abuse. James had tried to convince my mother that Sarah and my father were having an affair. He'd told the sheriff that Ruben Bellinger was sneaking around the manor at night. James had even believed that his seventeen-year-old stepdaughter was a spy. James didn't think I was on drugs. That's not why he'd looked through my phone. He'd started to think I might be a threat to him.

When I opened my eyes again, the air was thick with steam. My head rolled to the side, and my eyes landed on the bathroom mirror. There was something there. I immediately jumped out of the bath. Dripping and naked, I stood in front of the mirror, where two words were scrawled. *Leave Now!* I reached out a finger and ran it across the *L*. The message had been written in soap.

I grabbed a towel and headed out of the bathroom. I checked the closet, under the bed, and behind the curtains. There was no one hiding in the room. I spent ten minutes studying the back of the closet, searching for signs of a hidden door. There wasn't one, I was sure of it. I returned to the bathroom. The fog had dissolved and the message was slowly disappearing. I wiped the soap off the glass with a washcloth.

I paced the rose room for hours, waiting for darkness to fall. At around ten o'clock, I crawled into bed fully dressed. I wanted to be prepared for anything, and I didn't think I would be able to sleep. My whole body was buzzing with anticipation. Lark's father had said she came to the manor almost every night. She hadn't shown up the previous evening, so I was convinced she would make an appearance before sunrise.

I lay in bed, the hours passing, and yet no one arrived. Exhaustion was beginning to catch up with me. My eyelids drooped, and I felt myself sinking into the mattress. The next time I opened my eyes, I could see the sun just peeking over the mountains. A scrap of paper had been shoved under my door. On it was a hastily scrawled note from Miriam. Taped to the bottom was a key.

I've been told to take two days off.

There's another big storm on its way.

There may be power outages.

You can't be here on your own.

Get to town, and Sam will pick you up there.

She was right. It was starting to seem like Lark wouldn't be coming. And I couldn't be stuck in the manor with James.

Thirty-One

I threw on my coat as quickly as I could manage, grabbed my backpack, and crept down the stairs. Every time a floorboard creaked, I froze in fear. I turned each lock on the front door so slowly that it took minutes to get through them all. I opened the door a few millimeters at a time. But once I was out of the house, I ran faster than I'd ever run before.

The sky was hanging heavily over Louth. I'd been in town long enough to know that it meant more snow would begin falling soon. As I raced down the drive, I glanced back over my shoulder. The sun was beginning to rise, and the manor's windows were still dark. I picked up my pace and reached the bottom of the hill. Just when I was sure I'd made my escape, I heard the sound of an engine starting. A pair of headlights blinded me, and I shielded my eyes. Two doors opened and closed, followed by the sound of heavy boots on snow. Someone had been waiting for me. All I could see were the silhouettes of two men dressed in down coats. They were blocking the road to town. I spun around and started to run in the other direction.

"Hey!" one of them called out. "Bram Howland! Where are you going?"

"Damn it, stop her before she gets away!" shouted the other. I could hear someone sprinting behind me.

A few seconds later, a hand grabbed a hunk of my coat and jerked me backward. I managed to reach into my pocket and pull out my can of bear repellent. But before I could position my finger on the nozzle, a giant hand wrenched my weapon away. I looked up and saw Brian.

"Jesus!" he cried. "What the hell are you doing?"

"Get away from me!" I shouted. "Let go or I'll fucking kill you!"

Brian held me close to his chest with one muscular arm while he studied the can of repellent. He lifted it up to his face to read the fine print. "You have any idea what this shit could have done to me?" he demanded. Then he raised the can high in the air. "Look at what she just pulled out of her bag!"

Taking my chance, I stomped down as hard as I could on his foot, unzipped my coat, and wiggled out. I didn't even feel the cold as I wove around Mike and sprinted down the hill toward town. Then an arm slipped around my waist and yanked me off my feet.

"What is it with you?" I could feel Mike's steaming hot breath on the side of my face. "How come you've never liked us?"

"Fire!" I screamed at the top of my lungs, though I knew no one could hear me. "Help!"

Mike pinned my arms behind my back. "For God's sake, make her stop!" he ordered his friend. Brian pulled a bandana out of his coat pocket and stuffed it into my mouth. I kicked and flailed, but I couldn't break loose. They were going to murder me or worse. And there was nothing I could do to stop them.

"Please don't thrash around like that." Mike sounded annoyed. "We aren't supposed to hurt you."

I wasn't going to stop. I stood no chance against the two of them, but I was not going down without a fight. I delivered a mule kick to Mike's kneecap.

"Damn it!" he yelped. "I really didn't want to do this, but you're not leaving me any choice. Brian, get over here with those zip ties." A few seconds later, I heard a loud zip and felt a narrow band of plastic dig into my wrists. Panic squeezed all air from my lungs and I struggled to breathe while Mike squatted down behind me and pulled my ankles together. Then a second zip tie was employed.

"Load her into the back," he told Brian.

"Maisie's gonna be pissed," Brian said as he picked me up and laid me down in the flatbed of their truck. I couldn't fathom what Maisie had to do with this, but it didn't bode well. She was smarter than both of them put together.

Mike threw my coat over me. "If she wants to be pissed, she can do her own goddamn dirty work from now on."

Their doors slammed and the truck pulled onto the road. I lay on my back, my heart pounding. All I could see were the tree branches passing by overhead. I figured I had one shot left. When I saw power lines, I knew we'd reached town. I struggled to sit upright, hoping someone would see me and call for help. I'd just managed to lift my head high enough to peek over the side when the truck took a sudden turn and I fell and rolled across the flatbed. By the time I got back into position, I saw branches overhead once more. Then the truck rolled to a stop. We hadn't gone far. I spotted the side of a marble wall and figured out where we were. They'd taken me to Louth's cemetery. I knew I was in terrible trouble. No good comes to girls in graveyards.

Mike and Brian got out of the cab and opened the tailgate. A female gasped.

"What did you two idiots do to her?" It was Maisie, and as predicted, she was mad as hell.

"You told us to find her and bring her to you," Mike said.

"And when exactly did you hear me use the words 'zip ties' and 'gags'?"

"Sorry, Maisie, but she's mean," Brian practically whimpered. "She almost sprayed me with bear repellent."

"Get her out of there and cut those ties," Maisie ordered, and I almost passed out from relief. "We're supposed to be helping the girl, not torturing her!"

Within seconds I was free and standing on my own two feet. While Mike and Brian beat a hasty retreat, I looked around to get my bearings. Grace Louth's mausoleum stood nearby. When my eyes landed on Maisie, it was hard to believe it was the same girl whose bedroom floor was ankle deep in designer clothes. She was wearing jeans, snow boots, and a down coat. She looked just like one of them.

"I'm so sorry," she said.

"You're *sorry*?" I wanted to punch her. "I thought they were going to kill me. I nearly peed my pants."

"Dumb and Dumber weren't supposed to kidnap you. I've been trying to get in touch with you since yesterday. I sent them to the hospital to see you, but Sam shooed them away. Then I called the manor, and your uncle told me you weren't allowed to talk to anyone. I didn't have any way to reach you, but I knew there was a chance you'd come down the hill at some point. I asked Mike and Brian to keep an eye out and bring you to see me if you did. Are you okay?" She reached out for my hand and examined my wrist, gently rubbing with her thumb the red welt that circled it.

"I'll live," I said coldly, and yanked my hand back. "So those are your henchmen, I guess? Did you have them throw the rocks at Nolan's windows, too?"

"I had to do something," Maisie said. "You were in there alone with him."

"What the hell? We were eating soup!"

"I told you to be careful. I warned you to stay away from him."

"So you had your friends try to kill us?"

"They aren't my friends," Maisie said. "Mike is Ella Bristol's brother. Brian is her cousin. The third guy was a friend of theirs from school."

"And they're pissed because Nolan helped a girl get the hell out of Louth?"

Maisie's laugh was bitter. "That's what he told you, is it?"

I felt a chill. "What do you think happened to her?"

"I don't know," Maisie said. "Neither does anyone else in town. Not her best friends. Not her family."

"Hasn't she been posting on social media?"

"Someone's been posting," Maisie said. "But her family says there's no proof it's really her."

"Is it possible that Ella doesn't want her family to find her?" I asked. "With relatives like Mike and Brian, I'd probably run away, too."

"You're not taking this seriously!" Maisie shouted in frustration. "A girl could be dead!"

"I am taking it seriously!" I snapped. "But you have no proof of anything, and you just had me kidnapped. Based on what I know at this moment, if I had to choose between you and Nolan, I'd definitely take my chances with Nolan."

"Stop," Maisie ordered. "There's more."

"I'm only interested if you have facts, not just gossip. I know you hate Nolan. I'm sure he and his family did something super shitty to you in the past, but—"

"Nolan *is* my family." Maisie looked queasy. "He's my brother."

"What?" I said, not sure I'd heard right. "That's not possible."

"He's my half brother, if you want to get technical. Gavin Turner is my biological father."

My mind was blown. "Does Nolan know?" I asked.

"I don't know. He might suspect something. But no one knows for sure aside from me, my mom, and Gavin. A few of my grandparents knew back in the day, but they're dead now."

"It would be easy to prove. You'd just need a DNA test."

"Had one," Maisie said. "That's how we have the money. Gavin settled out of court. My mom got a giant financial settlement. All she had to do in return was keep her mouth shut and forget what he did to her."

My stomach dropped. "What did he do?"

"Eighteen years ago, his parents held a party at their summer house. My mother was one of the local girls hired to serve drinks. She was only sixteen at the time. Gavin was thirty. And though my mom didn't know it, he had a wife and a baby on the way. He convinced her he could help her get modeling jobs if she came down to the city. He even told her she could stay in an empty apartment he owned. She knew her parents would never approve, so she ran away. There were no modeling jobs, of course, and the apartment wasn't empty. Gavin was staying there, too. A week after she got there, Gavin got bored and kicked her out. She was too ashamed to call my grandparents. She lived on the streets for a few weeks until she found a way back to Louth."

I was stunned. "She was only sixteen. She should have gone to the police," I said.

"She did. Her parents made her. But that was long before Sheriff Lee's day. Even if some of the cops thought she might be telling the truth, no one wanted to take on the Turners. Besides, everyone knows that guys like Gavin Turner don't need to seduce anyone. The cops advised her to go back to school and forget that anything had happened. When she found out she was pregnant, she knew she had proof. That's what I am. I'm the proof."

I couldn't imagine anything more awful. "She's kept it a secret all these years?"

"One word, and my mom and I could lose everything.

But that's not why I haven't told anyone. You're the first person I thought might believe me." I saw a look of terror in her eyes. She was worried she'd gone too far. "Do you?"

"I do," I said. "I can't believe you've stayed quiet for so long."

"I find ways to let my rage out now and then. Thanks to Nolan, a lot of people in Louth are happy to help."

"You really think Nolan might be like his father?" That was the only part I was finding hard to swallow.

"No," Maisie said. "I think he's worse. Tell me this—since you moved to Louth, how many times has he gotten you all alone?"

I felt goose bumps rise on my arms. "At least twice," I had to admit. "The night I had dinner with him, he showed up at the manor when he knew everyone else was out."

"If you'd disappeared that night, what would people have thought?"

A junkie like me? "That I'd run away to buy drugs."

"Nolan knew that."

"So why didn't anything happen to me?"

"Did anyone see you with him?"

I thought back to the night in question. "Your mom saw us together," I said. "She ran out in front of his car. Then she banged on the window and shouted for me to get out."

Maisie nodded. "He couldn't take the risk that she'd remember seeing you in his car. The second time you were alone with Nolan, he took you up to that lake on the mountain."

"Yeah." It felt like Maisie was reading my mind.

"You got *really* lucky that time," she said. "Mike's grandfather saw Nolan's car heading there. He and his friend rushed up the hill after you."

If she was right, I was an idiot. But I still wasn't convinced. If Nolan was looking for an opportunity to hurt me, he'd had plenty of time before Henry Bristol had shown up.

"And let me guess," Maisie continued. "Nolan's offered to help you in some way. Did he say he'd give you money to get out of town?"

The surprise on my face was all the confirmation she needed.

"We think that's how he lured Ella, too. My guess? She isn't in Manhattan. She's at the bottom of that lake on the mountain."

I rubbed my eyes with the heels of my hands, trying to digest what she was saying. It just didn't make sense. Nolan had gone out of his way to stick up for me. He'd never tried to harm me, and as far as I knew, he'd always told me the truth.

"The person you're describing may be real, but it's not the Nolan I know," I said.

"It's all an act, Bram. Nolan's not normal. He's a monster like his father."

I believed what she'd told me about Gavin Turner, but Nolan?

"Have you told the sheriff about your theory?" I asked.

"Yes," Maisie said. "She suspects that Lark discovered something about Ella's disappearance. She thinks that may have been why Lark went to see Nolan the night of the fire."

I realized I needed to share what I knew. "If her theory is right, there may be a way to confirm it," I said. I pulled off my backpack and unzipped it. "Miriam Reinhart found this in a heating vent at the manor." When I held out the phone to Maisie, she seemed afraid to touch it.

"Is that what I think it is?" she asked.

I nodded. "It's Lark's phone. Nolan said she took his picture the night of the fire. That means she had the phone with her when she went to his house. If Lark discovered proof that Nolan harmed Ella, there's a good chance that the evidence is stored on this phone." I put my backpack on. "Let's go," I said.

"Where are we going?" Maisie asked.

"I want you to drive me back to the manor." I couldn't believe I was saying it. But if a girl's life was at stake, I had to hack into the phone right away. Until then, I'd respected Lark's privacy. I'd never gone looking for clues to the passcode. Now that it was a matter of life or death, I knew right where to start my search—the same place Grace's secret was hidden. The mural that covered the walls of the rose room.

Thirty-Two

The storm that Miriam had predicted rolled into Louth just as Maisie dropped me off at the end of the drive. The first flakes settled on snowbanks and drifted down between the trees. Soon every branch that had shaken off its last coat of snow was covered. The hedges had donned their disguises, and the whole world had disappeared beneath a fresh layer of white.

Ahead, the manor lay waiting. As the storm gained strength, the building came alive. Black clouds hovered in the building's windows, and its ivy coat writhed in the wind. The mansion was warning me that my mission was dangerous. But I couldn't run away. I had to find the password. If she'd discovered something dangerous, Lark would have left clues. The more I thought about it, the more convinced I became. Hidden somewhere in the rose room's mural were the six digits that could uncover the truth.

I found the front door ajar. Either I'd left it that way or someone had known I'd be coming back. When I slipped inside, the only sounds I could hear were the ones I made. The manor's monsters were sleeping. I crept to the second floor and down the hall to the rose room. I closed the door behind me and walked to the center of the room.

For the hundredth time, I located Grace Louth in the painting, sprinting down the hill to freedom. I traced the route Grace would have taken from the manor to the boat waiting in the Hudson River, knowing Lark would have done the same thing I was doing.

Patience. The name of the boat had eight letters. I tried the first six, and the phone rejected it. My eyes continued across the mural until I stopped at a familiar cluster of little buildings. A tiny storefront with a sign that read MAXWELL & MASON, GENERAL MERCHANDISE, LOUTH, NEW YORK. I squinted at a sign that was posted in the building's window. RIVER FESTIVAL JUNE 15.

I felt a rush of excitement. June 15 was the day Grace Louth had made it to freedom. If I changed the four letters in June into the corresponding numbers on the keypad, June 15 had the perfect number of digits. I carefully entered all six numbers. Again, the screen shook and spat it back out. I was about to move on when I remembered, *the year*. It had been 1890. My hands trembling, I tapped 061590 into the password screen. And just like that, I was in. I felt the blood rushing through my veins. Every cell in my body was vibrating with excitement. I went straight to Lark's texts and scrolled through the names until I reached *Nolan*. The last exchange between the two started at 10:48 on the night of the fire, with a message from Lark.

U there?

Watching Carrie. U?

Need fresh air. Can I drop by?

Sure.

So he'd told me the truth about that. Lark had initiated the texts. She really had wanted to get out of the house. I went back and scrolled through her other texts from the night in question. She'd chatted with her mom about buying a new pair of boots. Then she'd texted Maisie pictures of two pairs of boots to see which she preferred. Those were the very last texts Lark had sent.

Disappointed, I turned to Lark's emails. She hadn't sent a single email on the day of the fire. I searched her files and couldn't find any information about the manor, ghosts, or dead girls. Then I opened Lark's photos and immediately found myself face to face with Nolan. It had to be the picture he'd told me about—the one she'd taken the night of the fire. Nolan was smiling at the camera, and nothing seemed to be out of the ordinary. He'd posed for the photo in the library at his house, leaning against the table where the Turner family pictures were on display. Lark had snapped the shot on landscape mode, and it was oddly off-center—*unless*, I realized, the photo wasn't really of Nolan. Had she used him as an excuse to take a picture of something else? I zoomed in for a closer look. The only things that were in focus were two framed pictures—and both were pictures of the family patriarch, August Turner. I'd seen them myself when I was in the library. The first showed him in his prime, standing on the prow of a boat. The second had been taken decades later. It was the picture of an elderly August, dressed in a tuxedo, posed with his arm around Nolan's father.

I scrolled through the rest of the photos on Lark's camera. There were a few pictures of Maisie and dozens of Dahlia. But most of the pictures on the phone were close-ups of the manor's façade. There were over a hundred in all. Lark had documented every inch of the building's exterior. I studied the pictures, looking for some kind of clue regarding what she was looking at. I saw nothing but stone, iron, and ivy. But the photos meant something. They *had* to.

I flipped forward and stopped. Tucked in between the photos of the mansion was a picture of a little orange pill wedged between two wooden floorboards. I knew what it was—generic amphetamine salts. Exactly the pills Kevin from rehab had favored. At my school in Manhattan, they were the top-selling study aid. The drug made my heart race and pushed me to the edge of panic. I'd quickly learned to avoid it. But my uncle seemed to like that kind of high. James must have dropped the little orange pill somewhere where Lark had spotted it. If she'd taken a picture, she'd either known what it was or planned to look it up later. In either case, she must have figured out what James was on.

I closed Lark's photos and opened her browser. There were five tabs open. The first was an article from an old issue of *Condé Nast Traveler* magazine titled "A Life Restored." A full-page photo showed James and Dahlia standing on one of the manor's Juliet balconies, gazing into each other's eyes, surrounded by the wild ivy. The caption read, *James Howland and his fiancée, Dahlia Bellinger.* The story must have been written before they were married. James looked clean and healthy. They both seemed ecstatic. It was hard to believe that Dahlia would be dead less than a year after the photo was taken.

The article would have been several months old by the time Lark had opened the tab. Surely she'd seen it before. Had she been reading it the night of the fire? The article was filled with photos of the inn's décor. Many of them showed rooms from the north wing of the manor before it had burned. James's renovations had been truly spectacular. My heart almost broke when I saw the library that had been destroyed. Then, halfway through the article, I came upon an image of a wall of old photographs. I almost scrolled past before something caught my eye and I took a closer look. I recognized the pictures. They were the same ones I'd found in the storeroom—inside the box marked with an *X*. In the photo in the middle of the arrangement, another face drew my attention. Though the resolution was too poor to be certain, it appeared to be Nolan's great-grandfather August Turner.

August Turner seemed to be showing up everywhere. I went back and opened Lark's photos, scrolled to the image of Nolan in his family's library, and paid particular attention to the two framed photos beside him. One was a photo of August and Gavin Turner from the same party. The second showed August Turner on his boat. He'd been obsessed with sailing, Nolan had told me. I almost dropped the phone when two seemingly unrelated facts collided in my brain. August Turner had loved boats. And, as I'd learned in the *Columbia Daily Spectator*, April Hughes's mother had been a maritime historian.

A quick Google search confirmed that August Turner was the man who'd hired Bernice Hughes to run the maritime museum he'd planned to build on the Hudson River. *He* was the reason the Hughes family had been visiting

Louth. *He* was the one who had rented the manor for a whole week around New Year's Eve.

I grabbed the keys Sam had given me to the manor's storeroom and ran for the basement. I went straight to the storage room and found the box with the *X*. I pulled out the original of the photo I'd seen online. It was indeed a picture of Nolan's great-grandfather standing on the manor's grand staircase, a well-dressed crowd mingling in the entrance hall below. Engraved on the frame were the words "New Year's Eve, 1986." The night April Hughes died. The significance of the date hit me just as my eyes landed on a person who'd been captured in the background—a girl in a dark dress, her black braids twisted into a bun on top of her head. Someone in a tuxedo had grabbed her by the wrist, and she was trying to pull away. The guy had his back to the camera, and only the girl's profile could be seen. Still, I would have recognized her anywhere. The girl in the photo was April Hughes. And I was convinced that the young man harassing her was Gavin Turner.

I clicked back to the photo that Lark had taken of Nolan in his family's library. I now knew why Lark had taken the picture. She wasn't interested in the family patriarch. She'd been gathering evidence that Gavin Turner had been at the manor the night April had died. The photos weren't irrefutable proof, but they didn't leave much doubt, either. Lark believed Nolan's father was somehow involved in April's death.

I slid the phone into my pocket. I knew why Lark had broken into the manor the night of the fire. Once she'd confirmed that Gavin had been at the party, she'd come for the picture she'd seen on the wall. I was sure of it.

As I was preparing to leave the storeroom, a text arrived on Lark's phone.

Bram, it's Sam. Have you left the manor? The snow is getting bad.

I'll leave now, I wrote back.

I hurried toward the kitchen stairs. The snow had covered the windows, and Miriam wasn't there to build a fire in the fireplace. The room was cold and dark. I didn't see the man until he cleared his throat.

I froze, then switched on the light and found my uncle seated at the kitchen table. He looked exhausted. I could tell he was crashing. I still remembered the person he'd been— the one who'd been so kind to me when I was little. It hurt me to know I'd lost that uncle forever.

"Good morning." James sounded zombie-like. "Where were you just now?"

"The laundry," I lied, as calmly as possible. "My clothes are all filthy."

"Go back to your room. I'll bring your laundry up to you when it's done," he said.

"Why don't I make us something to eat?" I asked politely.

"No, thank you," James said. "I don't eat as much as I used to."

"I've noticed you don't sleep very much, either." I needed to broach the subject carefully, but I wasn't going to play dumb anymore.

James looked down at the table. "No," he admitted.

"Amphetamines, am I right?"

His silence was confirmation enough.

"Lark found out, too, didn't she? Is that why Dahlia made her move out of the manor?"

James sighed and nodded. "Dahlia thought Lark would be safer around Ruben. It was ridiculous."

"Were you on amphetamines back when Sarah died, too?" I already knew the answer. It explained everything. The unpredictable rages. Sarah's fear. The laptop that he'd hurled from the window. I just wanted James to confirm it.

"My father always told me I'd amount to nothing. He said I was too spoiled to ever put in a hard day's work. The day I announced I was starting my business, your mother predicted it wouldn't last. And you know what? She was right. A year later, I was heading toward bankruptcy. I thought the pills would help me stay on top of things and prove everyone wrong. Then, before I knew it, my life was spiraling out of control." James looked up at me. "Your mom says you've been asking questions about the tragedy. It's time you knew the truth. It was my fault. If I hadn't been high, I would have had someone come to the house to check the furnace."

"So my father died because you popped too many pills and forgot to schedule a maintenance call."

He winced. Hearing the truth seemed to hurt. "I'm so sorry, Bram. I tried to get better so I could make amends. I left for rehab the day of Sarah's funeral. That's why I was away for so long."

That was a lie. Any sympathy I'd had for him was now just fuel for my fury. "I didn't see you for years. You couldn't have been in rehab that long. You abandoned me."

"I was ashamed of what I'd done. After I got out of rehab, I couldn't bear to go back to Manhattan. So I came here to Louth. When I met Dahlia, I thought I'd been given a second chance. Once we got settled, I was going to ask you to come stay with us."

"But you didn't," I pointed out. I wasn't buying any more of his bullshit, but I had to keep myself under control. There was much more I wanted to know. "When did you start using again?" I asked.

James gestured to the refinished kitchen. "When this money pit sucked me in. I funneled every dollar I had into the renovations. I couldn't even afford the insurance premiums. When the pressure built up, I gave in to temptation again. I tried to hide it. I'd lie in bed next to Dahlia until she fell asleep, and then get up and roam the halls until dawn."

"You were the one making the noises Lark heard at night."

"She thought it was a ghost at first. That's when she became obsessed with the legend of Grace Louth. After that, Lark's problems snowballed. If I hadn't been using again, we could have gotten her help before she burned the house down."

I was on the verge of exploding. It took a moment to calm down before I trusted myself to speak. "Why do you keep insisting that Lark started the fire on purpose?" I demanded. "It doesn't even make sense. Why would she do something like that?"

James shook his head. "Maybe she believed in the curse. Maybe her father put her up to it. Who knows why the mentally ill do what they do?"

I wasn't going to let him get away with saying that. I had to set him straight. "For your information, Lark didn't come here to destroy the manor. She was looking for a photo that was hanging in the library."

"A photo?" he asked, looking up at me.

"It was one that had been taken at a New Year's Eve party in 1986."

James's expression changed. He knew exactly which one

I was talking about. "Yes, I remember that picture. It was destroyed in the fire."

No, it wasn't. It was in a box downstairs. He must have known that.

"Have you found out why Lark was trying to find it?" he asked.

I hesitated before I answered. James seemed to be digging for information, and I just wasn't sure why. I decided to give him a little, to see what he'd do with it. "There was a girl in the photo. April Hughes—the one who froze to death out in the woods. The picture was taken the night she vanished. It may have been a clue."

"And the photo's been lost," James groaned, acting as though he were physically pained. "What horrible luck. Have you told Sheriff Lee about any of this?" he asked.

"How could I?" I asked. "You confiscated my phone."

James hung his head. "I'm sorry about that, Bram. I'll run up and get it," he said. He pushed his chair back and stood. "Go ahead and make yourself some breakfast. I'll be back down in a moment."

I didn't move until I heard his footsteps on the stairs, when I took out Lark's phone and texted the pictures I'd found to Sam for safekeeping. Then I dialed a number and put the phone to my ear.

"Hello? Who is this?"

"It's your daughter," I said. "I just have a second. You told James that I've been asking about my father's death."

"My dear, James is your caretaker. He needs to know when you're showing signs of instability."

"Mom, do you remember telling me that James had been working too hard—and that was the reason why he'd forgotten to have the furnace checked out?"

"Yes," she said.

"Were you aware that James was addicted to amphetamines at the time?"

There was a pause then she answered. "Yes."

"Are you aware that the symptoms of amphetamine abuse can include extreme paranoia and delusions?"

"Yes, Bram, I am. What is your point?"

"My point is that you chose to believe a man you knew was addicted to amphetamines over your own daughter."

"I chose no such thing, Bram."

"I told Dad about something that happened once when I slept over at Aunt Sarah's. James had come home from a business trip early, in the middle of the night, and scared the hell out of her. She must have been convinced he was dangerous, because she made me hide in a closet. I think Dad went over to her house the morning they died to talk to her about what had happened. When I found the bodies at around eleven-thirty, Dad and Sarah were both fully clothed. They hadn't been having sex. They'd been having a conversation about James."

"That's what you thought you saw. You were never there, Bram."

I couldn't believe it. "What in the hell are you talking about! I've told you a hundred times I was there!"

"Damn it, Bram, you weren't on the security tapes!"

It was my turn to go silent. "What do you mean I wasn't on the security tapes?" I asked at last.

"Your uncle had installed security cameras outside the house, hoping to find out who Sarah was cheating with. The police watched all the tapes. They saw your father go into the house early that morning. They saw the maid arrive hours later, at around three. No one else entered or left the house in between."

My world went sideways. I put a hand on the table to steady myself. "Why didn't you tell me?" I demanded.

"Your therapist didn't think we should confront you with the facts. She wanted you to come to terms with the truth on your own."

And I finally was. What had never made sense was suddenly, unquestionably clear. It had taken five years to understand the truth. I turned around to see James standing in the doorway.

"I've got to go," I told my mom. As I lurched forward

and grabbed a kitchen knife off the counter, I fumbled Lark's phone.

"Bram!" I heard my mother shout as the device fell to the floor.

James picked up the phone and ended the call. Then he looked at the weapon in my hand and nodded sadly. "Is this really what it's come to? You're threatening me with a weapon?" he asked. "Your mother has been trying to convince me that you need medical attention. I kept assuring her that you would be fine once you got settled in. It seems she was right this entire time."

"You edited the security footage from your house. You knew how to do it and you had plenty of time. The leak wasn't an accident, was it? You murdered my father," I said. "You murdered Sarah."

He looked at me with such pity that I almost doubted myself. "Do you hear how crazy that sounds, Bram? You know better than anyone else how much I loved Sarah. I would never have done anything to hurt her. My dear, you are not well. We need to get you some help."

"No." I shook my head. "I am not going to let you do this to me again. I know what I saw that day. I know I was there."

"I called the sheriff when I was upstairs. She's already on her way," James said soothingly. "When she gets here, you can tell her everything you saw. Whose phone did you use to call your mother just now?" He looked down at the phone in his hand and then back up at me. "Bram, did you steal someone's phone?"

"Of course I didn't steal someone's phone!" But I couldn't tell him the truth. I couldn't let him know it belonged to Lark.

"I think you should let me hold on to it until the sheriff arrives," he said. "Stealing a phone is grand larceny. If we return it without any damage, we may be able to convince the owner not to press charges."

He took a step toward me, and I held out the knife.

"Okay, Bram," he said. "Take your knife and go upstairs to your room. Sheriff Lee should be here any moment now."

Thirty-Three

I stood on the rose room balcony and looked down. The only way out of the manor was over the side. There was little chance I'd walk away uninjured if I jumped. In fact, there wasn't much chance I'd be able to walk at all. Worst-case scenario, I'd hit my head on a rock buried beneath the snow and that would be the end of my story. James would never be brought to justice. I'd just be the latest Dead Girl, driven mad by the manor's curse.

There had to be another way out of the house. Grace Louth had found it the night she'd leaped into the river. April Hughes had slipped out of the manor without being seen. And Lark has been able to come and go as she pleases. I thought of the box of family photographs Grace Louth's mother had sent her the night she'd escaped—and all the strange photos Lark had taken of the manor's façade. I'd studied each one of them, but I hadn't seen anything. Maybe, it occurred to me, what I needed to find was something that couldn't be seen.

I reached over the balcony's railing and stuck my hand deep into the ivy. I could feel the vines wrapped around something icy cold. They weren't clinging to the stone itself. An old photo from Lark's scrapbook popped into my mind. The picture had been taken shortly after the mansion had been built and Frederick Louth had decided the manor looked too new for his taste. His gardeners had mounted a metal trellis to the walls. The photo had shown them weaving ivy vines through it. Once the vines had grown, the trellis had disappeared.

Could the picture in Lark's scrapbook have been one of the photos that Clara Louth gave her daughter the night Grace disappeared? Did the picture of the trellis hidden under the ivy show Grace how to escape?

Grabbing hold of the metal trellis with my left hand, I pulled myself up onto the balcony railing. The wind whipped around me while I felt for a hold with the toe of my left shoe. I climbed down slowly at first, terrified that the hundred-and-fifty-year-old lattice might peel off the wall. But it worked as well as it had for the girls who'd escaped before me. Yet as I got closer to the ground, one thing continued to bother me. If Lark had known the secret, why had she chosen to jump the night of the fire? Then I realized the answer was obvious. She hadn't jumped. Someone had pushed her over the side.

I was still four feet off the ground when I saw headlights coming up the hill through the snow. For a fleeting moment, I wondered if James had really called the sheriff. Then the car disappeared between the hedges and stopped. The driver turned off the headlights and cut the engine. The vehicle was hidden from view. I heard a door shut and footsteps followed. I dropped down from the trellis and crouched in the shadows as a figure in black walked up the drive to the house.

The front door opened. "I told you this was a bad idea," Gavin Turner growled. "Where is she?"

"Upstairs," James replied.

The road to town was no longer an option. There was a chance someone was waiting behind the wheel of the car hidden between the hedges. The only safe place I stood a chance of reaching lay on the other side of the woods from the manor. I sprinted across the lawn and slipped into the forest. I hoped to make my way to Ruben Bellinger's house.

The snow on the ground was already deep and growing deeper. Fresh powder clung to my coat and piled on my shoulders. Within minutes, I was completely covered.

Then the wind changed direction and snow blew into my face. The storm wanted me to stay. As I stumbled blindly through the forest, it became painfully clear that I would never make it to the Bellingers. I was going to die the way April Hughes had.

Right before you freeze to death, you see wonderful things. When I spotted the flickering light in the distance, I was certain I'd arrived at death's door. I'd lost sensation in my face and legs. My mind was wandering through childhood memories. I felt my father take my hand and guide me toward the little stone building in the middle of the woods.

Dahlia's mausoleum almost seemed lived in. The pool in front had frozen over, but a fire was burning inside. I pulled open the door, and a wave of warmth washed over me. I stumbled inside and collapsed onto one of the benches. I watched a puddle of meltwater form beneath me as I slowly returned to my senses.

Then the door opened, and my uncle appeared in the entrance with a kitchen knife in his hand. He pulled a phone from his pocket and put it up to his ear.

"She's in the mausoleum," he told the person on the other end. "We'll wait for you here."

James took a seat on the bench across from me, but he

couldn't stay still. I wondered how many pills he'd swallowed. As much as I wanted to, I was too exhausted to attack.

"Is Gavin Turner going to kill me?" I didn't see any point in mincing words.

"I wanted to help you. I really did. But you just wouldn't let me. Your mother always said you were impossible to deal with. I should have listened."

"So all of this is my fault?" I asked.

James shrugged helplessly. "I tried my best," he said. "But Jane was right. You are a very troubled child."

"Because you murdered my father."

"Your father was having an affair with my wife," James said.

"That's not true!" I screamed. "My dad went to see Sarah because I told him she was scared of you. When I found their bodies, they were both fully clothed. You were at the house that morning, weren't you? After I was gone, you made it look like they were having an affair. Then you edited the security tapes so the police wouldn't know you and I had been there."

"None of that proves that Sarah and your father were innocent," he insisted.

"James, you were high on amphetamines. You were paranoid."

"That doesn't mean I was wrong to suspect them."

I sat back, exhausted. There was no point in arguing. "My mother doesn't know what you did, does she?" Before I died, I needed to know for sure.

"I never told her. But then again, she never asked many questions. I think Jane was pleased with the way things worked out. As we both know, she was never well suited for family life."

"You seem to have some trouble with it yourself. You keep murdering wives."

"No, not Dahlia." James looked offended that I'd even suggest such a thing. "Her death was an accident. I loved her. If I'd known Dahlia was going to run into the north wing, I would have stopped her. The fire was out of control."

"You mean the fire you set because you'd thrown her daughter off a balcony and you needed to make it look like Lark had no choice but to jump?"

I saw the surprise on his face. I'd guessed right.

"Here's what I think," I continued. "I think Lark broke into the manor to find the photo of the New Year's Eve party. As usual, you were probably too high to sleep. I bet you caught her with the picture and figured out what she'd found."

"I was about to lose the manor," James said. "I'd sunk every dime into the restorations, and your mother refused to help me financially. The moment Lark showed me that New Year's photo, I saw a way out. I'd approached Gavin about investing in the inn, and he'd turned me down. The picture was leverage. He would save the manor—and do it on my terms. But Lark insisted on taking the picture to the police. She was bent on ruining me."

"Or maybe it had nothing to do with you," I said. "Maybe Lark just wanted justice for the girl Gavin Turner murdered."

James sighed. "That was decades ago. Everyone's moved on. No one even remembers what happened anymore. The girl's just a campfire story."

I felt my fists clench. I would have punched him if I could. "April Hughes was a human being, and Gavin Turner killed her."

"He didn't kill her." James made it sound like I was an idiot for suggesting such a thing. "He let her die. There's a difference."

"How do you know what happened?"

"He told me," James said. "They were at a party. She left to go to bed. He had a key to her room. But when he got inside, she was gone and the balcony doors were wide open. He thought she might have jumped, and he went to have a look. When he got outside, he spotted her running for the trees. He found her alive, but he'd lost interest at that point. So he left her out there in the woods."

The legend was nowhere as horrifying as the truth. "He killed April," I said. "What he did was no different from stabbing or strangling her."

"Yes, well, I have the whole conversation recorded, and I've made it clear what will happen if Gavin crosses the line again," James said. "Right now there's no need to involve the authorities. These sorts of problems have often been solved with gentlemen's agreements."

"Gentlemen's agreements?" I scoffed. "That's what you call making a deal with the devil?"

James's phone rang, and I saw that Gavin Turner's name was on the caller ID. "What's taking so long?" James demanded. I could hear it was a woman's voice on the other end. James's face went sheet white and he instantly ended the call.

"Get up," he ordered.

"What's going on?" I asked. "Was that the sheriff?"

"Get up." He dragged me off the bench and pulled me out of the mausoleum. "Walk." He pushed me forward.

"Where are we going?" I asked. We weren't headed home. I was the only person who knew that James had murdered my father—and attempted to murder Lark. He had to get rid of me.

"Just keep going straight," he ordered.

Straight meant across the frozen pool in front of the mausoleum. I stepped forward without even thinking. And fell.

The cold burned for an instant, and then every part of me went numb. When I surfaced and grabbed hold of the side of the pool, I couldn't feel very much at all.

"I salted the ice earlier," James explained. "But you couldn't have known that. It's going to look like a terrible tragedy. Still, I suspect that won't stop the locals from gossiping."

I gripped the ledge as hard as I could, but my muscles had seized up and I was powerless to pull myself up.

"Help me," I begged. I could hardly force the words out.

James squatted down at the side of the pool. "I'm so sorry it had to end this way, Bram. But I promise you, this is for the best."

I opened my mouth to speak, but I could no longer move. When the warmth began spreading inside me, I realized I was dying. And I realized how the scene would look to whoever found my body. They'd assume I'd fallen into the water and frozen to death. There would be no sign of foul play. James would never pay for what he'd done.

My body was lost to me, and I could feel consciousness slipping away. I thought my mind was playing tricks on me. A ghostly figure had appeared at the edge of the woods, her face hidden behind a veil. She moved slowly and silently behind James until she loomed over him. Then she pulled off the veil and let it fall to the snow. I watched her raise a finger to her black lips, warning me not to make a sound. The ghost's other arm hung by her side, a thick stick clutched in its fist like a club. She raised the wood and brought it down in one swift movement onto the base of James's skull.

Thirty-Four

"Do you know where you are?"

I was lying on my back, looking up at the ceiling, and the voice had come from the right. When I let my head flop in that direction, I could see I was tucked into a bed with blue sheets. A girl had pulled a chair up to my bedside. She was small and pale, with dark brown hair and big black eyes.

"Who are you?" I croaked. My mouth was parched and my throat hoarse.

"My name is Lark," she said, handing me a glass of water.

I stared at her over the edge of the glass while I gulped water down and tried to place the name.

"Your uncle married my mother. Do you remember what happened?"

I thought for a moment. "I remember James getting hit on the head by a ghost."

"That wasn't a ghost. It was me," she said. "James fell into the pool after I hit him. His heart was damaged from amphetamine abuse, and the shock of the cold water sent him into cardiac arrest. I'm sorry to tell you he died."

"He tried to kill me." It was all coming back.

"Yes." Lark picked up my hand and held it. "You've been unconscious for three days."

"You saved my life?"

"I wasn't the only one," Lark said. "Sam got worried when you suddenly stopped answering texts, and he called the sheriff. If he hadn't, Gavin Turner could have murdered us both."

I struggled to sit, and Lark jumped up to adjust the bed for me.

"Sam called the sheriff?"

"Yep, and since then, he's probably spent more time in this room with you than anyone else. The mums are from him. They were grown in his parents' greenhouse."

On the other side of the room stood a table with two vases overflowing with expensive flowers. Between them was a mason jar full of handpicked white chrysanthemums.

"The other bouquets are from Maisie and Nolan. They were both here this morning."

"Together?" I marveled. "At the same time?"

"Yeah. It's hard to believe that, until a few days ago, Nolan had no idea they were related—and Maisie was convinced that Nolan had murdered Ella Bristol."

"Did he?"

"No," Lark said. "Ella is in Manhattan. I was the one who asked Nolan to help her. He could have easily cleared his name at any time, but Ella didn't want her family to find her. Now that she's eighteen, she doesn't need to worry about being dragged back to Louth. Apparently, she and Nolan have been a thing for a while now."

"How does Maisie feel about that?"

"She's still wrapping her head around it." Lark laughed. "So she tried to convince you that Nolan was just like his father?"

"Yes. I wasn't convinced, but I would have looked into her claims."

"Sounds like you have good instincts. They tell me you never believed I started the fire, either."

"It didn't make sense," I told her. "It was like Grace's story. It just felt wrong."

Lark nodded. "Yeah, I know what you mean. I'd heard about Grace Louth my whole life. But the moment I saw her face on the mural, I knew the legend couldn't be true. When I started hearing noises at night, people kept saying it had to be a ghost. I wasn't convinced, so I decided to find out what really happened to Grace."

Lark's mother had told her about a box of unusual items that had been uncovered during the renovations. The construction crew working on the building had discovered the artifacts tucked under floorboards or hidden behind walls. Among the items were a box of old photos that seemed to have belonged to the Louth family itself—and a small, leather-bound three-ring binder.

"It's called a Filofax," Lark explained. "They were super popular in the eighties and nineties. That's how people organized their lives before smartphones. Filofaxes had sections for addresses and appointments. There were also calendar pages you could use as a diary."

"Oh my God!" I gasped. "That little leather notebook that was packed in the same box with the photos. It belonged to April Hughes, didn't it?"

"Yep," Lark said. "But I didn't figure that out right away. When I started the scrapbook, I was way more interested in the photos of Grace Louth and the manor. By the way— how long did it take you to notice the trellis in the old pictures of the house?"

I was embarrassed to say. "Too long," I told her.

"Took me a few days, too. Grace used the trellis to escape from the manor the night she jumped in the river. But she came back to the house after she was supposed to be dead. Grace was the 'ghost' people kept seeing in the days before her father's heart attack in the rose room. The trellis allowed her to enter and leave the manor without being seen. She stayed in Louth long enough to have her revenge. As soon as I figured all of that out, I knew for sure there had never been a curse or a ghost. And once I'd eliminated those two things . . ."

"You knew there had to be a logical explanation for the noises you kept hearing in the manor at night."

"Exactly," Lark said. "And there was."

"It was James, roaming the halls while he was high on amphetamines."

"Which was scarier than a ghost. I told my mom what I'd discovered, and she asked me to move back in with my dad for safety. She stayed at the manor. I think she really thought she could see James through his problem."

"So did my aunt, Sarah," I told her. "Two women died trying to help him."

"Yes, James and Gavin have left a trail of dead girls behind them."

We hadn't even gotten to Gavin Turner yet. "How'd you figure out what Gavin Turner did to April?"

"When I read April's diary, I noticed that the last few entries kept mentioning someone she called *G*. It was somebody she was clearly afraid of, and I assumed it was Grace Louth. She also wrote that she didn't want to make a huge deal out of it, since the museum was her mom's big break."

"When did you realize she wasn't talking about Grace?"

"It must have been the night of the fire. I remember more now, thanks to the phone, but a lot of the evening is still pretty fuzzy."

"I think I know how you figured out who G was," I told her.

"You do?"

"I think you were looking at an old issue of *Condé Nast Traveler* that had a profile of James and your mom. In the article, there was a picture of a photo from New Year's Eve 1986. It was hanging on one of the walls while you lived at the manor. You must have remembered seeing it."

A smile broke out across Lark's face. "That's right!" she said. "I knew New Year's Eve 1986 was the night April disappeared, and I remembered seeing a similar picture at Nolan's house."

"Which is why you went to see Nolan that night. You took a picture of a photo that showed August and Gavin Turner together at the same New Year's party."

"That must have been the moment I made the connection. Gavin Turner had been at the party with April. And *G* stood for 'Gavin,' not 'Grace.'"

"So you went up to the manor to get the original photo. James told me what happened next. He caught you on one of the balconies. You must have had the photo and the Filofax. You wanted to go to the police. He wanted to use the photo to blackmail Gavin into paying for the manor's renovations. When you refused to give it to him, he pushed you off the balcony. Then he started the fire to make it look like you'd had no choice but to jump. He didn't expect the fire to kill your mother—or burn half the manor down."

"So, James tried to murder me, too."

"I'm sure he didn't expect you to survive the fall. But you did, and when the firefighters found you alive, you kept talking about April Hughes. James let everyone think that you'd lost your mind. But the truth was, you *had* seen April Hughes that night—in the picture you'd gone to the manor to find."

Lark sat back in her chair. I could see tears in her eyes. "I wish James was alive so I could kill him again."

"There's no need. You did it perfectly the first time," I said gently. "I will never forget the sight of you in that white wedding dress sneaking up behind him. When did you decide to start dressing up like the ghost of Grace Louth?"

"As soon as I got home from Hastings," Lark said. "I realized my phone was missing, and I knew I must have dropped it that night. I had to get inside the manor, but I needed a disguise in case anyone spotted me. So I did what Grace Louth had done to get her revenge on her father—I came back to the house dressed up like a ghost."

"Then I showed up."

"That's right. I saw you coming that very first night— out there in the snowstorm using your phone as a flashlight.

I figured you were way out of your depth. At first I just wanted to scare you away. I tried doing little things that would freak you out without tipping off your uncle. I'd leave your door open or move your candle. But then one night, I heard you screaming in your sleep, and I realized I should help you instead. It wasn't until much later that I figured out you'd come to Louth to help me."

"I think somewhere deep inside, I always suspected that James had a hand in my father's death. I'd blocked out the memories, but there was some part of me that couldn't let him get away with murder again—or let you take the blame for what he'd done."

"So you came to Louth to clear my name."

"Yes," I said.

"Why haven't you tried to clear your own?"

She knew about what had happened to me in New York. "It's not possible. At the end of the day, it all comes down to 'he said, she said' and everyone believes Daniel."

I couldn't understand why Lark was grinning. "Not everyone," she said. "Sam and I did a little research while you were resting."

She pulled up a photo on her phone and passed it to me. It took me a second to realize that it was a picture from Daniel Lane's party. A group of girls were posing in front of the glass doors that led to the terrace. "Now watch," Lark said, swiping to the next photo.

This time the picture had been digitally enhanced. A misshapen shadow on the other side of the door had been lightened to reveal two different people. One had the other's limp body hanging over his shoulder. Both my face and Daniel's were visible.

I hadn't cried when it had happened. For months after the incident, I'd felt nothing but numb. I'd been so certain that nothing could save me and nobody cared. Now that I knew someone did care, I found tears running down my cheeks.

"Makes it pretty clear you didn't willingly go back to the bedroom with him, doesn't it?"

I was too overwhelmed to speak clearly. After a moment I asked, "Where did you get this?"

"The girl who took it posted it on Facebook. I made sure every person at your school got the enhanced version." Then she grinned. "And yeah, I sent a copy to your mom, too."

Epilogue

"So have you decided what you want to do with the manor?" Sam asked me.

I'd been as surprised as anyone else to discover that my uncle had willed the house to me. Now that it was May, the snow was gone, and flowers were springing up all over the lawn. I didn't need to use my imagination anymore. Sam had worked wonders on the grounds.

"I'm going to keep it," I said, admiring the newly open space where the topiary had stood. Sam and I had spent the afternoon chopping them down.

"That's a bold decision," he said, with a smile that told me he approved.

"Lark can live here until she goes off to college. You can stay here whenever you come home from school. There's more than enough room for everyone."

"Are Maisie and Nora going to lose their money now that they've told the whole world about Gavin?"

"I honestly don't think they care," I said. "They're welcome to move in, too. Maisie can turn one of the bedrooms into an enormous closet, if she likes."

"So it sounds like the manor's going to be an inn after all. You know, a lot of people in your shoes might hold a grudge against this house."

I shook my head. "No. I'm grateful," I said. "I wouldn't have all you guys if it weren't for the manor."

"And we're glad you came," Sam said. "It's just a shame your uncle won't have to answer for what he did to your aunt and your father."

"It is," I agreed. "But at least Gavin Turner's in jail."

"Poor Nolan," Sam said. "He should probably consider changing his name. They say a sixth woman came forward to accuse his dad this week."

"Good," I said. "Nothing will change if we stay quiet. That's what I told my mom. She called this morning and begged me not to go public with the news about James. She said she doesn't see any need to tarnish the family reputation now that James is dead and my name has finally been cleared."

"What did you say?" Sam asked.

I looked up at Sam and smiled. "I told her it's my story. And I want the whole world to hear."

ACKNOWLEDGMENTS

This book would have been a different beast if not for my editor, Krista Marino. It was a tame little creature when she first encountered it. Krista helped me give it teeth and set it free. Thanks to Lydia Gregovic at Delacorte Press for her insightful comments, which helped guide the book to the unconventional conclusion its heroine deserves.

Thanks as always to Suzanne Gluck and Andrea Blatt at William Morris Endeavor.

And a giant hug for Georgia, my butt-kicking, rock climbing, ghost-spotting inspiration.

ABOUT THE AUTHOR

Kirsten Miller lives and writes in New York City. She is the *New York Times* bestselling author of *The Eternal Ones, How to Lead a Life of Crime,* and *Don't Tell a Soul,* as well as the acclaimed Kiki Strike books. She is also the coauthor of the Nightmares! series and the Last Reality series with Jason Segel.